Crown and Blade

Lauren Dane
Anya Bast

ELLORA'S CAVE
ROMANTICA PUBLISHING

What the critics are saying...

ဢ

SWORD AND CROWN

5 Angels "SWORD AND CROWN five angels and says in part: The sexual tension between Rhea and Jax were scorching hot and erotically passionate. I took great pleasure in watching Rhea and Jax's story unfold, feeling their emotional turmoil and seeing how they were willing to try to overcome numerous misunderstandings, past betrayal and massive heartache. I found Sword and Crown to be a compelling story and I was hooked from the start." ~ *Fallen Angel Reviews*

"*Sword and Crown* has equal parts fantasy, suspense, action, eroticism and the most important ingredient—love found again. I have never gone wrong by picking up one of Ms. Dane's books and this was no exception. You will love *Sword and Crown*—I did." ~ *Joyfully Reviewed Reviews*

WHISPER OF THE BLADE

4 Rating "*Whisper of the Blade* was a fantasy taking place in a different world. [...] I found all three main characters to be well-written and extremely sexy. [...] I was so aroused that I found it hard to continue to read! Toys are definitely desired here. [...] I found the plot ran smoothly, and didn't think it dragged at any time. The characters, plot and sex in this book made it just wonderful to read. Overall, this was a fun and arousing fascinating read." ~ *Just Erotic Romance Reviews*

"Still, the characters are pretty well-drawn to a two-dimensional degree and likable, with the bonus of Emmia being a smart and level-headed heroine. *Whisper of the Blade* also has some very nicely written naughty scenes. [...] If you are looking for a well-written fluffy threesome sex romp featuring characters you won't want to throttle to death with your own hands, this one is probably it." ~ *Mrs. Giggles Reviews*

An Ellora's Cave Romantica Publication

www.ellorascave.com

Crown and Blade

ISBN 9781419958373

CROWN AND BLADE

ଔ

SWORD AND CROWN
Lauren Dane
~11~

WHISPER OF THE BLADE
Anya Bast
~131~

SWORD AND CROWN
Lauren Dane

ഌ

Author's Note

The Queen of Swords has been through many trials, many conflicts in her life. She has weathered them with strength and courage. She's lost loved ones and experienced pain but those experiences have made her stronger. She is realistic and pragmatic, she is a loyal friend and determined ally. She is also intelligent, rational and has a cutting wit. This card, this woman, is extraordinarily astute and forthright and does not play games or tolerate falsehoods. She looks beyond the face others present and sees deeply into their true natures. This makes many uncomfortable. Her blunt nature is often considered aloof or cold when really she is simply very discriminating about who she lets into her inner life.

The Queen of Swords is portrayed on her card in the Rider-Waite tarot deck as standing. Light glints off her sword and crown, showing the relationship between truth (light) her thoughts (crown) and her actions (sword) amongst the swirling air that governs her suit. Oftentimes she bears a third eye of intuition, a sixth sense of wisdom. Butterflies symbolizing change after incubation fly around her. She has been through hard times and has become stronger, she is able to cut through illusions with clarity.

Rhea is a Queen of Swords woman. She's a woman who's discovered strength and wisdom through the trials she's been through in her life. In *Sword and Crown* she's on the verge of a change. She must reconcile who she used to be as a young woman to the changed person she is today. Her world exists in peril and she must greet that as a woman with her past as not a burden, but armor.

Trademarks Acknowledgement

&

The author acknowledges the trademarked status and trademark owners of the following wordmarks mentioned in this work of fiction:

Holly Hobbie: American Greetings Corporation

Chapter One

ဆ

Rhea moved through the night air, the cool breeze caressing her bare flesh. Talent flared from her skin in indigo arcs and swirled around her. Pleasure pulsed through her, jumped from her to her partner—his magic uniting with hers. The darkness edged back until it was a mere shadow on the far horizon again.

Triumph roared through her at their victory. Until she looked up and saw Paul standing in the doorway, clutching one of his bottles of elixir. Eyes that had once gazed at her filled with love and adoration now held jealous bitterness.

And then she came awake from the dream with a gasp, trembling as the memories crashed back through her.

* * * * *

Walking across the campus to her ten a.m. lecture, Rhea ignored the interested stares. She always did. It was more than her voluptuous, nearly six-foot frame. More than the blue-black hair and the plump lips. It wasn't even the steely blue-gray eyes fringed by dark lashes.

No, Rhea Harris was overflowing with sex magic. Even when she tried to stifle it, she exuded raw sensuality. No glamour could hide what she was.

"Rhea," the assistant dean of the department met her outside the lecture hall.

That sensuality often attracted smarmy assholes like Tom Andrews. Men perpetually on the make, regardless of the wedding ring they wore on their left hands.

11

Rhea didn't bother to hide her annoyance. The prick had been hounding her for the last six weeks. She was sorely tempted to bewitch the bastard off a short pier. Instead she'd decided to try giving him as little attention as possible.

"Tom." Not even looking at him, she reached around him for the door. He moved to touch her body with his own. She really hated that sort of thing. "Hey, Touchy McFeely, back the fuck up."

He winced, shock on his face as she pushed past him to walk into the room. Every seat was filled and people stood up at the back.

At the front of the hall she tossed her bag to the side, pushed the lectern out of the way and perched on top of the desk instead.

"I'm Rhea Harris, the visiting Rex Scholar. And I don't tell you that to impress you or anything. Believe it or not I have to say that before every lecture I give. I don't know why, it's not like there's Rex Scholar products for you to buy in the bookstore or anything but there it is. I'll be talking for about an hour. Afterward, I'll take questions."

And she began. As always when she spoke about the intersection of science and magic, her deep passion for the subject took over and the entire hall was swept along. Didn't matter if she was in Los Angeles or Budapest.

"Humans are fond of talking about the unknowable, the paranormal. But everything has an explanation. Even if we don't understand things, there are laws which govern space and time. All magic is, is the manipulation of those laws by those who have a natural skill to do so.

"There is nothing mystical about magical Talent. It's like the ability to sing or paint. An artistic talent if you will. Magic is energy. We know from Newton and Einstein and countless other scientists that energy does not go away. It simply metamorphoses into something else.

"Psychics and other empathic people — those who are gifted in dealing with animals and other humans, those who wield great amounts of charisma and sexuality, those who sway with anger and fear — to an extent this is all magic or the manipulation of energy. There is nothing unknowable. There are many things we just can't explain right now."

She went on to talk about chaos theory and high-level mathematics as well as particle physics and their intersection with magic. Rhea loved giving people food for thought about how they accessed the world around them. Coming from a world where magic was commonplace, she wanted those humans she came in contact with to understand that a mystery was just a question that hadn't been answered yet.

At the end she saw them all queue up eagerly and waited for the inevitable.

"Ms. Harris, what makes you think we believe any of this crap? You're taking the university's money and conning people! This is a rip-off."

Rhea watched Ardent Doubting Thomas with amused eyes. There was a version of him at every single lecture. "You don't have to believe any of it. I'm not trying to sell you anything or recruit you to live on a compound. Relax, kid. It's just a lecture."

He looked as if he was going to pop a vein when she didn't rise to the bait. "I just believe people should be thinking critically about this stuff," his voice cracked.

"I agree. Critical thinking is important."

"But magic isn't real! If it's real, show us. Make that clock fly off the wall or something."

Rhea smiled at him. "I'm not a performing monkey. Look, kid, make up your own mind but remember that within the realm of human history there were those who thought the Earth was flat and any mention of astronomy was heresy. It's the question that matters."

"That's so true, Professor Harris!"

Rhea saw the girl all in pink and begged the universe for strength. Why were they all so *pink*? The girl probably dotted the "i" at the end of her name with a heart. And Rhea knew the girl was a Bambi or a Missi or something of that ilk. She probably had pink pens with sparkles and fluffy feathery crap on the end and a cell phone with rhinestones. Her boyfriend probably shaved his chest.

"What's true?"

"Well, you know, I was born when Mercury was in retrograde and that's like a science. Just like you said. It's not hair, er, what you said."

"Heresy. It's an opinion contrary to one generally accepted in any field or belief system. In this case, the belief that the Earth revolved around the sun and not the other way around was considered heresy. Those who insisted the Earth was round and not flat were called heretics. But really, Galileo and those like him were visionaries because they answered questions by asking them in different ways.

"And you're thinking about astrology. I'm speaking about astronomy. Astronomy is the study of space and the stars. Not star signs. But thank you for your confidence." And that was it, she'd exhausted every last bit of nice she had within her, which wasn't much to begin with.

"Oh."

Next up, the fluffy bunny in the Holly Hobbie dress and the dredlocks. "Ms. Harris, are you taking students? I'd love to study with you."

"I don't teach magic. I don't give private lessons. Either you have magic or you don't. But science, reason and logic — these are things that exist for all of us every day."

Holly Hobbie looked disappointed but still had the gleam of adoration in her eyes. Rhea made a mental note of the multiple exits so she could avoid the fangirls.

And on it went. The Aleister Crowley wannabe, the Goths, the pretty princesses, a few more fluffy bunnies and a few more doubting Thomases.

When the time was up she rose and waved, taking advantage of their surprise at her sudden movement to dash from the room.

She walked, head down, to her car and got out. Their energy, their desire, their adoration and lust pressed at her, made her exhausted.

* * * * *

A relatively quick drive from campus brought her back to the condo on the beach owned by the Rex people. Compared to the last place she lived, this was far preferable. The air was clean, and the saltwater dampened some of the negative energy that always tired her out.

Inside she kicked off her shoes and opened up the sliding doors on the deck, letting the sound of the ocean wash into the room.

"How'd it go?"

Rhea turned and rolled her eyes at Sarai, her familiar and best friend. Currently, she appeared to be a tall, lithe woman with cocoa skin and large yellow eyes but Rhea knew she could also take the form of a cat the size of a small pony. "The usual. That asshole Andrews came on to me yet again. Rubbed himself against me. Gah! Why do men do that? Blech! I'd like to know if it ever works for them. You'd think it would or they'd stop it. Wouldn't you? Then again, disgusting men in stained T-shirts hoot at women walking by on the streets over and over. One wonders, Sarai, what lies between their ears."

Sarai got up and brought a pitcher and two glasses back from the kitchen, placing them on the table outside on the deck. "I've made you some fresh juice. I can see the strain around your eyes. Drink."

"I'm all right. I just need to cleanse my system more often." Even so, the fresh juice made her feel much healthier. She'd taken in far too much synthetic and processed matter. It weakened her and left her vulnerable to those around her.

"Better?"

Reaching over, she rubbed her face along Sarai's jaw, seeking comfort, giving it in return. Rhea didn't have words to thank Sarai for coming with her when she was exiled. "Thank you for taking care of me. All of these years you've been here, without another of your kind. I'm sorry to have robbed you of your life."

Sarai looked at her through those big yellow eyes, not bothering to make them look human when it was just the two of them. "You're alone here without another of your kind too. You did not ask. I came to be with you. You are the sister of my heart and I'm honored to serve you now as I was then."

Familiars and Practitioners bonded when both were very young. In Rhea's case, she and Sarai had bonded when Rhea was three and Sarai was a mere kitten. Sarai had jumped into Rhea's arms and the bond had been formed at that moment. There hadn't been a day in Rhea's life where she'd failed to hear Sarai's voice or seek her advice or comfort. A sort of substitute for Rhea's mother, who'd always been a place of refuge for her.

The thought of her mother brought a slice of pain through Rhea's gut. Gone. All of them gone. Damn it.

"Rhea, I worry about you. You have to Practice more and more often to keep yourself unharmed by the energies of the humans. You're lonely. You have no roots." Sarai purred as she smoothed a hand over Rhea's hair.

"I have enough roots. But something is wrong. I can feel it. It drains me."

"Wrong how?"

"The balance is tipping. I see more thin spots than I used to. After Ra'Ken was destroyed I often wondered if the

Council could hold the Nameless back. I wonder that even more now."

Sarai didn't push any further. She knew it was pointless. There would come a time, though, when she wouldn't stop pushing until they went back. It was not only imperative for Rhea's health, but her birthright as well.

"You know, that hottie from next door was asking after you again."

"I can't. Don't start this." Rhea's eyes flashed.

"It was a fluke, Rhea. He clearly had some Talent. You couldn't have known. You had no problems before that."

"Problems? Is that what you call blowing out the windows in every building on the block? I can't risk it. I can't hurt anyone again."

Sarai closed her eyes against Rhea's pain. "It wasn't your fault."

"I so don't want to go over this with you again, Sarai."

"Fine. You know, I'm the one with fur but you're the one wearing a hair shirt. Get over it. How long will you let something you *had* to do define your life?"

Rhea got up and went back into the condo and put her glass in the sink. Hearing a knock on the door, she called to Sarai that she'd get it.

And opened it to face her past.

Jaac Sarne looked into the face of the only woman he'd ever loved and the only woman whose loss had ever mattered. Fifteen years without hearing her voice or her laughter. Her magic had gone and the world was a darker place without her. Literally.

She stood there in the doorway without speaking.

"Aren't you going to bid me enter?"

"Stop talking like that. No. Go away." She tried to close the door on him but he blocked it with his foot.

"I need to talk to you, Sa'Rhea. Please."

"Don't call me that. I'm Rhea Harris now." She spoke low and looked out past him, making sure no one had overheard the exchange.

"Who is it? Oh shit..." Sarai came to a halt when she caught sight of Jaac. In the stillness of the moment, Rhea took him in. He was the mirror opposite of his brother. Dark where Paul had been fair, tall and broad where Paul had been thin and athletic. Deep eyes as dark as midnight stared back at her.

"He was just leaving," Rhea hissed.

"No he wasn't." Sarai pushed past Rhea. Grabbing his arm, she yanked him into the apartment and closed the door, locking it. "You can't ignore this, Rhea. What are you doing here, Jaac?"

"The Nameless. It's back and the entire western shore has fallen. We need you, Sa'Rhea."

Shock, cold and hard, slammed into her. Shaking off the hand at her upper arm, she fell into a chair. "How many?"

"A lot." Jaac was quiet as he watched her reaction. Still so fucking beautiful that looking at her hurt his chest. And he'd thrown it away like a stupid boy.

"A lot? You still a scientist, Jaac? That's very astute of you. Precise. A lot."

The dry sarcasm in her voice surprised him. The Sa'Rhea he'd known had been sweet and joyful. "Ten thousand, four hundred and six. Is that better?"

She opened her eyes and that stormy blue-gray gaze held him fast. "Don't piss me off, beefy."

"Beefy?"

Sarai snickered.

"Look, Paul Bunyan, tell me what it is you were sent here to say. I have things to do."

Sarai really seemed to think that was funny and he resolved to look it up when he could. "We need your Talent.

There are no high level Practitioners left. At least none who can hold the Nameless back."

"And you come crawling to me? After shaming me and sending me away like I was nothing? *Now* I'm worth speaking to, when you need me?"

"We could have used the scrolls but they're gone now."

Immediately, he regretted his words when she flinched as if he'd physically struck her.

"You're an asshole, Jaac. I can't believe I let you in here." Sarai's voice lowered into a growl and her face took on a more feline shape.

Damn it, a familiar minx in fury mode. Perfect.

"I'm sorry. Okay? I didn't mean it. I know you...I know you had no choice. I believe your account of what happened." Sighing, he splayed his fingers out before his body and then pulled them into fists. "It doesn't change the fact that we need you desperately. You're the last of your line. Your father is too old."

"And my sister, Emmia?" Once she could have said "sisters", but no longer. "Your sisters?"

"Your sister may be strong enough with the aid of the scrolls but without them..." He shrugged. "The power holding the Nameless back has been weakening for the last fifteen years. Many of those remaining have been sent away to the Eastern Mountains."

"Who sent you here?"

"The Council. We need you. Please."

"My father? Yours?"

He sighed, nodding. "Yes. Both. Your father would have come but he's not in the best of health. He's been using most of his energy to keep the boundary up. The coastal cities are in danger but the wards are holding. For now."

Rhea went to look out the sliding glass door at the ocean. She'd yearned to be with her own people for fifteen years.

Wanted to hear the sound of the food sellers as they called out their afternoon bargains. Missed her mother's humming and her sisters' laughter, her brothers teasing each other. Not that her mother could laugh from her grave. She missed her Talent. She wanted to go home.

Sarai came to stand next to her. "You don't owe them anything."

"Not the Council, no. But the millions who are threatened now, how can I ignore that?"

"You can't, because you're you. Get a guarantee that the geas against you has been lifted. Make sure the family holdings due you as Paul's widow are awarded so you have a place to live after this is over. It's not greed, Rhea, it's common sense. You can't come back here, you're dying. There you can have your magic back and a living. Fuck the rest of them." Sarai said it quietly but Jaac heard anyway.

"You're dying?" The panic in his voice was obvious.

"Not from a sickness. The environment here drains me. I can't keep it all out without a severe bleed on my powers."

He wanted to touch her. Pull her into his arms and kiss the lips he dreamt of every night. "I can assure you your widow property. I have the paperwork with me. You've got enough of a settlement to live comfortably for the rest of your life. The geas was lifted when you agreed to leave, by the way. You're free to return."

Home. The mere thought of it took away the aches and pains of her day. If she lived alone with Sarai in her home—even if no one ever spoke to her—it would be better than dying a universe away. And she'd be able to save millions of lives and Practice again.

"I have to call my employers here and then we can go."

Chapter Two

∞

Holding a small bag and leaving the rest of her belongings back in her condo, she walked into the rift behind Jaac and back into D'ar, the capital city of Molari. *Home.*

Her magic rushed back into her the moment her foot touched the soil. So much, so fast that her back arched and a gasp broke from her lips.

Jaac was next to her then, holding her arm, steadying her. "Sa'Rhea? Are you all right?"

It filled her. More and more until she was sure she'd explode from it. Until she was sure she must glow with the power rushing through her cells. But the warmth of his hand on her arm, of his body against hers, holding her upright, anchored her until the intensity passed.

When she opened her eyes Sarai's widened. "Rhea, your eyes are..."

Jaac looked and laughed. "Your eyes are normal again."

Meaning that the gray was the dominant color once more. The slate blue-gray of a snow sky. Her magic was back and it showed in her eyes. Marked her as a high level Practitioner. And it felt good. Clean. And she realized how much she missed this feeling. Feeling at one with her environment. Feeling her magic course through her veins. Feeling nurtured and fed by the very ground she walked on. In the distance, the emerald spires of the capitol building jutted up into a sky more amethyst than blue. The air was clean and crackling with magic.

"Welcome home, Sa'Rhea. You've been missed," Jaac said quietly, squeezing her hand before letting it go.

21

Joy. For the first time in fifteen years she felt joy as she'd thought she'd never feel again. Her magic was back. At the same time, she felt the...wrongness in the air. A taste on the back of her tongue. Things were out of balance. "I can feel it," she murmured. "How did you let it get this bad?"

"I don't have an answer to that, Sa'Rhea. I've been counseling them to seek you out for a very long time."

She turned to him, surprised. "You're on the Council now?"

"Yes. After Paul...after his death, I stepped in." Not that his worthless brother had been useful anyway.

"Ah, I see. Well, let's get this show on the road, so to speak. I imagine we're to go to Council chambers?" The joy on her face was gone, replaced with an expressionless mask.

"Yes, there's a conveyance here." He pointed to the small car that waited across the park from where he'd opened a rift.

"Pretty sure of yourself, weren't you?"

He looked at Rhea. "I hoped that you still had your big heart."

It'd been broken, but she still had her sense of duty and kinship with the people she was born to protect and had served ably until she made a mistake. A mistake that cost her her family and her homeland.

Sarai sensed Rhea's pain and leaned in to nuzzle her softly. "We're here. And we'll make it all right."

"Go and see your family, Sarai. They'll want to see you. Come to our home when you can."

"You're sure they'll give it to you?"

"They will or they can face the Nameless alone. I didn't come here to play games. If I'm back, it's as a full member of the Hars Caste or not at all. My home seems a small price to pay."

Jaac stared at her.

"I'm not her anymore, Jax. That girl is gone. Rhea Harris would not have allowed herself to be scapegoated and shunned in the public square."

"Jax?"

"I like it better than Jaac. Anyway, let's go."

Sarai metamorphosed and bounded toward her familial home after a brief hug. She was emotionally tied to Rhea through the bond, she'd know if she was needed and come immediately. Rhea knew that and appreciated it.

Jax put a hand at the small of her back and guided her to the car that awaited them and helped her inside.

She leaned back against the seat, trying to ignore the brand of his touch, the way the simple stroke of his hand against her back had ignited her senses. "Tell me what the situation is on the Council."

"What do you mean?" Jax was careful. He knew the driver was listening. Then again, he wanted quite badly to run his fingertips down her neck, sliding his hand around the back enough to pull her to him for a kiss. He'd forgotten the way her body called to his. It had been why he'd stayed away after she married Paul. He needed to be careful in more than one way.

"I mean, who's in charge? Which caste is in charge? What has happened in the fifteen years I've been gone? Who is on my side? Who do I need to worry about?"

The last time he'd seen Sa'Rhea, she'd been weeping. Begging her father to save her from the exile order. That Sa'Rhea was such a sweet woman. Not much more than a girl really. She'd never questioned the love and loyalty of her family. Never imagined that they'd toss her on the altar of convenience and make the whole debacle with his brother — her husband — her fault. But they did. And in doing so they'd tossed away their strongest weapon against their biggest threat.

This woman, Rhea, was stronger and there was no air of innocence in her. And yet, that was more alluring. As he sat there next to her, he realized this was his second chance to be with her. He'd failed her before, yes, but he aimed to be the man she needed him to be. This woman wasn't a fragile girl to be taken care of. She would stand at his side. But first he'd have to convince her of it.

"Your Caste is still the ruling family. There was a power struggle for the first three years after you left. My Caste challenged yours." He paused, not sure how to proceed, but decided to just tell the truth as he knew it. "There was a shake-up. We're in the second position now."

He turned to her and took her hand. "You can count on me to be on your side. Always. If I'd been here when..." He shook his head at the memory, "Anyway, that's over. The Dashan Caste was opposed to bringing you back but they're still at the end of the table. Your Caste is divided. Your sister and uncle Treya are all supportive. Have been for years, by the way. Your father, well, he's recently come around but his brothers are opposed. The other Castes were never vehement either way. They'll fall where the power lies."

"My uncles know that I'll take over my father's chair when he steps down. They don't want to lose power. And the Dashans will never forgive Paul marrying me instead of their Aan." Then again, she'd have been better off without Paul. "So it sounds like the only people I need to worry about are my father's brothers and your family."

"My Caste isn't necessarily against you."

She looked at him and made a disgusted click of her tongue. "Don't shit me. I've had enough. Fifteen years in exile worth of enough. I wouldn't be here now if you all weren't staring obliteration in the face."

He blinked several times and didn't argue. Couldn't argue.

They pulled in front of the capitol building. She got out without waiting for her door to be opened. He followed, interested in what she'd do next.

Straight backed, she walked confidently through the halls, up the grand stairway and into the council chamber without even a glance at the men-at-arms at the doors.

The people inside, all members of the Ruling Council, stared at her. Some with relief, some with disdain, all with shock.

"I hear you have a problem you need me to solve." She walked to the head of the table, where her father sat with her paternal uncles to one side and her maternal uncle to the other. "Where's my chair?"

Her uncle Treya stood and smiled at her. "Welcome home, Sa'Rhea. Still the most beautiful woman this family has ever seen." He winked and she smiled, shaking her head.

"Thank you, Uncle."

Taking a fortifying breath, she faced the table again and her father and other uncles. "Well? My chair?"

"Wait just a second, young lady! You can't just come in here and demand a place at the head of the table!" Her uncle Arta's face was beet red.

"I can. And I will. It is my rightful place as a Hars and a Sarne."

"You are no Sarne!" one of the Dashans declared from the end of the table. There were murmurs of shock and assent.

Rhea put her hands on the table and leaned in. "I am. I married Paul in a legal and binding ceremony. I was born a Hars and I held my place well. I kept you safe from the Nameless for my entire life. Paul would not be dead if he hadn't tried to steal those scrolls. I did what I could to save him for two years as he slid deeper into his bottle of elixir.

"I paid for my title with blood, loss and exile for fifteen years. It's mine—without question—along with my holdings

25

and my seat at the head of this table or you can all face the Nameless alone because I'll leave right now."

She stood and waited.

"We've all signed the papers giving Sa'Rhea back her rightful inheritance. Including her place at the head of the table. Let's remember that. And the important thing, stopping the Nameless." Jaac's voice rang loud through the chamber as he tossed the papers on the table.

Treya pushed a chair at her. "Here you go, sweetie."

Nodding, Rhea sat down and moved closer to the table to grab the papers Jax tossed toward her. Looking through them quickly, she saw she'd been made right again. Had all her property restored including her bride price credits. The Sarnes must have hated that.

She put them aside and looked at the faces at the table. "I've had a long day, tell me what's happening."

Her father, who hadn't spoken a single word, watched her through half-lidded eyes. He'd missed her every moment of every day even as he'd done what he thought was necessary to end the ordeal. And now she'd come back and her life would be in danger. She was their only chance against the Nameless.

Her mother, his beloved wife, was written all over her face. Oh how he'd missed them both. He knew Chela would have never let him exile their daughter. Knew it was wrong even as he'd done it. Now the child he'd tossed in the air just to hear her giggle hated him. And rightfully so.

He outlined the situation, explained that those younger citizens with Talent had been taken to the Eastern Mountains to a stronghold there. Just in case. He knew Emmia would appreciate the solitude. The separation from the voices, the emotions that made living among her fellow citizens nearly unbearable.

"We've had Practitioners at work every moment of the day. But the job gets harder and harder the longer we wait. Since it took all those people, the Nameless has gotten much stronger."

"Without the scrolls, we're too weak to hold it back much longer." Rhea's former father-in-law said.

But she didn't rise to the bait. He knew, they all did. "I need some rest, a meal and someone to Practice with. Give me twelve hours and I'll go to the borderlands. The wards need to be strengthened so we'll start there."

"I'll escort you," Jax said, rising when she did.

Leaning down, she kissed her uncle again and let Jax lead her out without another word to anyone.

* * * * *

"Are you sure you'll be okay here?" Jax asked as he led her into the large entry of the house she'd once shared with Paul while they were in D'ar.

She didn't answer as she walked past him and into the main room. Her fingertips traced the hand carved back of the chaise. "It hasn't changed. Not one bit."

"My mother closed it the day you…left. We opened it up a week ago and had some cleaners come in and get rid of the furniture covers, tidy things up. Your old staff, every last one of them, is back."

She smiled as she moved to face him. "Really? Oh, I've longed to eat Mrs. Dakins' stew again, missed the scent of her fresh bread baking every morning."

Touched, he reached out and pulled her to him, and time slowed when her body touched his. His laugh died in his throat as he leaned in and brushed his lips over hers ever-so gently. Her taste teased him and he wanted more. So much more. "Sa'Rhea," he whispered.

She extricated herself from his embrace. "Rhea. And yes, I'll be fine here. This is my home. Even the last two years with your brother didn't ruin this place for me." She dusted invisible dirt from her clothing but he saw the slight tremor in her hands and knew she was as affected by him as he was by her.

He cleared his throat but her taste still hinted on his lips. "Your clothes are in the closets. I believe Emmia made sure your things were shipped here before she left for the mountains. She wanted to stay but there wasn't time. Anyway, you should still fit in them. Your body looks as good now as it did then. You're even more beautiful."

"What's your game, Jax?" she called back over her shoulder as she walked up the stairs and into the master suite.

"Game?" He followed her into the room. He sat on the bed as she went into the dressing area, closing the door behind her. Looking around, he saw the stamp of the old Rhea on the space. The room was bright and colorful. The books on the shelves were volumes of song and poetry. Little ceramic animals lined the windowsills.

She exited a few minutes later and left him breathless. She stood there, not in the jeans and T-shirt she'd returned with but a sumptuous eggplant-colored at-home gown worn by the women in highborn Castes. A flowing skirt with cuts along the thighs and a tight, high waist with a bodice open at the neck. The sleeves were short and he could see the silky, creamy pale curves of her breasts and the long, elegant line of her neck. She'd pulled her hair up into a loose knot and that only emphasized her eyes and her lips.

"I...you... No one has worn that color since you left. I think because they would have been a pale shadow of you."

Rhea saw the greedy heat in his gaze and her pussy slicked in response. She'd wanted him so damned much in her youth. For three glorious months she'd had him in secret. They'd snuck out late at night to meet on the shores of the lake and made love under the open sky. He'd been older, skilled, and had taught her a great many things. Oh how she'd loved him!

But then he'd rejected her. Gone to the central cities without telling her. A few months later Paul had begun to court her and she'd fallen for him. Paul hadn't had his brother's intensity or his passion but he'd adored her and in time, she'd loved him too.

Twenty-one years since Jax had looked at her that way openly, and she shouldn't want it but she did. She'd never stopped craving him. Even in the early years with Paul when she'd truly loved him, Jax had filled her dreams, her fantasies.

"So? What's your game?" She waved him to follow her and went down to the kitchen. When the cook, Mrs. Dakins, saw her, she squealed in delight and pulled Rhea into a tight embrace.

"Sweetest! Oh how I've missed you! Come and sit at the table there. I'll have a meal for you both in just a few minutes. There's fresh juice there in a pitcher with some glasses."

Rhea smiled. "I've missed you too. Any fresh bread?"

Mrs. Dakins blushed, pleased. "Of course! I knew you'd be coming back, didn't I? There's lemon cake for dessert too. Now go on and sit, you look a bit tired."

One of Rhea's favorite things about the house was that it wasn't the large manor that they'd lived in, in Ra'Ken. This house was smaller, intimate. There was a formal dining space but Rhea had filled it with bookcases and couches and chairs instead, thinking one day it might be a playroom for children.

But the kitchen had always been a favorite room. The tall fireplace dominated the room, giving heat to the whole house in the winter months. The floors were a polished reddish tile, making the room seem cozy. Large windows dominated one wall and Mrs. Dakins had always had pots of herbs growing in the light there. Rhea took in the space as her fingertips stroked over the tabletop, smoothed from years of use.

It was jarring, the way things hadn't changed in the house but she'd done so much changing herself.

"What do you mean, Rhea?" Jax asked, pulling her out of her thoughts.

"Why you? Why did you come to get me? Why are you here now? What's with the kiss in the sitting room?"

"I came to get you because it's what I've wanted to do for fifteen years. I argued for it because I hoped you'd trust me and I wanted the person who came to ask for your help to be someone you could trust. I never thought you should have been exiled to begin with. And I kissed you because I've wanted to for twenty-one years. You taste even better as a woman."

"Is that why you left without telling me? Because I didn't taste good enough?" One of her eyebrows slid up.

"What happened to that sweet girl, anyway?"

"She killed her husband as he attempted to steal priceless scrolls to sell for more elixir and whores. That same night, when she was imprisoned in the capital city, the Nameless came and razed the entire city of her birth. Not only did she lose her husband but her mother, brothers and two older sisters. Then her own father turned on her and exiled her to save their collective skins. She took on the responsibility for the fuckups of the Council and those in charge. For everyone who should have protected her but failed her and then exiled her to cover up their neglect. She lived alone without anyone but her best friend in another universe that killed her slowly every day of the last fifteen years. Being sweet gets you stomped on, Jax. Being wary keeps you alive."

Mrs. Dakins tsked as she put a plate heaping with food before Rhea and another down for Jax. She kissed the top of Rhea's head. "You're back now. Wiser and older, and you'll not let them mess with you this time, I'd wager. Now eat up."

Rhea's eyes were amused as she thanked the cook and grabbed a slice of bread, beginning to eat.

"I left because you scared me." If she could be so painfully honest, so could he. "The way I felt for you terrified me. I was twenty-two. Gods, so damned young! I had a life and a whole lot of women ahead of me and you were there suddenly, filling my every damned thought. You were eighteen then, you'd just grown into your body. Long, leggy, your breasts, well, they still look damned fine. Anyway, the way you looked at me, the way your body reacted when I touched you..." Pausing, he closed his eyes briefly before continuing. "So eager to let me love you. You wanted to learn from me, to please me and be pleased. I suppose part of it was your magic, but mostly it was just you.

"I ran because I couldn't face it. And when I got back, you'd moved on to my brother of all people. And he loved you. And you loved him. So I stepped back and into my lab and jumped into as many beds as I could. And in doing so I wasn't here to watch Paul's descent."

She nodded, not speaking. Knowing that if she did, she'd lose control. And control was all she had at the moment.

A comfortable silence settled between them as they finished eating. Finally, taking a deep breath, she allowed herself to look at him. "I need to sleep. I've been up a very long time. I haven't Practiced in fifteen years. I didn't have all my magic on Earth. So I'll need some help. Who will I be working with?"

Okay. She seemed to just be ignoring all he'd told her. So be it. For now. But Jax meant to have her. This time for good. He'd bide his time but not forever.

"Me."

"What?"

"I'm not good enough to work without the scrolls, but almost. Together, you and I should be very strong. Better than you and Paul were when he was well. Sex magic is a secondary trait in my family, you know." Lucky for him, even

31

though having a primary Talent at sex magic was rare, it was among the secondary Talents that ran in his family. Meaning he wasn't strong enough to Practice alone but he was excellent with a partner.

She stood. "Fine. I'll see you in ten hours." She turned without another word to him, thanked the cook and went upstairs to sleep.

He watched her walk out of the room and sighed heavily.

"Well? You going to lose her again, you fool?"

Surprised, Jax looked over at Mrs. Dakins. "I…no, ma'am. Not if I can help it."

She narrowed her eyes at him for a moment and then nodded quickly. "Good." And turned her back to get to work.

* * * * *

All Rhea could think about once she slid into her bed was Jax. The way his hands felt on her, his mouth. Gods, the first time he'd spread her thighs and loved her with his mouth. That thought made her wet and achy. The girth of his cock as he slid into her body, stretching her, filling her up. Nothing and no one had ever felt that good. At one time she'd tried to tell herself it was just youth. Paul had been loving and giving for the first two years they'd been together. He'd been a good lover. And when she arrived on Earth she'd taken many lovers, faceless and nameless, just to try to fill the empty spot inside herself. No man she'd ever been with had come close to making her feel like Jax had.

She could admit to herself that she had been forever changed by Jax. That he was written into her so deep he was indelible. But the pertinent fact was that he'd abandoned her and thrown her love away and it would not pay to forget it.

It took Rhea a good long time tossing and turning before she remembered she had her magic back and spelled herself to sleep, hoping it would be dreamless.

When she awoke some eight hours later, Sarai was back, lying against her in the bed in her minx form. Rhea got out from under the blankets carefully and went into the large bathroom and took a very long shower and dressed for travel. It was the predawn deep purple of night outside. A color she was once so very sure she'd never see again.

"When do we leave?" Sarai asked sleepily, sitting up to stretch when Rhea came back into the bedroom.

"You don't have to come, Sarai. You can stay here with your family. They must have missed you. How are they?"

Sarai conjured up clothes for her humanoid form and padded downstairs behind Rhea. "They're all well. My mother sends her love to you. And of course I'm coming. That's what I do. That's what *we* do. I hear Jax is going to be your partner."

"I'd forgotten how quickly news travels around here." Rhea spoke over her shoulder and then turned, smiling, to see her cook up and already at work. "Mrs. Dakins, what are you doing awake already?"

"I'm making you a breakfast and packing some food for the trip. I'm coming along as well."

Ushering Rhea to the table, Mrs. Dakins put a steaming mug of coffee before her. It had been a pleasant surprise indeed to find that Earth had coffee too. "You don't need to do that. I was just telling Sarai to stay here with her family. I don't want you endangering yourselves to come along to the borderlands with me."

"And I believe I heard Miss Sarai tell you she was coming because that's what she does. As do I. You'll need to eat while you're there. I'm your cook. You're a smart girl, figure it out." A plate filled with food showed up on the table for each of them and a basket of fresh rolls followed.

Jax strolled in and sat in the chair closest to Rhea. "Morning. Or night. Whatever. How are you feeling today?" He nodded his thanks to Mrs. Dakins as she put food before him.

"We've got a whole caravan coming to the borderlands, apparently." Rhea's voice was wry. She used her sarcasm to hold back the gulp of air she'd wanted to take when he came into the room. Paul had been handsome in a boyish way, almost pretty. But Jax was all manly man with his predator's walk. His eyes were the deepest midnight blue and he had a well-trimmed beard. Ebony hair trailed down his back, caught in a leather tie at the nape of his neck when it wasn't braided at the temples. His shirt was sleeveless and he wore leather bands at each biceps, marked with the runes of his Caste. He'd been a scientist of fairly high renown but Rhea had never met any other scientist who made her toes curl the same way.

"Well, we'll need a cook and I never imagined Sarai would stay here without you." He winked at Mrs. Dakins and she laughed.

Rhea put her hands up in surrender. "Okay, thank you both. It should be safe. Sarai, if it gets dangerous, open a rift and take her out of there." That would be very last resort, a rift could go anywhere if opened near the wards.

"I'll open a rift and shove her through. I'm not leaving you. We've gone through this a thousand times."

"Ugh! You know, I hear that some people have familiars that are obedient. I get the cat with attitude."

"I heard that, human." Amusement lit Sarai's eyes.

"And I don't get thanks?" Jax teased her.

"For what?" Her eyebrow rose.

For soon delivering a fucking that will make you beg for more. "For accompanying you to the borderlands."

She waved her hand at that. "BFD. You'll ride in a car with some beautiful women, stay in a castle that's older and more revered than anything here and eat gourmet food for a few days while we rebuild the boundaries and wards."

"BFD?"

"Big fucking deal. I learned several useful phrases in my decade and a half on Earth."

"Wonderful," he said, tone laced with sarcasm.

In truth, he liked all the mannerisms she'd surprised him with so far. He liked getting to know this new side to someone he thought he'd known so well before. So the trip down would be nice and getting her alone would be even better. And he'd get to see her naked. Touch her, love her the way he'd longed to for twenty-one years. What was fresh bread and a moldering pile of stone compared to that?

They stood after eating and got ready to leave. They'd be unable to open a rift with any level of accuracy anywhere near the borderlands. The unique magic of the place coupled with the magical wards to hold the Nameless out canceled out that kind of inter-realm travel there. So they'd take one of the larger transports for the half-day's drive.

Rhea got in and wrapped herself in the plush blanket to ward off the early morning chill. Sarai curled up and went back to sleep and Mrs. Dakins rode forward with some of the other staff who were coming to the borderlands with them, including two burly guards.

Jax settled himself next to Rhea and breathed her in. The color had returned to her skin and he could see the magic pulsing through her. They'd create powerful magic together, he knew that. She was one of the strongest Practitioners he'd ever met, and definitely the most Talented. She was immensely powerful and it was a major bonus that her medium was sex magic and he'd be her partner. Sex magic was rare enough and mainly confined to three Castes of the Twelve, and none alive had more Talent than Rhea did.

"Tell me about your life. What did you do on Earth?" He fisted his hands to keep from reaching for her.

"Not much to tell."

"What did you do for a living? Where did you live? Your abode was so small compared to your home here. It took me a while to find you. It's a lot harder to lock there. Did you have a man?" He asked the last as casually as he could.

"I was a scholar of science and magic. I traveled a lot, all over the world, lecturing. Not a bad living really. They provided me with places to live. It's harder to lock because your magic is dampened. The longer you stayed, the weaker it would have become."

"A man? Did you have one?"

"More than one. I was there for fifteen years. A virtual menagerie if you must know. I kept them all on shelves and pulled them down when I needed a vigorous fucking."

He started and then narrowed his eyes. "Mmm hmmm. And were any of them special to you?"

"Do you mean did I play with one more than the others? They were all special, Jax. I'm just that magnanimous."

He tried to look annoyed by her ridiculous truncation of his name but in truth it pleased him.

"And it's not like it matters now anyway. Even if I did have a man back there, I'm here now."

Well he wanted to know if he was going to have to erase the memory of some beloved from her time on Earth or not. She was so evasive and contrary.

"Are you married?"

He laughed. "No. The only woman I ever wanted to marry has been very far away for the last fifteen years."

"Watch out. Sarai can be very violent during sex, you know. And children are out because you can't breed across species. Other than that and how she likes to groom you when she's sleepy, you two have a chance."

Sarai's ear flicked up and her pelt jumped in a few places until Rhea snorted and broke into laughter. A yellow eye opened and stared at Rhea for a few long moments. Heaving a heavy sigh, Sarai closed her eyes again and went back to sleep.

Jax let her evade, for the moment. But he'd be back. Rhea was his. He'd missed his opportunity all those years ago but he was a smarter man now and one who was willing to seduce her back to his side. Once he got her there, he planned to keep her there.

* * * * *

Rhea tried to pretend that Jax's presence didn't affect her, but the heat of his body seeped into hers and his scent filled the air. *And gods how she wanted him to touch her.* Relief filled her when they began to descend into the long valley that marked the borderlands between the central coast and cities and the western shores that lay just outside the warding walls.

There was another set of wards just to the south of the western shores. Obviously it'd been breached if the Nameless had been able to flow in and decimate the entire population.

A large keep sat on a bluff overlooking the water and lands to the south. Bleached white towers rose toward the amethyst sky proudly. Large walls stood around the keep and a lush garden, untamed and overflowing, roiled through the inner courtyards. The keeps were magical bastions against the Nameless from the time when it had roamed more free and deadly and they'd needed constant vigilance. The Nameless had been contained and then it stayed away from the cities long enough that people got lazy. And then it had devastated tens of thousands in one night.

With that thought on her mind, she got out of the car, and the wrongness in the air hit Rhea like a punch. It felt unnatural. The normally clean, crisp smell of the sea was masked by something foul in the distance. The breeze that came from the water hung thick instead of light. The taint was palpable.

"It hangs like smoke in the breeze. The stench of the Nameless." Looking around warily, she searched for physical signs but saw none. Yet.

Jax came to stand next to her while their things were unloaded and taken into the keep. "Yes. It's out there."

"And it knows we're here." Rhea could feel the cold regard of that eye of evil. She'd felt it twice before. Once when she turned eighteen and did her first full-fledged Practice. She'd come face-to-face with it in the ether. Several months before Paul had died in fact, and not too very long before she'd been exiled. For some reason the Nameless had appeared with a great well of strength and it'd taken her and others using the scrolls to push it back and close the boundary lines.

Rubbing her hands up her arms, Rhea warily looked out over the shoreline. The pristine, white sandy beaches and the small fishing boats in the harbor below were signs of normalcy. But she felt the end of that normalcy coming. Dread, cold and heavy, sank through her.

"Shall we go inside? We'll prepare and begin work. I feel we don't have long." Jax's face was serious and Rhea turned to him, nodding.

Inside the keep the echoes of generations of magic reverberated through the hallways. It was impressive and awe-inspiring to be there, to be one of those whose magic would protect the people of their world. She only hoped she wouldn't fail them.

"We've prepared the uppermost chamber for you." Mrs. Dakins met them at the base of the grand stairway. "Your bags are there and have been put in the adjoining suites."

Jax turned to Rhea, holding out his arm. Taking a deep breath, she reached out and laid her hand on it and let him lead her up.

Outside the doors to the main chamber, she let go. "I'm going to go change. I'll be in in a few minutes."

Standing in front of the mirror in the suite adjoining the room where she'd Practice with Jax, Rhea looked at herself. A frisson of fear slithered through her. Would she still have her power? Would she be what she was before? As strong? Could she Practice still after so long without her magic?

The need to Practice again was strong within her, along with the need for connection with a partner.

Sarai helped her out of her clothes and Rhea bathed in water laden with ritual herbs.

She donned a loose white robe and with one last look in the mirror, headed through the doors into the other room.

Jax was waiting there, kneeling on the bed.

The echoes of magic past swirled about her like dust motes. The doors and windows opened to a battlement that faced the walls of wards. The gauzy curtains blew gently on the breeze. Up there, inside the keep, the air wasn't as fetid as it was down below.

The bed Jax rested on dominated the room and had been carved from a single tree that was hundreds of years old. Rhea had Practiced in this room once when she'd been a lot younger. It had been more a trial run with her magic than anything else.

The expectancy was heavy this time, the stakes much higher.

Her bare feet walked over the cool, smooth wood as she made her way toward him.

He was beautiful there, ebony hair loose about his neck and shoulders like a spill of midnight. Shirtless, his broad shoulders and chest made her stomach clench. His thighs bulged from his position, so muscular and thick. He wore nothing and it was impossible not to take in the line of hair leading to his erect cock. Magic pulsed from him, catching her magic's rhythm in a seductive answer.

"Rhea..." The unspoken hung in the air like a spell and she shook her head sharply, not wanting him to speak it. Wanting this to be magic and magic only. She could not afford to open herself up to him. The memory of loss was still too sharp to bear.

He knelt there looking at her, eyes greedily soaking up her every move as she walked toward him. Her skin was beautiful, glimmering with magic as he caught glimpses of it as she moved.

He'd never seen a more beautiful sight as this woman he loved. He'd thought he loved that Sa'Rhea of his youth, but no. He'd loved the idea of her. This Rhea was his woman. A woman who'd endured and was strong and a bit remote. A woman who'd be a true partner.

After they beat the Nameless back.

Dropping her robe, Rhea reached out to take the hand he'd held out to her and joined him on the bed. Her body was lush, fecund and filled with magic. The sex arced from her and wove a spell around him.

Once both their hands joined, they moved close, bodies just touching, and began to Practice.

Magic moved through different mediums. Anger, fear, joy. But most powerful was sex magic because it encompassed all of these things and radiated from two Practitioners. The peak of sex was the peak of the spell.

There was usually companionship between Practitioners of sex magic. In this case, it was more. Jax wanted her desperately.

Leaning in, he heard her murmuring the beginning of the spell. His lips touched the column of her neck and she purred at the contact. The magic expanded and began to fill the room.

The undertow caught him, drove through his body, his senses. His cock hardened impossibly as he rolled his hips, driving himself into the softer flesh of her belly. Hands sliding up the soft flesh of her torso found her breasts, palming the nipples.

Opening up his own Talent, he pushed it hard into hers. Their magic, united, brought a gasp of pleasure from her lips. Her head lolled back and he brought his lips down her neck to her nipple.

How could he have forgotten her taste? The salt of her skin, the sweet essence of her flesh and the tang of her magic locked into his senses like they'd never left his mind. Her nipple, hard and eager, pressed against his tongue. Her back arched as he dragged the edge of his teeth over the sensitive flesh.

When her hands moved up his biceps and into his hair they left a tingle in their wake.

The spell began to build, the intensity of it discernable on the air, like heat from the ground on a hot day.

He pushed her back and climbed between her thighs, between those incredibly long legs. Her eyes were glazed and faraway as she gave herself over to Practice. As the vessel for the Talent, she'd weave the magic and her partner would drive the pleasure for the magic to ride through and be delivered.

Kissing up the inside of her thighs, his lips just barely skimmed over her heated pussy. From his vantage point he looked up the line of her body and watched her nipples darken and harden.

His hair skimmed over her legs and belly, her fingertips rested at his temples. He devoured every inch of her with avarice. With mouth and teeth and tongue, with fingertips and palms and the entirety of his body rubbing against hers.

Twenty-one years he'd wanted this. Wanted her under him and over him, wanted her around him. That would come soon. Forcing down the intensity of his need to be inside her, he went back to trailing licks and kisses up the backs of her legs and toward her core.

Spreading her to his gaze, the sight of her cunt, cocoa brown and glistening, swollen and ready, slammed into him. Certainly, he'd never needed anything more than to lean in and taste her.

Suddenly she sat up on a gasp. The room darkened.

"It's here."

The wall of magic they'd been weaving tighter wavered. Weakened. Fear replaced pleasure and the spell began to break down.

"Rhea, focus." Jax's voice was urgent. He felt her trying to regain control but it wasn't working. If she failed, they'd die and make the Nameless even stronger.

He pressed her back to the bed and kissed her hard, lining his cock up and pressing into her deep and hard.

"You're mine. I control your pleasure, Rhea. That thing does not get you. Now I'm going to fuck you like you've wanted me to for two decades. You got me?" His voice was a low growl in her ear and he felt her body respond, felt her magic stop wavering and begin to flow out again.

She was so tight and hot he didn't know how long he'd last. He wanted it to be hours, she felt so good around his cock. He knew he'd have to fuck her a few hundred times more before he got anywhere near sated with her.

Holding her wrists above her head, he thrust into her cunt relentlessly. Sweat trickled down his spine, his orgasm began to build at the base of his balls. She writhed beneath him, making soft sounds of whimpered pleasure around the spell she whispered.

Grinding his pubic bone into hers, he felt the swollen bundle of her clit. She rolled her hips up with a gasp and the Talent streamed from her, stronger. The room was no longer as dark and the stench had lessened. He moved his attention back to her, to making her come.

"Come for me, Rhea. Your pleasure is mine, give it to me." Leaning down, he took a nipple between his teeth and she thrust back at him, rubbing her cunt against him, straining against his body to get the friction on her clit.

He was so close his control hung by a thread as she arched and writhed, and suddenly a cry broke from her lips as her pussy clamped down on him. Orgasm claimed her and a last burst of magic overflowed from them both when his climax exploded from the head of his cock.

In the aftermath he collapsed against her, face buried in the crook of her neck. Her pulse pounded under his lips. He stayed, buried deep within her, her pussy still spasming around his cock, until he began to soften.

"Thank you." Her words were quiet.

He rolled to the side and looked at her. "It wasn't very finessed of me. Next time we'll make it better. I'll take my time. I only got the barest taste of your pussy." He grinned.

"Thank you for helping me focus my magic." Her lips were pursed, he couldn't tell if it was ire or she was trying not to laugh. "If you hadn't taken over like that it would have broken through."

She sat up and when he reached out all he got was air. Frowning, he watched her pull the robe back on and he got up to follow her outside onto the battlement.

The horizon was dark.

"It's still out there."

"Damn it."

"The wards here are as strong as we can make them. We need to move inland, continuing to strengthen them elsewhere."

"That's not going to work forever."

Rhea felt the cold regard of that darkness all the way down to her soul. "I know. We're going to have to face it in open battle before this is over."

"You aren't ready for that."

"Not right now, no." Turning, she went back inside.

"We should work together more after a break. Work on concentration. You've been gone for fifteen years. Your power is still so very strong, but you were unfocused. If you hadn't been as strong, it might have broken through."

Rhea nodded absently as she looked out over that dark horizon from her place near the bed. "Yes. And we should leave at first light tomorrow. Go to the next keep. And the next, to continue to strengthen the wards."

"It's stronger now."

She turned and faced him. He saw the fear shining in her eyes. "I know. The lives of the ones it took have made it stronger." She shook her head to clear it. "But it seems like there was something else too."

"Come back to bed. Let me love you slow this time." Jax reached out to touch her but she stepped away.

"Jax, there's to be no recreational sex here. We have a job to do. We Practice together but there's nothing to be gained with play."

He narrowed his eyes and stalked into her space but she didn't back up. "This isn't play, Rhea. I made a mistake then. A big one. But I aim to make it right between us."

His head dipped for a kiss but she put her hand on the center of his chest to hold him back. "There's nothing wrong between us, Jax." She stepped neatly away. "Now, I need to work."

He watched as she walked just outside the room and brought her bag back inside with her. Sitting on the bed, his eyes followed her movements as she sprinkled salt in the four corners of the room and came back to the center.

Eyes closed, she struck three wooden matches at once, the acrid scent of the sulfur harsh against his senses. She breathed it in and slowly breathed out again.

Her long body folded itself gracefully as she sat on the floor. Magic began to pulse around her. He felt it beat against his skin. Panicked at first, he relaxed and let it flow against his skin like a warm caress.

Rhea opened herself up and cast her consciousness out into the ether. It was the first time she'd done it in twelve years. The first few years on Earth she'd been able to but as her magic was drained away she'd lost the ability. Still, she kept herself tethered to Jax, felt his reassuring presence back on the other plane.

The Nameless was there, just outside her reach, in the corner of her vision. She held her place, conquering her fear of failing as she drew her power from the air. The Nameless gave her its regard and she felt it cold and dark. In response, her strength grew as she soaked up the energy on that plane and slowly let herself fall back into herself.

The light had paled. Long shadows played on the floors and walls and Jax lay there on the bed as he watched her.

"You were gone so long. I would have worried but your body was so relaxed. I felt you along my spine. I just knew you were all right." He swung his legs off the bed and went to her, holding out a hand to help her up.

Stiffness held her muscles and she hissed at the feeling as she stood. "I'm too old to sit on a hard floor for hours."

"I'll have a hot bath run for you, shall I?"

She began to refuse but changed her mind. A hot bath would help her muscles and enable her to relax before she ate dinner.

"Yes. Thank you. Please tell them I'll be in shortly. I just want to put my bag back in my room."

"You can sleep with me, you know. I'd like that."

She sighed. "Jax, this isn't going to happen. We're friends. Nothing more."

He snorted. "You keep telling yourself that, Rhea. When it finally happens between us, when the walls come down and it's more than Practice and it's real, it's going to be incredible. Just Jaac and Rhea, not to save the world, but just you and me. I'll wait for you to come around. It'll be delicious when you do." Winking, he turned and walked out into the hallway, whistling.

Pissed off, she slammed back into her suite, changed into a casual robe and tied her hair up before heading to the bathing chamber.

Jax smiled the whole time he arranged for her bath and their dinner. Oh he'd break down her defenses all right. He'd felt her as they Practiced, he knew what they shared was more than just magic to her.

* * * * *

The room that held the large tub was steamy and fragrant. Immediately, Rhea began to relax as the scent of coconut reached her. Mrs. Dakins taking care of her with a bit of kitchen magic. Smiling, she dropped her robe and stepped into the water.

She knew what had to be done. As she lay there, letting her muscles relax, she realized they'd have to call the population in the area surrounding the keep back to the capital where they'd be safe. Until they could get the Nameless under control it would simply be too dangerous to let them stay there.

After a long soak she went back into her room and changed, heading down to dinner.

She sat at the table and Jax pushed a glass in her direction. "Drink, you're bound to be dehydrated after this afternoon."

Nodding, she took several long drinks of the cool fruit juice and ate silently for a few minutes, refueling before speaking.

"We're going to have to call the people here back. Away from here and toward safety." She sat back before starting another course.

He looked concerned. "They aren't going to like that."

"The people here whose lives are in danger or the Council?"

"It's a political nightmare to try to get people to leave their homes like that. We got the wards back in place. Don't you think it's an overreaction to call them back?"

She blinked at him in disbelief. "Overreaction? Like those who died in Ra'Ken perhaps? Or those ten thousand four hundred and six who used to populate the entire western shore? You don't believe what you're saying, Jax. You can't. You felt it today. Those wards will hold, yes. For tonight, for the next week maybe. But if it comes back and pushes like it did today and we aren't here, what then?"

Savagely, she tore a piece of bread and used it to mop up the gravy on her plate. "Look, I know it's a political nightmare. I'm not doing this lightly. But I can't not make this recommendation, Jax. They have no protection once we go if these wards fail."

"They won't do it if he doesn't back you up." Sarai sat down at the table and began to eat.

"I can't make his choices for him. I can only make my own." Rhea stood and went to the sink to rinse off her plate.

Before she walked out of the room she turned and looked at him once more and was startled by the intensity in his eyes. "We should move to the next keep first thing in the morning. If we're to have them fall back to at least the next wards toward the capital, we need to get the orders out now."

She left without waiting for an answer.

"She's putting me in a difficult position." He looked up into Sarai's yellow eyes.

"She's wanting you to do the right thing, Jax. The only real difficulty is talking yourself around doing it. She's not..." Sarai broke off with a shake of her head.

"What? Tell me, Sarai. Surely you know I still care about her deeply."

"It's not mine to tell."

Chapter Three

ॐ

Rhea awoke as the sun rose. Her second morning back. Things should have been easy. Joyous even. A homecoming with people happy to see her, but no. She got ominous threats of death to tens of thousands, if not millions, and political undercurrents she felt but didn't understand completely.

Getting out of bed she went to the windows and threw them open to the morning air. It was then she saw the trails of people moving inland. Toward the capital. A sigh of relief broke from her.

Dressing quickly, she grabbed breakfast and went to the cars, where everyone was waiting to go. She saw Jax and nodded as she got in.

"Thank you for backing me up." She settled in and he sat beside her. Far too close for her peace of mind.

"It's only to Ma'ken. More wards there and no signs of weakening. And it's voluntary. Those who want to stay can do so. I sent home word last night and workers are in the city below helping those who wish to leave."

Reaching out, she squeezed his hand quickly, but the warmth of his skin radiated up her arm. She knew he'd taken a political risk and she was relieved he'd chosen the lives of their people over political expediency. Gods, how he got to her, even then, with such a silly thing. Only it wasn't silly. It was important and he thought so too.

Jax watched her as the miles passed. Her reaction when she realized he'd gone forward with the evacuation gave him hope. He'd broken through one more barrier.

As they drove, they spoke of their lives over the last fifteen years. She fascinated him. Her intelligence had grown and her knowledge of magic and the scientific foundations of Talent impressed him. After they'd stopped the Nameless, he planned to ask her to teach at the university with him. He thought she'd make an excellent teacher to the younger Practitioners. She had a way of speaking about magic that seemed so straightforward and uncomplicated. He liked that.

The next keep was inland several hundred miles and when they arrived after many hours' driving, Rhea sat forward in her seat. The horizon was dark. The air crackled with negative magics attempting to short-circuit the wards.

"Let's get inside and working right away. I think we made it not a moment too soon." Rhea practically jumped out as they came to a stop, and began to give quiet orders to the staff while Jax had their things carried inside.

This keep wasn't as old as the last. The location was remote but the wards were aided by the mineral deposits in the mountains that flanked the plateau the keep stood on.

She went up the stairs and headed into a room adjoining the Practice suite and he did the same.

Running the water for the cleansing, she poured the herbs and flowers into the water. Words as old as time left her lips as she stepped in and immersed herself and then stood, the water cascading down her body.

The robe was white, shot with silver thread. The silver magnified the magic. Her familial runes marked the edging of the silk. Her bare feet showed with each step toward the Practice room, where she knew Jax would be waiting for her.

Her heart quickened at the thought.

They could have Practiced anywhere, but Practice rooms were furnished and sanctified in a way that protected the people within as well as amplified the power to carry outward.

Jax watched as Rhea walked the four corners and opened the space. He felt the stagnant air and the oppressive feel of the Nameless flow outward as she worked. He appreciated her addition of the cleansing magic to ritual. Her hair was loose and still wet from her ritual cleansing. It slid around her shoulders as she moved. His hand tightened in the comforter on the bed as the sense memory of it floating against his skin hit him.

She turned and came to him and he saw the power shimmer against her flesh. A gasp broke through his lips as she dropped the robe and stepped to him.

Shaking his head, he held his hand out to stay her and went to her instead. "I want you standing," he murmured against her collarbone. "For now." He maneuvered her so that her back was to the bed and took a moment to breathe her in as she centered herself and opened herself to her Talent.

Magic began to flow out of her in a warm stream as her eyes closed and her lips parted. The spell wrapped around him, around his own Talent, and he dropped kisses over her neck and the hollow of her throat. His hands found her breasts and palmed her nipples. Those swollen points pressed into his touch and her magic intensified as he rolled and pulled, tugging them.

Her taste called out to him and he leaned down and flicked his tongue across first one nipple then the other, pressing her breasts together, moving back and forth rapidly. Her power rose, filling the room, the murmured words of the spell echoing outward.

Graceful hands slid up his biceps and into his hair, holding his head to her, taking strength in how he gave her balance, kept her from falling.

Bowled over by her effect on him, he fell to his knees before her. He didn't want to distract her then but he made a promise that after the spell was through he'd tell her how beautiful she was there. He looked up the line of her body to see her head tilted back, breasts high and proud—the curves of her body called to him to touch her, love her.

And so he did. He waited, letting his own Talent build until the timing was right for him to plunge it into hers. With that transfer established — the connection between them, their power mingled, emotion flowing between them — he brushed his hands up the silky skin of her legs. Up over the curves of her thighs, thumbs brushing against the neatly trimmed hair that shielded her pussy, and her hips rocked forward.

The seductive scent of her desire rose from her body in waves. Savage triumph roared through him. He'd conquer her bit by bit. Each time they Practiced together he'd break her defenses down more and more until she had no place left to hide from him.

Pushing her back onto the bed, he pulled her ass to the edge and stayed on his knees between her thighs. He had been rushed the last time he'd had the opportunity to taste her pussy and he wasn't going to be this time. He planned to take it slowly. Enjoy each and every fold of flesh.

His thumbs pulled her open and he stared his fill as he slid the pads up and down the wet lips of her sex, and her body squirmed even as her power expanded as her arousal rose.

Unable to resist any longer, he pressed a thumb inside her as he leaned in to take a long lick from perineum up to the swollen button of her clit. His body tightened as her taste sang through his system. His senses filled with her essence. Her pussy tasted like magic and he had to have more.

A twist of his wrist and two fingers pressed into her and a third tickled her anus while his tongue flicked, licked and teased her clit.

A ragged sob of need broke from her mouth and her magic swelled to such an extent he felt it hot against his skin. He was the channel so it could leave her and move outward. On the outer edge of his consciousness he felt the Nameless rise and press back. As her partner, it was his job to keep her focused on Practice, to build the medium — pleasure — on which she could deliver her spell with her Talent.

Shoving her thighs wider, he went back to eating her pussy and felt her gain control.

Damn it, she was so wet and hot. He held her juicy pussy to his mouth, serving himself of her body. Her breath caught, he knew she was close. He added a third finger and sucked her clit into his mouth, slightly grazing it with his teeth. Her back arched and a ragged moan came from her and a bass hum echoed as the burst of her climax powered her Talent and the Nameless was pushed back a bit more.

Standing quickly, he took his cock in his hand and slid into her slick, hot cunt in one thrust. Her inner walls fluttered and clenched around him as he hilted himself deep within her.

Her eyes came open and she reached out and grabbed his biceps. Pulling herself up, she took a long lick up the wall of his chest. The muscles leapt at her touch. His cock pulsed at the sharp bite of her nails as they dug into the flesh of his upper arms.

Because she was so tall, they fit there like that. Wrapping her long legs around his waist, her cunt opened more and he slid in even deeper.

"Fuck me," she slurred and her head dropped back, sable hair pooling down the curve of her back, breasts arched toward him so tantalizing he had to lean in to take a nipple between his teeth.

And then he began to thrust. Dragging himself almost all the way out of her body and then pushing back in, the wet embrace of her body nearly undoing him before he even got started.

Taking a deep breath, he focused and centered his power, sending it in a steady stream to her, aiding her even as he devoured her body. Over and over he thrust into her, his own pleasure gathering at the base of his spine and spreading outward, through every cell of his body with electric ferocity.

Her nipple beaded against his tongue as he undulated his hips, fucking into her hard and deep. A soft, needy cry whispered from her lips when he bit down. *Ah, she liked a little pain with her pleasure* — he smiled at the discovery. Tucking that away for the time he'd be able to love her without the pretense of Practice, he refocused on the task at hand.

Releasing her nipple, he grabbed her hair in one fist and pulled her mouth to his, breathing power into her as he tasted her lips. Their tastes mingled, the salty sweet tang of her pussy and the velvet taste of her lips, as her magic left them. His own magic accented the mélange of flavors, deep and rich. Her fingers tightened on his biceps and dimly he felt the Nameless stumble back even more.

Sucking her tongue into his mouth, he took one of her hands and slid it down to her pussy. Fingers entwined with hers, he found her slick clit and played over it and felt her inner walls respond, rippling around his cock.

As her orgasm began to build she felt it within her, felt it fill her up until she threatened to overflow. She tasted it — her desire of this man inside her — metallic on her tongue. The scent of it filled her nostrils but she pushed aside the panic and used it to add extra strength to her spell.

The Nameless was different here. Smug, for want of a better word. Oh she'd knocked it on its ass all right. But it wasn't banished like it should have been. Her Talent had re-knitted the wards where they'd weakened but there was something wrong that she couldn't quite put her finger on.

Better to think of that than how much she never wanted this moment with Jax buried balls-deep in her to end. Wet sounds of just how much she enjoyed the time with him echoed through the room. She didn't think she'd ever been so wet in her life as when he touched her.

His cock was thick and long and he filled her to the point of too much. So much the intensity of feeling rode right on the edge of pain, but it hurt just right. His hair swept forward and caressed the skin of her arms and over the sides of her breasts.

Wrapping his Talent inside of hers, she grabbed her climax and rode it, let it send her spell out into the air around them as her back bowed and the last words of her spell burst from her lips.

"Fuck..." Jax gasped as her cunt gripped him in climax and his balls pulled up tight and orgasm shot from his toes and scalp and out the head of his cock. Everything he had, everything he felt, poured into her.

After several long moments he let his weight carry them both to the bed and pulled her tight against his body while he regained his breath.

* * * * *

Rhea allowed herself the comfort of his body and the cadence of his heartbeat until she regained her senses. Exhausted from Practice and from the sex, she pulled healing breaths in through her nose and meditated while she let herself recharge.

After some minutes she sat up, still a bit shaky. A warm hand at the small of her back supported her. For a moment she despaired at how much she wanted to lean into him, let him help her. Take the comfort he offered.

But that was a dead end. He'd abandoned her once before and she had no intention of letting him do it again. She'd survived far worse than feeling a bit alone and she wouldn't trade a big heartache named Jax for a few days or weeks of comfort.

"There's something different." Standing, she reached for the robe she'd dropped and wrapped it around herself, shielding herself from him if only in a minor sense.

He felt no such compulsion and came to stand with her at the windows, still naked, half-erect cock teasing her senses. The heat of his body, the scent of his skin, married with her own scent, their sex hanging in the air, seduced her, and she leaned out to take a breath of fresh air.

"Different how?" Jax leaned against the windowsill and watched her through very alert eyes. An arrogant smile played at the corner of his lips. The bastard always was sure of his own allure.

She crossed the room to be away from him. "I don't know. It's not going away like it should." Shaking her head, she fought for the right words. "It could be that I'm not as powerful now but I don't think so. We generated a hell of a lot of power today and yesterday. It should have erased all weakness from the wards. Should have pushed the Nameless far, far away.

"And we did knock it on its ass, no doubt. But the wards are still weak. Even here with the mountains as an amplifier. It doesn't make sense."

"Let's return and report this to the Council. They should know what's going on."

Sighing, she turned and shoved her hair into a knot. "Fine. But in my opinion, we need to be moving along the entire borderlands to deal with these wards. This is our first line of defense. If it fails..." Rhea shrugged.

"All right. I agree with that assessment. But we'll need to get direction on that anyway. So let's go back and talk to them and then we'll be free to keep moving. And perhaps on our way back from the frontier wards we can strengthen the secondary wards and the ones around the capital." His eyes took note of her slightly shaking hands as she clutched the robe to her body. It didn't escape his notice that she'd practically leapt across the room when he sidled next to her. Oh yeah, she was going down. When she finally broke and let him in, he'd relish every moment.

Until then, though, they had to deal with a very real problem. Because she was more powerful now than she had been fifteen years before. Most Practitioners became more powerful with age so it wasn't like that was a surprise. But her perception that something was different with the Nameless was disturbing and he only hoped the Council listened to her because she was their big weapon. Most likely their only weapon.

"Let's go now. Not wait until tomorrow."

Her sense of urgency caused panic to flow through his system. He bowed his head. "Of course. You get cleaned up and I'll go get everyone ready to leave. If we drive straight through we can be back just after daybreak tomorrow. We'll leave most everyone at the halfway point so we can get right back to work when we finish with the Council."

"Thank you," she murmured and went back into the connecting room, closing the door gently behind herself.

Cleaning up quickly, she dressed and grabbed her bags and headed back downstairs.

She paused for a moment before she reached the bottom of the grand staircase. Jax stood in the doorway, directing people as they repacked the transports and readied to leave. His features were set in a hard line, dark hair pulled back from his face, hands on his hips. Lean hips, flat stomach, clever fingers. His skin was so hard and hot. A flush broke over her and her hand went to her throat as she devoured the sight of him.

His head snapped around and his gaze locked with hers. The hard line of his lips softened into a wicked smile. Oh he knew exactly what she was thinking. And he liked it. Even so, Rhea couldn't stop herself from smiling back at him and shaking her head as she finished taking the stairs.

As she walked toward Jax, someone immediately came to take her bags.

"I'll take you up on that promise in your eyes when we get back to D'ar." His voice, a silky undertone, caressed her senses. Sexy bastard.

"In your dreams." She snorted, walked outside and got into one of the transports.

Chuckling, he nodded to Sarai, who watched him from the other side of the yard.

* * * * *

The drive back to D'ar was quiet. Once they'd gotten away from the mountains, Jax had been able to get in contact with the Council and set up a meeting for first thing the next morning.

She dug in her bag and pulled out a black velvet pouch.

"What's that?" He nodded his head toward the pouch.

She looked at him, not even realizing he'd been watching her. "Tarot cards. I brought them back for Emmia. They're special. A reader, a woman with probably more magical ability than anyone I encountered on Earth, gave them to me three years ago. She told me I'd need them to see clearly. I have the feeling she meant now."

Rhea pulled down the small console and laid out a soft cloth. Taking a deep breath, she shuffled the deck over and over until it felt right. And then she laid out her own spread.

Nine of Swords—beware isolation. Reach out for help close at hand. She sighed.

Queen of Swords—survival. Reason. Seeker of justice and giver of wisdom. Also a woman who's been hurt and remains wary, sometimes to her detriment. *Okay, I'm getting it. Thank you, universe. Sheesh.*

Ace of Wands—a gift of beginnings. Ability to achieve goals. Reject inaction.

The Chariot—victory. And yet, a message to continue to seek answers and not turn away when puzzled or challenged.

Six of Cups—faced with memory. Be sure the memory does not control you or keep you from moving on.

She put her head back on the seat and closed her eyes. Yeah, she was getting the message. The real question was whether or not she could bear to make the right choices.

"Is it bad?" Jax asked softly, his fingertip trailing up her arm.

"No. Yes. Oh fuck, I don't know. I think it's more about me personally than this thing with the Nameless. Anyway." She sat back up and put the cards back in order before sliding the deck into its velvet bag. The purple cloth followed and both disappeared into her duffel.

She knew he felt her close up but thankfully he just shrugged instead of pressing. She might be tired but she knew he'd be back to the matter later on, he had a gift for knowing when her guard was down.

"Why don't you sleep a while? We'll get into the city at first light and won't have a lot of time before the Council meets. You need to rest."

She nodded and allowed him to wrap a blanket around her. She curled up in the seat and closed her eyes, thinking she wouldn't be able to sleep, but it found her quick enough and she fell into a dreamless rest.

* * * * *

Jax watched her as she slept, mesmerized by the rise and fall of her chest. Of the way her hair looked like midnight against her skin. One of her hands was open just beneath her cheek. In that one unguarded moment he saw a bit of the Sa'Rhea he'd known in their youth.

When he'd felt her eyes on him as she came down the stairs, his whole body had come alive. Turning and meeting her eyes, seeing her flush and the hand at her throat, he'd known he'd win. Known that eventually he'd break down those defenses and she'd let him into her heart again.

Because Rhea wanted him. Not as a Practice partner but as a woman wants a man. He still affected her as deeply as she him and he held onto that like a life preserver. He would have her once and for all and he'd spend the rest of eternity making her glad she let him in.

But for the time being, he'd continue to slowly seduce her. And try to shield her from the political shitstorm that brewed back home. His advice to evacuate had not been met with a lot of support at the bottom of the table. Luckily, he knew his father would always back him and, surprisingly, Rhea's father had backed her as well. But her paternal uncles would prove troublesome, Jax knew.

He worried that she'd be attacked. That some would say she wasn't strong enough anymore. Although what good that would do them, even if it were true, he couldn't see. Rhea was their last, best hope.

Still, protectiveness edged through him as he put her head in his lap and ran his fingers through her hair, giving in to his need to touch her.

* * * * *

Rhea awoke to Jax's voice in her ear. "We're here, angel. We've got about an hour before the Council will convene so they're dropping us off at my house. You can clean up and get breakfast and we'll walk over together. Sarai can go visit her family or stay here, it's up to her. All right?"

Rhea realized she'd been sleeping curled in his lap and sat up slowly. She didn't want to go to his home. She felt off balance with him enough as it was. But her home was a ways from the Council Chambers and from the looks of it his was right across the square.

"Swanky."

He looked at her oddly.

She laughed and got out of the car, stretching. "Swanky means really nice. Richly appointed."

He grinned. "Ah. Well, thank you then." He pointed the way up the steps of a very grand townhouse.

The double doors opened up and Rhea froze for a moment.

"Sa'Rhea, it's good to see you again at last."

Heart in her throat, Rhea looked up into the face of Paul and Jax's paternal grandmother.

"Katai." Unable to say anything else, she went up the steps quickly and into the embrace of a woman who'd been her biggest ally in the Sarne family. The only one who'd tried to help her with Paul.

Katai drew her inside and they sat on a small bench in the front hallway. Jax stood with Sarai and they watched Rhea weep. Jax knew his grandmother and Rhea were close but he apparently didn't know the half of it.

"Sweet girl, I've missed you. Stop your tears now. It's over." Katai kissed the top of Rhea's bowed head and patted her back slowly. With her other hand she passed Rhea a handkerchief to dry her tears.

After some time, Rhea sat up and looked into the older woman's face. "I can't believe you're here."

Katai laughed. "I'm not that old!"

Rhea blushed. "I didn't mean that! I meant I was sure you'd be away in the Eastern Mountains, where it's safe."

"She refused to go. She lives here with me."

Rhea turned to look at Jax, surprised. "Really?"

He laughed then. "What? I love my grandmother. Why shouldn't she live here with me?"

"It was that or with my son and daughter-in-law." Katai's voice made it clear what she thought of that idea. And Rhea couldn't blame her. Her former in-laws were obsessed with position and rank. Their home was the kind of place one could never feel comfortable in.

"I've had some breakfast prepared and a hot bath drawn for you in the guest suite, Sa'Rhea. There are clothes there for you as well. Sarai, darling, it's wonderful to see you too."

Sarai hugged the older woman and stood back at Rhea's side.

"I'll go freshen up and be down in a bit. It's good to have you back again, Katai. We'll visit when all of this is over." Rhea pressed a kiss to Katai's forehead.

"Let me show you where the guest suite is." Jax moved to the stairs.

"Rhea, I'm going to go visit my family for a few hours. I get the feeling that we'll be leaving again after you meet with the Council. I want to try to convince them to head east." Sarai's face showed concern but her words were calm.

Rhea nodded. "Good idea. I'll see you in a bit."

Jax led her up the stairs and down a quiet hallway. He opened the door at the end and stepped aside. "This is it. The bathroom is through there. I...I hope seeing my grandmother hasn't upset you too much. I thought you'd be happy to see her. She's always spoken so fondly of you."

Rhea touched his arm softly. "No, it's fine. Thank you. Katai is very special to me. She was the only one who listened to me. The only one who tried to help with..." She shook her head once, hard, and stopped speaking.

"With Paul. I'm sorry I wasn't here."

"Me too." She stepped into the room and closed the door softly.

Chapter Four

ဢ

The two of them entered the Council Chambers right as the session began. Rhea walked to the head of the table with such ease that, if Jax hadn't known her, he'd have guessed she'd done it every day for years.

He took his own chair a few down from hers.

"I demand to know why you've ordered an evacuation! You'll cause panic in the streets. Chaos!" her uncle Arta shouted in a shrill voice.

Rhea took a sip of her coffee and leaned in. "The Nameless is stronger than I've ever seen it. The wards are weakened significantly at both keeps we visited. For now they'll hold. But until we figure out just why..."

"You'll cause panic!"

Rhea sighed. "Let. Me. Finish." She looked to her father and he nodded once, sharply. "As I was saying, the citizens are in danger and will continue to be. We need to figure out why the Nameless is able to wield so much power. And then we need to beat it back and defeat it. *Then* those people can go home."

"Maybe you're not up to the job." Her other uncle, Stephen, said this with a smirk.

"You'd better hope you're wrong, Stephen. Because you sure as hell aren't up to it."

The room silenced as they all turned to stare at Rhea's father, Timus.

Jax's father nodded and soon most of the room nodded with him.

Rhea told them all about what she'd felt and that she worried about the difference in how the Nameless seemed to attack the wards.

"We believe that the population at the across the borderlands should be pulled inland toward the capital, where the wards are much stronger. Rhea and I will move to the central keep next." Jax sent her a supportive look that she appreciated greatly.

"We'll send out a voluntary evacuation notice and set up camps at the base of the mountains. I've also called up some of our other Practitioners to head to the keeps farthest out to work on the wards there. It can't hurt and it may help. For now, we'll keep those we've sent eastward there. But it may be that we send for the strongest to help in the end." Timus looked at his daughter and she sighed.

"The end is coming. I can feel that much." And the truth was, Rhea felt that someone at the table was betraying them but she couldn't figure out why or how. But the way the Nameless seemed to know her and the way it attacked the wards, changing its focus each time in direct reaction to what they'd been doing, was as if it somehow had inside knowledge. That shook her.

"Then let's be sure we're the ones standing."

She nodded at her father. "If that's all, Jaac and I need to be on our way."

"You can't just leave now, son! At least have dinner with us before you go." Jax's mother's voice still drove Rhea insane all these years later.

"We can have tea now but we've got to leave within two hours. This is urgent, Mother. Rhea, would you like to come?"

It took all she had to hold back a snort of derision. "Uh, no. Thank you though. Just come by my home when you're finished. I'll go and get some supplies at the market while you're out."

And Jax watched as she left, back straight, and utterly alone.

* * * * *

But she wasn't lonely. She walked out into the city she'd once loved and caught a trolley down to the public market.

And there it was. The smell of the food stalls, the calls of the different merchants. More than the sky or her house, it was this that made her feel like she was home.

She shopped the stalls for the different supplies she'd need as they went to the different keeps. Sesame seeds, yellow to enhance sex magic, and black to dispel evil. Elder leaves to scatter around the Practice room to ward off evil. She bought henna to stain her hands for protection. Lastly, she found thistle to protect against dark magic attacks.

She walked back to her house through the teeming streets of the city and marveled to be there. Was overjoyed to hear the language of her birth, see the style of clothing she'd yearned for, the colors that indicated caste and rank.

Jax waited for her at her door and without many words they moved into the back of the house to open a rift that would get them half a day's drive closer to the next keep. They'd left most of the other people and all vehicles but one at the halfway point. They'd be prevented from getting any closer by the protective magics around the keep but it meant an entire day's drive would be split in half and they wouldn't be so exhausted by the time they arrived.

And they traveled for the next ten days. Shoring up the wards when they could, falling back when they had to. More and more they ended up sending any local populations toward the capital.

At each keep they came upon, the wards were weakened. Not so much broken as thinned, even brittle in some places. Each time they Practiced they had to approach the strengthening of the wards differently. It was as if the

Nameless had taken on human sensibilities, and that scared Rhea to the marrow in her bones.

Worse, Jax kept at her, worming his way back into her life. Their magic intensified each time they Practiced together. He was always *there*. Helping her, listening to her talk about magic, telling her what had happened in their world since she'd been gone. He'd put himself into her life in a way that she was suddenly unable to imagine it without him. And that was dangerous. Her defenses against him were weak. They weakened more by the day and it was harder and harder to remember why she resisted to begin with. The idea of sleeping next to him every night was appealing, she admitted it to herself. Letting him touch her outside of Practice... Gods she wanted him to kiss her, hug her, caress her. It drove her insane and she knew he knew it, which made her even more crazy.

But the situation became more and more dire and they Practiced pretty much daily, which only made her want him more. His damnable, smug attitude and the knowing look on his face only agitated her more. That and resisting him when she knew that ultimately it was futile.

* * * * *

High Plains Keep was one of the newer fortresses. Built when Rhea's father was a boy, it filled the gap between the mountain keep they'd been at just before and the next one, five hundred miles to the east.

It sat atop a flat-topped mountain that overlooked the valley below. When they first arrived it felt peaceful. They'd eaten a late dinner and had gone to bed to recharge before the next day, when Rhea and Jax would Practice at dawn.

But Rhea had awoken several times during the night, feeling the sense of darkness in the air spreading, getting heavier and heavier. Finally she gave up and went down to the cozy sitting room where the fire still burned.

"I thought I'd find you in here."

Rhea turned to see Jax walk into the room. He wore loose sleep pants with an untied robe over them and no shirt. The hard, tanned flesh on his chest taunted her. She picked up a mug of tea to keep from reaching out to him.

Still, he sat next to her, not quite touching but very close. Close enough to smell his skin.

He nodded his head in the direction of the velvet bag that held her tarot deck. "I've never been one to read the cards. My mother used to. But she hasn't...in a long time."

"Since her precious Paul was killed?" The depth of anger in her voice surprised them both.

But Jax just nodded. "Yes. She's sort of given up since then."

"Yeah, because she didn't have any other children or anything. Oh and because she did everything she could to help me rein your brother in, bring him back from the brink. Oh wait! No she didn't. She ignored it like they all did."

"Whoa!"

Her teeth clicked together as she locked her jaw. Standing she nodded once. "I'm going back to bed."

He moved quickly, blocking her exit. "Why don't you tell me? It's eating at you. You hold it to yourself like some kind of fucking millstone. Or do you like the misery too much, Rhea?"

She froze. "How dare you? Where were you, Jaac? Where were *you*? Too busy fucking your way through co-eds at the university, I'd wager. While your precious mother and father played blind. Don't you judge me!"

"Then tell me, damn it! I know I failed you but I don't know the whole story. Stop holding it so fucking close it's like a lover."

"You think you're ready for it, Jaac?"

"Jaac? What happened to Jax?"

"You can't have it both ways." Her voice was flat and he narrowed his eyes.

Grabbing her upper arms, he moved her back to the couch, careful not to hurt her. "We're going to do this once and for all." He got on all fours over her, his arms caging her.

Glaring up at him, she clamped her lips shut stubbornly.

"I've got all night, Rhea. But you know you want to tell me. Unburden yourself. Let me in! I'm not trying to have it both ways. I'm trying to understand. Won't you please help me understand?"

Suddenly it all uncoiled inside her gut. The burden was too heavy and she wanted done. "The first few years with Paul were wonderful. He was young of course, immature, but he loved me. He was my Practice partner and I was stronger. That was a fact. He knew it when we got married. He said it didn't bother him. But he began to start these stupid, petty fights. The jealousy," she closed her eyes a moment, "he began to work on his magic all the time. And I encouraged it because it made him stronger and it seemed to give him a goal. But it didn't last.

"The elixir started first. He told me he needed it to be as strong as I was. But it didn't make his Talent stronger. It never does. The elixir, the fights, his behavior, it all got worse, and money started disappearing from our accounts until I had to begin to freeze and hide things. I put him on an allowance. I became his mother. Certainly more than yours was ever willing to. Gods, your mother was fucking worthless."

He winced at the vehemence in her voice but didn't try to deny it. He knew she wouldn't lie. Saw the truth, *knew* the truth, even if he didn't know the specifics.

"He'd lose his temper when he'd run out of money. I begged your parents for help. They ignored it. Said it was a phase. Advised me to downplay my own Talent to help his esteem. Like I could! The Nameless could just walk right in because your brother couldn't handle that his wife was more powerful. Even when I went to them, my face bruised and swollen from one of his insane, elixir-fueled beatings, they pretended it wasn't a problem.

"So yes. Your brother stole from me. Stole from my family to buy more elixir and pay for whores. And I caught him stealing those scrolls! He sneered at me, taunted me that he was going to sell them to set up a house for his newest tart. I sent out a spell to stop him but he sent one out too. It was unwieldy and I tried to stabilize it – *to save his life*! But it...he..." A sob broke through and he moved back, touching her softly, but she shook her head. "He tried to kill me. I counteracted his spell with my own to try to save him and he used the scrolls on me and all the power...it just exploded on him, destroying the scrolls and killing him."

"Why didn't you tell them?"

She blinked back tears. "I *did*! I told the magistrate when I was brought before him. Your parents denied that I'd ever come to them for help. That night, in jail, that's when...Ra'Ken...the whole city...my mother and my brother and sisters. If Emmia hadn't come to help when she'd heard I was arrested, she'd be gone too."

"My parents denied it?"

"Yes. That day in the square, you were there, Jaac! I tried to tell them all but my father handed down that sentence and sent me away. They never tried to help me. Not when they could have saved Paul, not when they could have saved me."

He'd asked for it. Bullied her to tell him, and the truth of it was worse than he'd imagined. Guilt and shame at his family's behavior flushed his skin. His own part in the mess coiled low in his gut. She was alone and he'd done nothing to help her. His hands clenched and he forcibly relaxed. If his brother had been alive, he'd have beaten the hell out of him for harming Rhea in such a way. His parents would have to be dealt with as well. He didn't relish that but it had to happen. Especially as Rhea would be with him. "Oh gods. Rhea, I...I don't even know what to say. I'm sorry. I failed you. And my parents, how could they do that? It's like they're strangers to me."

She stood up and tried to leave but he grabbed her arm and pulled her back. Pulled her tight against him, needing her more than he'd ever needed her before. Wanting to establish their connection and claim her right then. "Where are you going?"

"To bed."

"Not without me, you're not. You've resisted me long enough. I am not Paul."

"No you aren't. He married me. You ran away. When I needed you..." She shook her head, refusing to finish the sentence.

"When you needed me I wasn't there. Is that what you were going to say?"

"I'm tired. I need to sleep."

"No. Damn you. I made a mistake. I wanted you too much. I had to stay away. Each time I saw you, even after you'd married him, I wanted you. I didn't care that you were his. I had to stay away. I didn't know he'd fallen so far. It doesn't matter now. I can't change the mistakes I made. I can only make the future better."

"Fine. Now let me go."

"No. You want me, Rhea. As much as I want you. Damn you, I *love* you. I always have. We have a second chance. Do you know how rare that is?"

"My body wants you. You've always been able to make me want you like that. But I'm smarter now. I can use my head and not my heart. So fuck me, Jaac. Let's go." She pulled her gown up over her head and stood there, naked, skin glistening in the light of the fire.

He knew what she was doing and it wouldn't work. She thought if she could make it seem like it was just a quick fuck he'd back off or be hurt and she'd protect herself that way. "It's not going to work, Rhea. Don't mock it. It's more than that and you know it."

"You gonna control my feelings now, Jaac?" She prayed he couldn't hear the tremor in her voice. She held her hands in fists at her sides, hoping he couldn't see them shaking. She couldn't afford for him to see how much she craved his touch. Needed him not just in bed but in her life.

He narrowed his eyes and used his body to push her back into the room, kicking the door shut behind him. "I'm going to control something. But you and I both know what your feelings are. You may not like it, but you love me. And by the time the sun comes up you're going to say it. I've taken it easy on you, knowing you had to work through it your own way. I gave you time to come to me but I'm done waiting now. The time for patience is over and the time for reckoning has arrived, Rhea. I aim to take what's mine."

The look he bore was feral, intense and possessive. Instinctively she took a step back, even as her hand went out to touch his face. He leaned into her caress a moment before sliding out of his robe and shucking his pants.

He stood there, gloriously naked, cock hard. His chest moved with shallow breaths as his pupils enlarged until black was all she could see. Reaching back, he pulled his hair free and it fell around his shoulders and down his back. A tide of barely leashed masculine sexuality rushed from him, knocking the breath from her lungs and bringing her hand to her chest above her heart.

"I know. I feel the same way every time I look at you." He circled her, his body just close enough that she felt his heat, still not quite touching hers. "So beautiful. Still young, in the prime of your life." He reached out then, a fingertip trailing down the line of her spine. "I can't wait to see what you'll look like in middle age. When you're sixty or seventy and your hair finally begins to silver…gods, you'll be stunning. I want to grow old with you, Rhea."

She didn't want his words to make her feel this way, damn it!

He chuckled. "It rankles you, doesn't it? Knowing I can see right into your soul."

"Don't be so fucking sure of yourself!" She spun to face him. "You're a pretty face and a nice hard cock. Don't make more of it than it is."

Quicker than she expected, his hand shot out and cupped her neck, pulling her to him. His lips met hers in a kiss that devoured, devastated. Her body was electrified by contact with his.

Their magic rose, warm, thick like honey. His cock burned against the flesh of her stomach, that sensitive place where thigh met body. Pre-cum seeped from the head, first hot then cool against her skin.

His tongue swept into her mouth like it belonged there. He didn't just kiss her, he *possessed* her. Dominated her. Pulled emotion from her despite the fact she didn't want to give it to him. There was no place to hide from him with his hands on her, his lips over hers, tongue sliding sensuously against the inside of her mouth.

Desire drowned her but anger rose too. Anger that he could make her react to him even though she didn't want to. She wanted to stay behind the walls she'd erected. No one could hurt her there. Exposed now, in his arms, she was raw and open and vulnerable.

She tried to push away and he broke the kiss but continued to collar her throat with a gentle hand. "You can't hide yourself from me, Rhea. I *know* you. I'm not letting you go. I'm not going away."

His gaze bored into hers, the intensity of emotion panicked her.

"I've got you on the ropes, Rhea. Just give in to me."

His arrogance rankled but at the same time comforted. He did know her, in a way that no one else ever had. But he took it away. Took that knowing, that comfort of being known, and left her alone.

"You left me." Planting her palm against his chest, she pushed away from him. "You know me so fucking well? You walked away from that! You don't deserve me."

She bent to grab her nightgown but she found herself tackled, her back on the soft rug in front of the hearth, his body holding hers with his weight.

"I was a fool! But I've paid for it every day of the last two decades, knowing you were in Paul's bed every night and then knowing I'd failed you. I thought about you on Earth, wondered if another man got to hold you and love you the way I wanted to. I was young and stupid."

She tried to get out from beneath him but the subtle move of her hips brought him into the cradle of her thighs. His cock slipped between slick labia and pressed against her gate. She felt the throb, throb, throb of the head as it rested just inside her.

"I can't trust you." Her voice was soft. He heard the fear in it.

Slowly, giving her a chance to refuse, he pressed into her pussy, watched her lips part and her eyes widen.

"I'm not that scared boy anymore. From the moment you opened that door a month ago and I walked back into your life have I let you down once? Stop trying to find ways to keep me out, Rhea."

A soft grunt came from her lips when he hilted fully within her. Her thighs widened and the magic flowed again between them.

"I want to look into your face when you come. When we Practice, there's always the magic there. You hold it between us like a screen, a mask. But I want you to find release while looking at me. Know I'm the one who's making you feel that way."

"Shut up and fuck me," she murmured, rolling her hips. Her fingernails dug into the hard muscle of his shoulders as her legs moved to encircle his waist.

She meant to try to keep him out with sex. Smoke and mirrors. Thought she could toss a fuck at him and he'd forget about the rest. He saw her ploy ten miles away. Still, he'd let her get comfortable, and enjoy it all the more when he sprang the trap.

"Is that so, Rhea? You want me to fuck you?" He underlined the sentence with a particularly hard thrust. Her breasts bounced and he grinned. "I like that. I like that a lot."

His lips skimmed over her collarbone, tongue flicking over the hollow of her throat. Her taste, sweet and heady, slammed into his system. She was integral to him in ways he couldn't even articulate. He just felt them, knew she was absolutely essential to his body, soul and heart. And he'd been showing her that, telling her that, and what lay between them at that moment was the final chapter. He absolutely knew he'd win because he loved her. He may not deserve her, she was right about that, but he loved her and he'd spend every moment of the rest of his life to work to deserve her.

His mouth slid over the skin of her chest and down to first one nipple and then the other. She arched with a soft cry as the edge of his teeth scraped over the sensitive tip. Round and round his tongue circled her nipple, teasing it harder and harder as he took his time fucking into her hard and deep.

He resisted the lure of taking her fast. He wanted to thoroughly win her over and so he'd take his time.

When he pulled out her half-lidded eyes sprang open and she tried to reach him to pull him back into her. "Jax!"

"Oh no, Rhea. I have plans for your pretty cunt right now. I'll fuck you again very soon." His eyes rolled up to meet hers as he licked a trail down her stomach, keeping her thighs wide open with his body between them.

Settling down between her legs, he pressed her knees up and out, spreading her wide open to him. "Now this is breathtaking." Her pussy lay pink and glistening wet to his eyes. To his mouth.

A mouth he lowered to her humid flesh. A bright flash of her Talent burst through the room, through him, riding his spine. In their youth there'd been a hint of this raw connection between them and their magic, but nothing at that level. When they'd Practiced together it had been different, controlled and channeled. Now it was just them, and the wild sex magic between them crackled and slithered through them both. Her control wavered and he saw victory within reach.

The taste of her, sticky sweet with the tang of her musk, seduced him, shot straight to his cock. He speared into her gate with his tongue. She writhed beneath him, attempting to roll her hips, but he held her immobile as he ate her pussy with abandon.

Wetter and wetter, her body heated. The scent of her drove him crazy, burned into his senses until all he had was her. There was room for nothing else in him. "Hold yourself open for me, Rhea. Wide. I want to lick every bit of you I can get."

With shaky hands, she moved quickly to comply. The flat of his tongue pressed up through the folds of her pussy and over her clit. Her entire body shuddered and a groan from deep in her gut broke from her. Beneath the pressure of his tongue, her clit swelled and hardened. Slowly but with insistent rhythm, he swirled the tip of his tongue around her clit and then, with a featherlight touch, flicked the underside of it over and over.

Her thighs began to tremble and her moans became breathy. He let go of one of her legs and pressed two fingers inside her, hooking them to stroke over her sweet spot.

She nearly sat upright the first time he did it but settled back, arched and moving restlessly under his mouth and hands. He briefly entertained making her beg and confess she loved him but he was too greedy for her climax and pushed her over, saving her confession for later.

Her hands gripped his head, fisting in his hair as the air whooshed from her in climax. Honey, scalding hot and delicious, rained on his hand and lips.

Riding it out, his mouth worked on her until she finally relaxed back against the carpet with a sated sigh.

Crawling up her body, he hovered over her lips. "Don't go anywhere just yet, Rhea."

An eye cracked open and she allowed herself a small smile at his audacity and in appreciation of his talented mouth. "Not going anywhere. My legs don't seem to be working just now anyway."

One of her hands snaked down and grasped his cock. He was so hard he throbbed in her hand and hissed at the sensation as she squeezed gently.

She shoved him onto his back and rolled onto him. Her hair curtained around their faces and he leaned up to touch his lips to hers.

"Have your wicked way with me, why don't you?"

"What a lovely idea." Pressing kisses across the edge of his jaw, she reveled in the way the bass of his groan vibrated through her. He smelled damned good—like magic and masculinity and sex on legs. It made her wet anew just breathing him in.

His pulse beat steady under her lips as they skimmed over the hollow just below his ear. She loved the way the prickle of his beard tickled her lips. He was so big beneath her, even though they'd both been angry she'd never feared him, always knew he'd treat her carefully, even as he pushed at her emotionally.

His powerful torso flexed between her thighs as she kissed, licked and nibbled down his chest. There was something incredibly sexy about having such a big, bad man under her power.

His magic created spice on his skin and her tongue tingled as she licked over the jumping muscles of his abdomen, scraping her teeth over him.

"You feel so good, baby. Your hair is like silk. Your lips, gods, I've never felt anything so fucking good in my life. Suck my cock, Rhea. Please."

Shimmying further down his body, she settled between his thighs. She took her time looking at him. Flat stomach, narrow hips that flared out to wide shoulders. His hair spread out around his head. Damn he was gorgeous.

Leaning down, she whipped her head, bringing the caress of her hair over his cock. He gasped and she looked up into his eyes, smiling as she reached out and grabbed his cock.

Moving her head, she took a long lick from his balls to the weeping slit of his head. The salty taste of him echoed through her senses. In the times they'd Practiced together, she hadn't been able to go down on him. It seemed decadent to be able to take her time with him, to taste him, drive him up slow and steady.

Her mouth moved down over his cock, taking him in as far as she could and backing off again. She did this over and over, feeling the change in his body, the electric hum of his magic as his pleasure moved toward peak. This kind of sex, with a partner who was matched magically and Talent-level-wise, was incredible. And she'd only ever experienced it with him. It was like all the other times she'd been with men were watery shadows of what she and Jax were together.

And that terrified her.

Pulling off him, she took a gentle nibble just below the crown and licked her way toward the root until she reached his balls. Her fingernails gently scored that sensitive flesh and he hissed, his balls drawing tight against his body. Her tongue gave just the right amount of pressure as she licked over him and then found her way back up his cock and around the crown.

She didn't want to think about how he made her feel. Didn't want to think about how good it was to give him pleasure, about how much it meant to her that she affected him so deeply even after all the years that had passed between them.

Sure hands slid up her arms and one moved to hold her neck, collaring her throat as she took him fully into her mouth again. He arched and thrust, meeting her. She knew his control was whisper-thin at that point as the muscles in his belly tightened to hold back.

"Stop, gods, stop. I want to come inside of you," he gasped out at the last moment, pulling her back by the shoulders.

She moved up to lie beside him but he stood quickly, picking her up and carrying her to the couch. He sat and dropped her astride him. "I want to watch you rise and fall on my cock. My own personal goddess."

Gaze locked on his, she reached back and guided the head of him to her gate and slowly sank down. There weren't words for what it felt like to be filled by him like that and so she sighed, replete.

One of his hands found her breast, palming the nipple, and the other slid up into her hair and pulled her down to his lips for a kiss. Nimble fingers rolled and pulled her nipple until she gasped softly and his tongue invaded her mouth. Hot and slick, he chased, teased and seduced hers.

Seeking to even the playing field, she pulled up and nearly off his cock and then pressed back down with a swivel.

Breaking the kiss, he looked deep into her eyes. "Rhea, you mean everything to me. I've been empty all these years. I tried to fill it with work, with faceless, nameless women, with power. Nothing completes me but you. Right here, right now, even with the danger on the horizon, I am home. In you, I am a full person. Give yourself to me. Let yourself love me, Rhea. I won't run this time. I swear to you on my life. You can trust me. You know that."

The passion in his voice made her breath catch even as the sensation of his cock slicing through her cunt deepened the intensity of the moment. He invaded her physically and emotionally—a dual assault, and she was weak. He'd worn her down over weeks and weeks of being with him when they Practiced and on the road—reforging the closeness they'd had in their youth only with more depth born of decades of learning from mistakes.

The words were there, burning the back of her throat. Her heart filled, her eyes brimmed with tears. Fear froze her in that moment.

"Let me love you," he whispered softly, his lips just above hers, his kiss deceptively gentle and soft. But he was there and she was in a corner emotionally and she had nothing left to hold him out with. He had proved she could trust him. He'd been at her back the whole time. Taken risks with his own power, his own family, to back her up time and again with the evacuation orders. She'd been evasive and rude and cold over and over and he'd still been there afterward. He hadn't left. He still remained. Constant.

And therein lay his allure. More than his physical beauty or the thick cock deep in her pussy—it was constancy that he provided, something she craved deeply.

Her mouth opened to speak and he watched her lips but he didn't say anything else. He didn't want to push her that last inch and she knew it. She also knew he'd never give up until she let him back in her heart. And the fear melted into something else, something deeper.

"Damn you."

He chuckled softly. "I got you. I'm under your skin, little lady, and I'm not letting go. So give in already."

"Gods, you're an arrogant bastard." She slid down on him harder and rolled her hips forward, smiling savagely when he groaned. "We've got each other, I think. Gods help me."

"I'm really close to coming here, Rhea. Will you just admit you love me already so I can? And we can go to sleep for a few hours and fuck again once or twice before Practicing again." His voice broke and she watched a bead of sweat break out on his temple and slide down his face and neck.

"So fucking sexy." She leaned in and licked from the place where neck met shoulder to his temple, tasting salt and magic.

His laugh was genuine and cocksure and suddenly it was easy to say because she felt it. Totally unfettered. "I love you, you bastard."

He froze a moment and then yanked her mouth down to his, kissing her with a ferocity she hadn't seen from him before. The hand on her breast moved to her clit and he flicked it while moving his hips to thrust back into her cunt.

Her breath was his breath. Her pleasure was his pleasure. It flowed between them hot and sticky until a mingled cry burst from both as climax broke. He came deep inside her body as she climaxed around him.

Cries of pleasure were swallowed and fed back as their mouths remained locked in that kiss. Her magic, freed by her admission of love, flowed out of her in a rush and filled the room. Sensing it, he carried it and it drained from the keep out into the air.

Breaking the kiss, she looked around. "Is it me or does it feel lighter?"

He picked her up and strode toward the door and up the stairs to her bedroom, not stopping until they were both in bed, under the blankets.

"It feels lighter for a hundred reasons but yes, I think we've cranked out quite a bit of magic tonight. That kind of wild magic may have been so effective because it wasn't what the Nameless expected. And I love you too, you shrew." He planted a kiss on the tip of her nose and snuggled her into his side.

"So romantic."

Caught by surprise, he laughed. "It's a good thing you're so beautiful and hot in the sack or all that sarcasm would turn people off."

She smiled in the dark. "Yeah, good thing. Now shut the fuck up and go to sleep, beefy, we have work to do in the morning."

Chapter Five

ℬ

Rhea's eyes fluttered open as her body rocketed into extreme pleasure. Sitting up, she found Jax nestled between her thighs, mouth on her pussy. His hair spread over her thighs like a blanket.

She let herself fall back to the mattress. Let herself go, be free to enjoy what he offered. It felt almost as good as his tongue on her clit.

After she came, he kissed his way up her belly and found her mouth, where she received him with joy. When she tried to push him back and grab his cock he batted her hands away playfully.

"We've got to work in about half an hour. Save it for then. I just woke up and you were in my arms and I had to taste you." He moved so that she was nestled against him, his heart beating sure and steady in her ear.

"Well, I'm not complaining."

"Good. I was worried."

"That I'd complain? Lookie here, beefy, I complain, it's what I do. But I'm not gonna turn away your mouth on my pink parts any time soon."

He laughed and stole a quick kiss. "Well, I meant I was worried that perhaps you'd be sorry about last night."

She sighed and spoke to the wall of his chest rather than look into his face. "I should feel sorry. But I don't. And I suppose that makes me feel guilty. And I feel guilty that I don't feel guilty."

"Angel, I love you but I have no idea what you're talking about." One of his hands stroked through her hair.

"All of those years I thought about you. I did love Paul, truly I did. Even at the end when he was violent and intoxicated and had turned into another person. But I wished for you. Sometimes I'd dream of you. Worse, he'd be making love to me and your face would be there. I wasn't totally his. I've often wondered if he knew that."

"Can I look at you, please? I want to see your face."

Nodding, she let him move her back. She looked up into those deep midnight eyes and his masculine beauty made her pulse speed.

"My brother loved you. And if I know you, and I think I do, you gave your all to him. You stuck with him until the very end. Even as he tried to kill you, you tried to save him. Rhea, I'm not sorry I was on your mind, but I am sorry I wasn't there to help. I can't change that. I stayed away because I wanted you so much. I would have seduced you in a heartbeat and it would have destroyed my brother, and you as well because that's not who you are."

"The guilt over that is gone now. After a time," she shrugged, "I accepted my hunger for you even as I knew I was the very best wife I could be to your brother."

"And now we're finally together where we should have been all along. If I hadn't gone away you wouldn't have been exiled. It's my fault."

Rhea sat up and sprang out of bed. "Are you only with me out of guilt? Because I don't need your guilt. What happened made me into a stronger person. I understand what's important and that I've got to fight for it. I wouldn't be this person today if we'd been together. I don't want your pity, Jaac."

He followed, backing her against the wall. "Jaac huh? What happened to Jax? I thought you were done trying to hold me out. I'm with you because I love you. I have always loved you. Even now I want to be inside you. I want to touch you every moment of the day. When I'm not with you I'm thinking of you. Sleeping in a room just feet away from you these last weeks has been torture. I want to marry you. Start a family with you. Even if you are a very prickly woman."

"Marry me? Beefy, your family…well, I've been there and done that and I'm not in any hurry to do it again. Except for Katai, who is marvelous. Why don't we take it slow? You can start with the being inside me part and we can maybe talk about the marriage stuff in a year or so. You can have the milk for free any old time you like."

Confusion marred his features.

"It's a saying on Earth. Now I need to bathe for Practice. We need to use the power of dawn today. I can feel it." Stretching up a bit, she kissed him quickly and ducked beneath his arms and headed into the bathroom as he stood and watched her retreat.

Her taste was still on his lips as he ran his tongue over them and headed into his own chamber to cleanse and ready for Practice.

* * * * *

Jax thrust into her body, watching, mesmerized, as her breasts bounced. Her head hung off the side of the bed and her lips moved with the spell.

Leaning down, he licked over her throat and her magic turned up in intensity. Her cunt wrapped around his cock, hot and wet, pulling him back on each upstroke. He'd Practiced with lessers before, with people who possessed small bits of sex magic, but this was different. This was even different from the day before when they'd Practiced. Now that she held nothing back, their united magic was amplified. They were more powerful now that they'd unified in their personal lives.

And the Nameless felt it. Through Rhea, Jax felt it stumble back against the slap their magic produced. He felt the wards strengthen as she wielded her magic more effectively than she'd done before.

But at that moment, he continued to fuck deeply into his woman while she fought for the future of their people. Turning his thoughts back to channeling her magic, he felt that her spell was nearing an end and his fingers found her clit, pressing against it the way he knew she liked.

At the deep tremors in her pussy, his orgasm unleashed. The last words of the spell sighed from her as she found her own climax around him.

Rolling to the side, he kept an arm around her waist as they both caught their breath.

How could his brother not have been proud of how strong Rhea was? Jax wanted to brag about her to everyone they came across. He'd mourned for Paul a long time ago, knowing part of the story from his grandmother. But hearing it all from Rhea the night before had been the final bit he'd needed to close the book. He'd have to deal with his parents when they returned to D'ar. After her comments about not wanting to marry him because of his family, it was imperative he deal with it. For her sake mostly—he certainly couldn't expect her to share his life with such a huge betrayal unaddressed. And for his own, because his mother had attempted to paint a different picture of Paul's end.

"Wow," she murmured some minutes later.

"Mmm hmmm. We should eat a morning meal, get your strength back up. And then I want you to rest all the way to the next keep."

"Bossy." She stretched her long body and stray magic floated into the air like dust motes.

"I like you this way. Before you ran out five seconds after the spell ended. If I wasn't boneless right now, I'd take you again."

"Well then, why offer? I'm supposed to believe you're all studly when your pecker is all wrinkly after one fucking? I thought you were all big, bad man?"

He would have been offended. He was on his way when she cracked open an eye and snickered.

"Oh, you're in big trouble later on."

"Promises, promises." She got out of bed and, without her robe, walked into the bathroom.

Damn, the woman looked good leaving a room naked.

Breathing deeply of their mingled scents—sex and magic, man and woman—he grinned and headed into the bathroom behind her.

"Got room for me in there?" He poked his head into the large shower stall where she stood, wet and glistening.

"In where?" An eyebrow rose.

Chuckling, he got in and crowded up against her. The friction of her soap-slicked body against his was delicious and even though he'd thought it impossible, his cock began to show interest.

"I like this side of you. You're so serious, it's nice to see you playful. You're usually only this way with Sarai."

He took the sponge from her and began to soap up her back.

"Sarai is my best friend. She's the only person other than my mother who I've always been able to trust. She left her home to come with me to a place that she was never able to freely exist in."

He scrubbed shampoo into her scalp and she leaned back into him.

"I'm honored then, that you feel comfortable enough to joke with me." And he was.

She didn't respond but let him continue to take care of her, and that spoke louder than words anyway.

* * * * *

"That was some bit of magic you two put out." Sarai grinned as Rhea and Jax walked into the kitchen half an hour later. "It feels better already out there. My teeth aren't on edge anymore."

Rhea took a deep breath and nodded. "I think this keep is safe. We don't need to evacuate the locals here. There aren't many of them anyway and it's near the rice harvest so I'd hate to interrupt that."

"I'll call and let the Council know. The good news, for a change, will be received well, I'd wager." And he leaned down and kissed her temple before walking out of the room to use the phone in the space they'd used as a makeshift office.

Annoyance warred with pleasure on Rhea's face as she watched him from where she stood, listening to the sound of his voice. Finally she rolled her eyes and gave in to the smile her lips wanted and winked at Sarai.

Mrs. Dakins hugged her tight. "Oh, you're together then? At last?"

Rhea nodded slowly as she drank her coffee. "Yes. Whatever it means when all this is over I don't know. But for now, we're together."

"Jaac is not a man to fuck and run. Not this Jaac. That boy is as dead as Sa'Rhea," Sarai said quietly.

"Do you approve, Sarai?"

Sarai's mouth curled into a smile. "Of course! I've wanted you to hurry up and admit you loved him since the first keep. But you're stubborn. Nice thing is that he's just as stubborn and you couldn't chase him away."

"I know. I like that about him. Even if he is bossy."

"I'm glad to see you happy. You deserve it." Sarai lowered her voice. "And I have to tell you I can't wait to see what his mother does when she hears."

Rhea's face was horrified for a moment and then she laughed. "Oh, my. Well, poor woman. I can't imagine she'll be very pleased to hear it. Hopefully Jax will wait until this is over so we can take it slow and deal with it in a way that won't cause too much trouble."

Even as she said it, she doubted it. Jax was a take-charge guy and she had the feeling he was going to be calling his parents very soon about her. She'd hesitated in telling him the truth of what had happened with Paul for so long because—despite the fact that she loathed her former in-laws for lying and leaving her to hang for their son's misdeeds—she knew Jax loved them.

And of course he was doing just that. In a very businesslike tone, she heard him inform his parents that he was in love with Rhea, always had been, and intended to marry her once this whole business with the Nameless was over with. He also added that they'd have a lot to talk about when he returned to D'ar.

Halfheartedly, Rhea cursed her luck that Earth and Molari shared so many conveniences like phones. But if they didn't, she wouldn't have chocolate or coffee so she scratched that thought.

He walked back into the kitchen, helped himself to breakfast and sat down next to her.

"The Council is relieved and quite happy to hear that we've been successful here at least. We're to go on to the next keep and assess the situation there. They got a report from the badlands that the power has been out in the surrounding towns along the river. The weather's been acting up too. Weird electrical storms."

"Shit. Let's go. That's what happened in Ra'Ken before the Nameless broke through."

He put a hand on her shoulder to stay her. "Eat first. You've been Practicing every day, Rhea. That's a lot of stress on your body and spirit. You need to keep your strength up. It'll take us seven hours to get there, another half an hour won't make a difference one way or another. I've already had the staff begin to load up the cars."

It was a relief, having someone else take care of the details. She let herself lean on him a bit and continued to eat even though her appetite was gone and worry ate at her. She knew he was right. Using her magic day after day was taking its toll on her body.

Mrs. Dakins clucked around and plied her with food, making sure they had plenty of juice and ate high protein meals while they traveled as well. It was nice to be taken care of.

In the car, Jax pulled her into his lap and gently massaged her temples until she fell asleep.

And that's when the dreams began.

One after another, each dream was of the Nameless. Of death and destruction. She could not shake the dreams, instead got sucked into a maelstrom of misery and fear of failure. The Nameless knew things about her magic. About their plans to defeat it.

Finally Jax woke her, shaking her hard and shouting her name. She clawed her way free of the dream state and sat up, groggy.

"Gods, Rhea! Are you all right?" He knelt before her and she realized she wasn't in the car. She was in a bed.

"What the hell happened? Are we at the keep already?"

"Already? Rhea, you've been unconscious for two days. I've been arguing with the Council to bring you back! They kept saying no."

Rhea heard the anguish in his voice.

"I thought I'd lost you. So soon after getting you back." He buried his face in her hair.

"The Council knows I've been unconscious for two days and they wouldn't send help or have me come back?"

"Your father wanted you back there but your uncles voted him down. Said you'd be more useful here when you awoke. They convinced everyone else you were the best hope.

They did say they'd send someone if you hadn't awoken by this evening."

"I'm all right now. The Nameless caught me in a dream. I've been there all this time." She shook her head. "It's not just some *thing*. There are people behind this. I felt that. And someone in the Council is helping them."

Jax froze and Sarai leaned forward. "What do you mean? How do you know that?"

"I felt it in the dream. It knows things about our strategy. How else would you explain how it meets us on every damned front? And no one could have gotten into my dreams without some bit of me. Sarai, call your mother right now. Have her go to the house. See if any of my personal effects have been taken. She'll smell if anyone other than me, you and Jax have been there."

"You can't mean this! If anyone on the Council is cooperating with the Nameless, they'd be helping with genocide! I can't believe it, Rhea. I can't." Jax stood up and began to pace.

"We need to Practice."

He spun. "It hasn't been here since you've been out! We're winning, Rhea. Why are you looking for problems that don't exist? Are you just looking for a reason to be dire?"

"No, we aren't. The Nameless was in my dream with me. But now that I'm free it is too. Now let's get moving before it's too late. We're on borrowed time, Jax, and you're lying to yourself."

She stood, expecting her legs to be shaky, but they weren't. She walked past him and into the bathroom where Mrs. Dakins was already laying out her robe and had run a bath with herbs in it.

"He'll come around. It's a shocking thing to learn someone you know and most likely trust is cooperating with the enemy." Mrs. Dakins clucked around, putting everything just so.

Rhea drank the glass of juice the other woman handed her and shed her clothing, getting into the bath without saying a word. His denial shouldn't have stung, she'd probably have done the same in his shoes. But it did. He thought she'd *wanted* something bad to happen? Like it was a part of her nature? She knew better than most what it felt like to confront the reality that someone you loved and trusted betrayed you. But his thinking she wanted something dire to happen hurt and hurt deeply.

Dunking herself three times, she stood and got out, quickly eating the sandwich Mrs. Dakins provided.

Robed, she headed back into the Practice chamber and waited for Jax.

He came in shortly and approached her, circling in a way that made the hair on the back of her neck rise, along with her nipples. He'd better hurry up and get over his snit because she wasn't going to fuck a man throwing a tantrum or blaming her for someone else's perfidy. She'd do her duty and Practice but there'd be no recreational sex.

She grounded herself, feeling the earth at the foundations of the keep, drawing power through it and up into herself. Slowly, surely, she uncoiled that power as the warmth of her Talent coursed through her and out into the air. Even though he was being a baby, Jax still rang her bell.

He kissed the back of her neck and she closed her eyes and began to speak, trusting him to put aside his emotions and do his job.

"You're angry with me," he murmured and she felt the warm wetness of his tongue trail across her shoulder.

Ignoring him, she drew more focus and continued to build her magic. Soon, she lost herself to it, falling into the tide of her Talent, of the sex and desire that drowned her senses as she worked her spell. She felt lips and hands, dimly heard him speak, but she let the Talent intoxicate her.

"I know you've gone off to your special place deep in yourself to work this spell. We'll work this out later on." His hands skimmed over her skin from her fingertips to her shoulders, across her collarbone and down to the other hand. He let himself get caught in the undertow of her magic, hitched a ride on it, became her anchor.

Large hands palmed her nipples, pulling back so that his fingertips pulled gently and then pinched until she gasped. Her nipples hardened and swelled, darkening and begging for his mouth. He complied, needing her as much as she needed him.

Her taste, as always, was a siren song. Luring him, seducing him, making him feel like he needed to fall to his knees and wallow in her essence. No other woman, not ever, made him feel a shadow of the way Rhea made him feel and respond.

And this woman was pissed off. He knew her well enough to tell. She hadn't looked at him very long and had fallen into herself and the Talent very quickly to avoid dealing with him.

And he knew why and despaired of it. He hoped like hell she was wrong.

Kissing down her body, he picked her up and put her on the bed, moving to straddle her body. As he did, his cock dragged heavily over her skin, torturing them both.

Spreading her thighs, he'd bent his head to taste her when her back bowed and she sat up. He felt it then, the Nameless coming, pushing hard at the wards.

"Rhea, focus!" But he knew it was more than that. It was too much. The membrane of the wards bent inward and stretched. He felt the strain on them, as if suddenly the very air around them was stretched too thin and tight.

Her eyes cleared and she jumped up. "It's too late. We've got to get out of here." Pushing past him, she yanked her robe on and ran into the hallway, raising the alarms.

"Rhea!"

She turned and stared at him for a long moment as he pulled on his pants. People began to rush down the stairs, carrying things out to the transports. He heard the engines turning over and the civil defense horns blaring through the valley where the river was. Most of the population had been evacuated several days before and he hoped they'd moved their asses to the next wards.

"It's too late, Jax. It knows! Damn you! Someone is helping and we're fucked if we stay. We cannot stop it." Still in her robe, she turned and raced down the stairs, urging the small staff to keep calm and get out of the house.

Reality hit him and he grabbed his duffel and followed her out into the night where he felt the Nameless, dark and toxic, in the air. He realized Rhea was right, it was too far gone. Maybe, if there had been other Practitioners there to help, it might have been possible to check the attack on the wards, but with just the two of them it was hopeless.

He jumped into the conveyance and they drove quickly away. They'd have to drive at least two hours before they could safely open a rift. In an emergency they could risk it but you couldn't be sure where you'd end up—in the middle of a mountain or at the bottom of the sea.

She grabbed the portable communicator and dialed her father. "It's breaking through. We're heading to a safe rift point. Get people back to the capital now. And watch your back because there is a spy at the Council table."

"What? Are you all right? Gods, Sa'Rhea, I wanted to come to you when you were in the dream but I couldn't undermine you with the Council. I wanted them to know I believed in how strong you were." Rhea heard the thread of panic in his voice and the idea of forgiveness suddenly wasn't so foreign.

Rhea explained what was happening and her suspicions about the spy or spies.

He sighed. "I've had the same suspicions over the years. I'm sorry to say so but I've felt that Paul had been working with spies and that was the real reason behind the scrolls being stolen. I wish I'd been more clearheaded when...well, I'm sorry. Not that it matters now. But I am."

"Get back here. We'll stage a last stand. I'll call back Emmia and the other Practitioners. We'll need every single weapon we have to stop it. Do you have any suspicions about who may be behind this?"

"Even though I believe the Sarnes would be overjoyed if I perished, I do know they love Jax, and for that reason I don't think it's them. And frankly, Father, it can't be anyone much lower at the table because they wouldn't have the information."

She knew she'd probably hurt Jax with her comments but the truth was the truth. His parents were lying bastards and totally capable of something like this. But not at his expense.

"My brothers?"

"I'm sorry, but yes. That's who I'm leaning toward right now. Don't tell them about bringing the Practitioners back from the Eastern Mountains. If they're innocent I'll apologize myself. But if they aren't we can't take the chance. This is bad. It's very powerful."

"Get to a safe rift distance and get back here right away. Straight to Jax's house. Do not speak to anyone else until you get here. Be safe, Rhea. I lost you once, I don't want to do it again."

She hung up before she started crying.

Sarai took the phone and dialed. She listened to her mother for long moments and hung up. "It appears your pillowcases were taken. In addition to those of us who belonged in the house she smelled your uncle Arta and someone else she hasn't identified yet. She's going to go to the Council to see if she recognizes anyone."

Rhea didn't dare look in Jax's direction. Knowing she'd been right didn't bring her any solace.

Jax touched her shoulder but instead of leaning into him, she stiffened and then moved further away. He felt it like a slap.

"You know, no one is perfect."

Her jaw clenched but she kept quiet. Sarai looked at him like he'd gone insane.

"What? She's so fucking perfect? No one gets to make a mistake?" Jax's voice rose.

"Is that your idea of an apology?" Sarai growled.

"Stop it, both of you! Do not talk around me." Rhea moved out of the forward-facing seat and next to Sarai.

"I'd apologize but she's too fucking self-righteous to accept it."

Rhea winced like he'd physically struck her. And he watched her draw into herself and wished with all his being he could take the words back.

"You can't run away from this, Rhea. How can we have a relationship if you do this every time I make a mistake?"

"You're right." Her voice had that flat, emotionally reserved sound again, and all his internal alarms sounded.

"What does that mean?"

"It means you're right. We can't have a relationship. I'm clearly too self-righteous for you. Add that to my terrible penchant for wanting something bad to happen and I'm clearly not fit." Her eyes met his and he saw the depth of pain there. Realized his error. It wasn't his inability to believe the worst in his fellow Council members, it was his thinking she wanted something bad to happen. She'd done what was right at a great cost and he'd called her self-righteous. Hadn't even apologized.

He scrubbed his hands over his face. "Rhea, I'm sorry. Let's start this over. I'm sorry I didn't believe you. And I'm sorry you took my words to mean I thought you wanted bad things to happen. I shouldn't have said it, I didn't mean it. I was shocked and, well, there's no excuse. And I suppose I was hurt that you'd suspect my parents, and I took out my frustration on you. It was wrong. But we do have a relationship, Rhea. I love you and you're mine. We have to be able to fight and get through it. People who love each other can have disagreements and work past them. In case you failed to notice, we're both pretty strong personalities, this won't be our last fight. I swear to you I'll be more careful about how I phrase things in the future. But I want you to trust one thing over everything else—I love you and I believe in you and us."

"I'm so tired of people thinking the worst of me. I'm not the one who stole those scrolls. I didn't lie and get someone exiled. I didn't give information to the Nameless. I have done nothing wrong and yet I get blamed. Usually by those who *have* done something wrong. That's not love, Jax."

It was one of the most revealing things she'd ever said to him and it felt like a gift. Hope bloomed in him that she'd share even a small part of herself with him. Sarai watched him with narrowed eyes but her claws had retracted—a good sign.

"I'm not blaming anything on you. Even before I knew the whole story I knew you wouldn't have killed Paul without absolute provocation or as anything other than an accident. And I've spent the last fifteen years working to get you back here. I wish it hadn't been this as the cause, but I'm not sorry it brought you home. To me. Please. Can't we get past this? I love you, Rhea. I do."

He held her gaze, begging her to see his sincerity, while he sent out a prayer that she'd forgive him.

"I'm so tired. I'm going to rest until we get to the rift point. My father is calling people back from the Eastern Mountains but he's not going to tell my uncles. I can't apologize for suspecting your parents, Jaac. Their lies sent me into exile. I lived in misery for two years with Paul and then lost everything but Sarai because they're liars. The only reason I don't think they're behind this is your involvement. I do believe they love you and wouldn't do anything to hurt you."

He sighed. She was trying to avoid him again and he wasn't going to have it. "Sarai, trade places with me please." He got up, threatening to sit on her if she didn't shove aside. Reluctantly, Sarai moved into the seat he'd been in and he plopped down next to Rhea and grabbed her into his embrace before she could move away.

Gently but firmly he tipped her chin so she was looking him in the eye. "I understand why you suspected my parents. I'm sorry they caused misery on your part. But I'm not them. Now," he brushed his lips over hers once and then another time because even when she was hurt and pissed off, she tasted good. "Now, darling, we are going to get past this. If you don't forgive me, I'll continue to bother you. I'll make a terrible nuisance of myself and sing beneath your windows at night. Plus you'll have to have sex with me in order to Practice and I'll leave love marks all over your neck. You'll look like youth after her first kissing party. And we both know I can do it. So save yourself the annoyance and embarrassment and admit that I'm an idiot but one you love, and forgive me."

When she rolled her eyes he knew things would be all right. "Gods, you're a big, giant tool. A tool of mythic proportions. I couldn't fall in love with an insurance salesman? No, I get Paul Bunyan with super testosterone power. Special."

"Who the hell is Paul Bunyan? An old lover?"

Sarai burst out laughing. "You'll have to look up Earth lore when you get back home. Now don't do this again or I'll have to gut you."

Rhea allowed him to bring her into his lap and put her head on his chest as they drove.

They arrived at the rift point and, as they got out of the car, Rhea nearly fell to her knees. She truly felt the dark presence of the Nameless once she was in the open air.

Sickness coursed through her as there was one less barrier between her and the Nameless. "The wards have broken. It's coming."

All around them, the people who'd been in the conveyances as they'd fled the area around the keep and the refugees who'd convoyed out began to open rifts, and those without the magic jumped through. The vehicles would be abandoned there, they were unimportant in comparison to their lives. Jax opened a rift of his own and Rhea grabbed her bag and walked through, hand in hand with him.

And walked into his front hallway. His valet waited there, looking dire but able. He took Rhea's and Jax's bags and moved quickly to put them upstairs.

Katai came down the stairs and hugged both Jax and Rhea. "Thank goodness you're here safe. I've been out of my mind with worry since Timus dropped in." She turned to Sarai and the others. "Rooms have been prepared for you. Rest now. Unless you're hungry? There's a meal waiting in the kitchen if you are. Timus has asked that everyone stay here or rift back to your homes and not contact anyone just yet."

Running on adrenaline that was about to exhaust, most of them decided to sleep first and then decide where they'd go.

There were five sets of warding walls around D'ar. All of varying types of magic. Different spells were cast in varying layers. Spells to repel evil, protective runes, physical impediments that were magically strong were all woven together to make walls that were physically and metaphysically impenetrable. Although Rhea felt an overall sense of weakening against the Nameless, she was sure they'd all be fine for the next several days at least.

"You've been unconscious for days and you've just brushed against something so awful there aren't words for it. Come on, I want you to eat and then you're going to bed." Jax led her past his grandmother and pushed her up the stairs. Just outside his bedroom he asked his valet to bring up a tray of food for both of them and made sure Sarai had been given a room close to Rhea.

His room was large and masculine, just like him. And she noted that it lacked even a small feminine touch and relaxed. She wasn't stupid enough to think he'd been a monk all the time she'd been gone. Still, she didn't like to think there'd been one regular woman in his life.

He turned her, noting she still wore her Practice robe. "Let's get you tucked into bed. I don't like how pale you are."

"I'm going to clean up a bit first. I need to wash my face and brush my teeth."

Reaching out, he pushed open the door to the large bathroom adjoining the bedroom. "Go on then. I'll get some clothes laid out for you. The food should be up shortly. If I know your father he's going to be back here in a while to talk strategy. And I need to talk to my parents as well."

"Hold that thought, I'll be out in a few minutes." She didn't have the energy to deal with his parents right then.

It was the spicy scent of curry that drove her to hurry. Poking her head out of the bathroom, she made sure they were alone and went to join him, climbing next to him on the bed where the food tray sat.

"Oh man, this looks so good. I bought some curry at a food stall when we were here last, but this is a million times better." She dug in, pouring the meat and veggies over rice and breathing in deeply before she scarfed it all up.

He stared at her and she blushed. "Sorry, I didn't realize how hungry I was."

Starting, he blinked and then laughed. "Oh no, angel, I wasn't staring at you because of how you were eating. I'm glad to see you with an appetite, you're losing a lot of weight."

"So?"

"You're fucking beautiful. I just can't believe my good fortune to have you walking naked out of my bathroom and scrambling up into my bed. I've imagined you in this room a thousand times. Reality is much nicer."

She watched him move the tray after he made sure she was full. She stretched provocatively. "Well, you do say the nicest things."

"You're exhausted," he said faintly, watching the rise and fall of her breasts.

"True. And you know what the best tonic is?"

"Turn over."

She froze at his tone, suddenly laced with command. With a half smile, she obeyed, moving to her belly.

He moved to straddle her and she jumped when a warm stream of fragrant oil pooled in the small of her back. Out of the corner of her eye she saw him put the bottle on the bedside table.

A grunt came from her lips when his hands moved up her back, taking the oil with them, kneading her sore muscles. Pressing, sliding, massaging, those fingers and the heels of his hands moved across her back, over knots of tension, working the exhaustion out of her. As he worked Rhea began to feel lighter, more relaxed, warmer, even as her body began to soften and bloom, readying for him.

At that point his touch wasn't so much sexual as ministering. He took care of her, showing her how he felt with his hands. That touched her more deeply than if he'd just said it. As his thumbs slid up her spine, tears sprang to her eyes and a sob began to build deep in her gut. But it was a positive release of emotion and she let go and when she did the sob turned into a happy sigh of laughter.

Still drunk with feeling, she looked up at him when he turned her over. Lips brushed over her forehead and then her lips. "Close your eyes, angel. Relax and let me make you feel better."

She obeyed, letting her eyes fall closed. His hair caressed her neck and arms. Nimble, clever fingers slid over the mounds of her breasts. The oil on them made warming friction. He teased with that slick touch, taking the nipples between slippery thumb and forefingers. Her breath began to come shorter and shorter and her libido crashed back through her with a delicious wave of sensation.

Her thighs fell open in invitation. *Touch me.*

The sweet-smelling oil slicked his hands as he stroked down her belly, avoiding her pussy. Instead he moved down her body and massaged her thighs and calves and over each foot, including her toes. He knew all the right places to apply pressure, each pass his thumbs made over her instep shot straight to her clit.

Still, all she could do was smile lazily. She felt relaxed and pampered. His body shifted again and his hair brushed over her thighs as his hands pushed them apart. She sighed happily and he chuckled briefly.

His thumbs brushed up over her labia, swollen and wet for him. Unable to resist, she rolled her hips in the direction of his mouth. And when that warm, slick tongue slid through the folds of her pussy and skittered up and over her clit, she cried out softly.

After she tried to reach him, he put her hands at her sides. And so she received, hands open there on the mattress as he ministered to her. Worshipped her with mouth and hands.

And his mouth pushed her, tongue lapping over juicy flesh, taking her in, flicking over her distended clit and then pressing it into her body. Orgasm floated just out of her reach but lethargy kept her from working to grab it. Instead she waited, open, for it to descend upon her and through her.

Each movement of fingers and then tongue pulled it closer, drawing it into her cells, making a home for it in her body. Her breath began to speed until she sobbed, gulping air.

One hand rested on her breast, pinching and rolling a nipple, and the other fucked two fingers into her. He slid a pinky finger down to tickle against her rear passage and she gasped. Sensation rushed through her.

His lips made an O and encircled her clit, sucking it into his mouth. Orgasm, lazily circling, slammed into her body with near violent force, filling up her cells in a wash of pleasure, and she let it pull her under.

Muscles twitching, clit throbbing, her body soaked it up. The endorphins were somehow essential and life-giving and she felt near to normal for the first time in days.

Turning her back over, he put her hands above her head and bent one of her knees up, entering her from behind. The weight of his lower body held her in place as he leaned on his elbows, hovering just above her ear.

The angle dragged the meaty head of his cock over the swollen bundle of her G-spot each time he thrust into her.

Her hands grasped the edge of the bed and she held on as he took her. Muscles relaxed and loose, the warmth of her body lulled her, pleasure wrapped around her senses.

"You're so beautiful. I've never seen a more gorgeous sight." His breath stirred the hair near her ear where he whispered.

His stomach slid against her ass and the small of her back. The oil still slick between them, the scent of almonds began to mix with magic and sex. It pulled her back under — the sound of their union, the scent, Jax's groans and murmured words of love. The rhythm of his body into hers over and over, filling her up and taking that fullness away — each time he pressed back in her body joyously received him, each time he pulled nearly all the way out she felt bereft.

They created a language there, beyond words — cock to cunt. The sensation of his body entering hers was somehow terribly monumental. Not face-to-face with him, her eyes were closed as she thought of the way he moved, of his smile and the glint of those deep blue eyes when he began to seduce her.

His hunger for her seemed bottomless and it lifted her, made her feel revered. Loved.

It hit her then in a way it hadn't before and a sob tore from her lips.

Jax heard it and pulled out, turning her over. "Baby? Did I hurt you?" Concern for her wrinkled his forehead. Still crying, she shook her head and pulled his lips to hers for a kiss.

But he pulled away from her lips and kissed softly over her cheeks and wet eyelashes. Gentle, oh-so gentle, he tipped her chin up and kissed her again. "What is it? I thought we were okay?"

She smiled through her tears. "We are okay. It just hit me—exactly how okay we are. I love you, Jaac."

He froze, a look of love on his face that sliced through her reserves. It wasn't that it made her his, she knew she'd always been. But all parts of her could finally agree to that, accept it. Her heart swelled in her chest.

His lips curved into a smile. "You do, huh? Well good. You don't know what it means to me to hear it from you. And not in response to me. I'd do anything for you. Just let me love you, all right?"

She nodded. "Now, you need to get back to work."

He laughed and moved closer, pulling her thigh up over his and entering her again. This time it was slow, as if he couldn't bear to not be deep inside her body. Instead of thrusting, he gently rocked.

Their foreheads touched, leaning against the other's. Her leg wrapped around him, calf against the hard muscles of his ass. The wall of his abdomen rippled as he rolled his hips.

"You're incredibly sexy," she said, almost shyly.

He blushed. "You think so?"

She laughed. "Uh yeah! Hello? Look in a mirror once or twice? I'm sure your bed hasn't lacked for company, Jaac."

He leaned in and kissed her quick and hard. "Yes, but none of them was you. And speaking of sexy, Rhea, you're magnificent. Overflowing with sex and magic, tall and voluptuous. I want to fuck you every waking moment and I'm sure I dream about it too."

"Smooth." She tried to suppress a grin, wildly flattered. Her hands smoothed over the bulk of his biceps. Moving her head, she gave in to temptation and sank her teeth into the muscle there.

Jax groaned softly as a shudder worked through him. "Gods, yes."

"Oh yeah? You like it a bit rough, Jax?"

Rhea shoved him back, rolling with him so that he stayed buried inside her.

"Where you're concerned, I like it all. Don't overdo it, you were unconscious for two days."

She arched, her head falling back. Her hair teased the backs of her calves. Reaching around, she found his balls and dragged her nails over them, delighting in his hiss of pleasure.

Flexing her thighs, she rose up and slid back down the shaft of his cock. Over and over.

His hands skimmed up her stomach and cupped her breasts. "How about you, Rhea?" Clever fingers pinched just shy of pain. Her nipples swelled in his hands and her head came back up.

Her teeth caught her bottom lip and she dragged her nails down his chest, leaving marks in their wake. Savage satisfaction slid through her gut at his pleasured moans. Possessiveness wasn't a familiar feeling but this man was *hers*.

Leaning her body down as he continued to cradle her breasts, she bit the muscle of his chest just above his heart and then licked quickly to each one of his nipples.

"Fuck...Rhea, I've got to come. Please."

Staying bent over him, she grabbed the tendon where neck met shoulder between her teeth and levered herself back onto him, fucking herself onto his cock over and over.

The angle was delicious, even better when one of his hands snaked down and his fingertips found her clit. He did little more than press into her as she rode on his cock, grinding herself onto his hand as she did.

Climax began to build deep inside her as she moved on him, felt his cock harden.

"You feel so damned good inside me," she whispered around the skin of his neck.

"Aw, Gods, Rhea." His voice was hoarse as he began to move his hips, thrusting into her, meeting her movements back. "Yes. Oh yes, baby. Fuck me. Your pussy feels so good."

Tightening herself around him was the last straw, and orgasm struck with near blinding intensity. She heard his groan as he thrust one last time, hard and deep, his cock pulsing as he came into her.

"I love you, Rhea." His words were sleepy as she collapsed beside him. She felt him pull the blankets up around them. Seeking his warmth, she rested against his body, her arms wrapped around the ones he held around her. Her last thoughts as she fell asleep were happy ones, unfettered by guilt or grief. It'd been a very long time.

Chapter Six

ॐ

She awoke to low sounds of arguing in the hallway outside Jax's room. Sitting up, she stretched, amazed that she felt so good. The massage and that hot sex must really have been a tonic.

There was no way she was going out there in her current state. Quickly she got out of bed and headed into the bathroom and showered quickly. Braiding her wet hair back, she put on the at-home gown Jax had left in the bathroom for her and, in her bare feet, she braced herself and left the room.

The hallway was empty so she moved toward the voices downstairs. Walking into the drawing room, she saw her father there with Jax's father and her uncle Treya. Her father froze a moment before his face crumpled and he headed to her.

"You're so beautiful. You look much like her. I'm sorry, Sa'Rhea. I thought I was doing the right thing and then I wanted you safe and, Gods, I'm so sorry. Please forgive me."

Her father stood before her, tears streaming down his face. She saw two paths, forgiveness and a lessening of her burdens or the continuation of her grudge but still having to work with him on the Council. The part of her that was her mother's chose the first path and she opened her arms and he stepped into them.

And she knew it had been the right choice as her heart felt free.

Sometime later she stepped back, not missing the touched look on Jax's face. Her uncle smiled and kissed her cheek.

"You're looking pretty hale for someone who was essentially in a coma for two days."

"So maybe she wasn't."

Rhea looked at her ex-father-in-law with distaste. "I'm not going to engage in this with you." Turning to her father and uncle, she filled them in on her dream and the collapse of the wards.

"We've got reports of three other wards falling. If you and Jaac hadn't called for evacuation of the population tens of thousands would be dead now."

His words meant a lot. "What do we do now?"

Mrs. Dakins came in with a tray of tea and sandwiches. Jax raised a brow and nodded at Rhea and then the food and she rolled her eyes but made herself a plate, poured a cup of tea and went to sit down. Protectively, Jax moved next to her, drinking his own tea.

"I've called back most of the Practitioners we sent to the Eastern Mountains. The remaining Practitioners of all levels are gathering here in the city now. We'll need them all, from healers to the weather controllers. The Nameless is moving in this direction. We've gone and brought back all refugees from the staging areas, they're all here behind the grand wards. There are teams out now, rifting and moving around to report on the progress of the Nameless."

There was a commotion in the hallway and suddenly a knot of people pushed into the room. A cry came from Rhea's lips when she saw her sister there, standing with Petra, one of Jax's sisters.

Emmia's guarded eyes caught her sister's and they both stood still for a long moment. Knowing the pain of Emmia's gift, she held herself back when she wanted to embrace her baby sister. Emmia's empathy meant that she had to deal with the tide of emotions of not just everyone in the room but those in the house and even on the street outside.

"Emmia, I'm so glad to see you well. I've missed you very much."

Emmia dropped her eyes for a moment. Her hands caressed the hilt of the blades she carried on each side of her body. The long rope of her hair lay in a braid that trailed down her back.

"And I you. Welcome home."

Rhea knew that would be all she got. While she knew her sister would give her life for her, they were not close in any traditional sense. Both had walls around themselves for different reasons.

Timus looked at his daughters, the ones who'd survived. Strong. The eldest tall and essentially feminine. His baby, standing there in trousers and a baggy shirt. He knew her arms were muscled and lean from her sword work. Both had eyes that were wary and not very trusting.

Still, he loved them both so much he ached to think their lives were in such danger.

Petra pushed her way into the room and hugged Jax. Turning to Rhea, she cocked her head. Rhea's stomach tightened. Petra was the feminine version of Paul. Lithe and very delicate. She had fair hair and lighter eyes. Petra had been a child when Rhea had seen her last.

"I had a vision, Rhea. It's coming and it's bringing men."

Seeing Rhea's confusion, Jax put his hand on Rhea's arm. "Pet's Talent is her vision." Pride was clear on his face.

A Seer. A rare and powerful gift.

"I told you to stay east!"

Petra turned and looked at her father. "I saw so many things. Forward and backward."

He paled.

"Petra, what do you mean?"

"The Nameless is coming. And it has an army of men. My mother has helped. Paul helped. My father knows but he's not involved." Petra met Rhea's eyes. "I'm sorry I couldn't help you before."

"You were ten when I was exiled. It's all right."

Rhea looked at her father and then to Jax, whose lips were in a tight white line. Rhea felt awful for him.

Jax looked to the guards near the door. "Go to my parents' home and arrest my mother. Search her carefully and put her in one of the special cells." He turned to Petra. "Anyone else, Pet?"

"Arta Hars and his son."

Timus sighed deeply. "Arrest my brother as well. Keep in mind he's telekinetic, and my nephew is telepathic. Send in one of the Blanks for my nephew. Special cells for them too. They're to have no contact with each other or anyone else."

The special cells were constructed so that no magic could be performed inside them without a key—the key being the genetic code of special jailers called "Blanks" whose Talent was that they gave off no discernable mental signature. Only they could rift in and out.

The guards left. Rhea saw the strain around Emmia's eyes. She knew the strain of being around this many people all on high alert and brimming with adrenaline was a lot to bear. "Why don't you go home and rest until we need you?"

"You'll need my blades." Rhea knew it was her sister's way of making sure they'd send for her.

Rhea nodded. "We will. I have something for you. Will you wait a moment?"

Her sister nodded and stepped into the hallway when Rhea moved past her and up the stairs to Jax's bedroom. She rustled through her duffel until she found the black velvet bag and the purple cloth.

Near the front door, she held them out to Emmia. "I brought these for you. The cards were given to me several years ago. I've always imagined giving them to you and so I think they're meant to be yours."

Emmia took them, her hands sliding over the nap of the velvet for a brief moment before tucking the gifts into the inside pocket of the baggy coat she wore. Emmia smiled softly and touched Rhea's arm gently, a rarity. And just that quickly it was gone and she turned and left.

When Rhea walked back into the drawing room her eyes immediately sought out Jax. Her chest constricted as she saw the pain on his face. "Jax, why don't you deal with your father? We'll work in here." Oh how she wished she could bear this for him.

He sighed, hugging his sister to his side. "Father, we need to talk." Leaning into Rhea, he kissed her softly. She gave him what comfort she could, touched that he'd seek it from her.

Once they'd left the room Timus turned to one of the guards. "Do not let Chan leave here without my permission."

Petra entered the room as they pulled out maps of the extensive warding walls around the capital.

"Tell us about this army, Petra."

"From what I saw it's not a large group. Not even a thousand men. But they're Practitioners of dark magic and they don't expect to be caught. They have scrolls."

"Paul."

Petra nodded. "Yes, I think so. And now my mother."

"She made a deal with them for our lives. My sisters and me and my father. Arta approached her a year ago. My mother knew about Paul but she didn't know the extent of what he'd done. My father was trying to stop her. I don't believe he helped at all."

"Except in his silence as my daughter's life was placed in danger repeatedly." Timus' anger shimmered around him. "And he sat silent while she was exiled!"

"And you did it knowing her innocence!" Jax yelled back as he came back into the room from the doorway where he'd been standing.

"And where were you? You claim to love her so much, Jaac. You stood there in the square with your family as she was sent through that rift." Timus stood, fists clenched.

"STOP IT! I'm not a bone to be fought over or a club to bludgeon each other with. I won't have it. In case you forgot, we've got an army of dark Practitioners and the Nameless barreling our way."

Jax looked at her and let out the breath he'd been holding. "You're right, angel. My father has told me my mother had plans to drug me and smuggle us all out of the city tomorrow night. He believes that's when the Nameless will arrive."

"How can we trust him?" Rhea wished she didn't have to ask but she did.

"We can't. But we can trust that he wants to try to save me and Petra." Jax's pain was clear in his voice.

Rhea nodded and went back to the maps. "We can't just wait in here. If the Nameless gets this far, it's all over."

Petra pointed to the outermost city wards, about forty miles away. "Here. They'll use the scrolls to breach here."

"Then we will be waiting."

"We can use these mountains here as cover for our own troops and most of the Practitioners. We'll need their magic to hold the next line of wards and lend you magic as you try to drain the Nameless."

"Negative magic?" Panic settled into Rhea. Trying to drain something as big as the Nameless with a negative spell to pull its power into herself was a big risk. Positive magic was something she could control, something she was sure of. But negative magic wasn't often used for a reason. It was dangerous and difficult to control.

"I don't like it either but what other choice do we have?"

"I don't suppose you saw the end of the battle?" Rhea looked to Petra.

"You know that's not how it works."

"Yeah, but I thought I'd ask anyway."

"Where is your father?" Timus asked Jax, his voice considerably calmer.

"He's upstairs. He's offered to help. I believe he will if for no other reason than to try to save my mother."

"We don't need that traitor!" her uncle Treya spoke for the first time.

"We do. He's got strong magic and he's a firethrower." Rhea shrugged. "Look, I don't like him. I didn't like him before and I really don't like him now. But this is bigger than me. This is the existence of our people. We need every weapon we can get."

Jax looked to Timus. As the leader of the Council, it was up to him in this case. After a long silence, Timus nodded shortly. "Broker a deal. If he helps us we'll spare the life of his wife. But they'll both be exiled. If we survive."

Jax swallowed and Rhea felt his relief. "I'll go then. I'll have him kept under guard and out of contact with anyone."

Petra hugged Rhea. "Thank you. You didn't have to do that."

Rhea looked at the empty doorway that Jax had exited through. "Yes I did."

* * * * *

After they'd worked out a plan, Timus left with most of the guards. They'd assemble the people they'd need and begin to rift out to the last ward to take their positions. It would have to happen slowly so as not to attract too much attention. They were pretty sure there were spies in the city.

Timus planned to go to the jail to interview his brother and had had Rhea's other uncle brought in for questioning.

Sarai went to her family to enlist their help. Minxes had their own kind of magic and their aid would be important.

Petra went to rest and, after the room had emptied, Rhea turned to Jax, who stood and looked out the windows.

"I'm sorry."

When he turned, his face bore a look of surprise. "You're sorry? My parents aided the thing that has tried to erase humans from this world for generations. They knew my brother helped it and did nothing to help you! You were exiled because of my family. You must hate me."

She shook her head and went to him. Reaching up, she cupped his cheek. "I love you. You bear no responsibility for your parents, Jax. What they did, they did. Did you know before tonight?"

"No! Rhea, how can you think that?"

"I *don't* think that. Didn't you just hear what I said?" Gently, she rapped her knuckles on his skull. "I thought you had a genius-level IQ."

"You still love me, huh?"

"Fucked up, felonious family and all. And Petra's okay at least."

"Felonious? I take it that's bad? You're going to have to give me a lexicon of all the Earth references you make." His smile was hesitant but genuine. "Thank the heavens Shandi stayed east. She's going to be devastated when she hears about our parents. And your family isn't perfect either. Arta is crazy and your father is a pompous ass."

"He is a pompous ass. But he gave us his blessing before he left. And Shandi is too young to be here anyway."

"Blessing huh?" He moved closer, banding an arm around her waist and pulling her flush with his body. "Does that mean you're going to make an honest man of me and marry me?"

She raised a brow before leaning out to lock the door. "No. I think we should live in sin for a while. I've done the marriage thing before and it didn't work out that well. Jax, I don't have a good track record, I seem to kill my husbands."

"Oh, only one." He winked but got serious again. "My brother was a wastrel and a cheat and wife beater, and apparently a traitor too. You did what you had to do, Rhea. I'm hard to kill anyway."

Her shock at his comments warmed to amusement. They were both clearly twisted people. "If you cheat on me can I cut your balls off?"

Wincing, he moved her back to the couch. "Hey, no discussion of my balls in anything less than an affectionate manner. And I have no plans to cheat on you. With you here at home, married to me or not, why would I need anything else?"

She sank to her knees between his thighs as he sat on the couch. Her hands undid his belt and pulled open the fly of his pants. "I knew you weren't wearing underwear."

"Your father came into the house and demanded to see you. I grabbed the pants near the door and put them on. Fuck!"

He stopped speaking as she sucked the head of his cock into her mouth, sliding her tongue around the ridge of the crown. He tasted faintly of her body.

His balls, heavy, lay in her palm. Tension from the whole last several hours strung through his thighs and stomach.

Each time she moved her mouth back down over him she took more of him. That tension released and his muscles jumped as they flexed and relaxed.

Her tongue pressed down the center of the shaft, over the throbbing vein there and back up, the tip digging into that extra-sensitive spot just beneath the slit on the head.

The salty tang of his pre-cum teased her senses. She felt powerful there, his cock in her mouth. Completely in charge of the pleasure of this potent man.

Pressing the pads of her fingers into the spot just behind his balls, she was rewarded with a deep groan and the jerk of his cock. She hummed her satisfaction around him.

"Yes, oh yes. Like that, angel."

She wanted to laugh at his calling her that. But it was poignantly sweet and so she let it warm her insides instead.

"Make me nice and wet. Oh that's the way."

Rolling her eyes up, she met his gaze. The blue was so dark that with his pupils so wide it was hard to see where one stopped and the other began. Hunger etched his features. His lips slightly parted as his chest heaved to pull in breath.

"How sexy are you there? Mouth wrapped around my cock, hair around your back like a cloak? Your ass swaying in that gown that marks your rank and makes you look like a queen. Get up, angel. I'm going to fuck you."

Blinking, she pulled off him with a soft *pop* and he helped her to stand.

"On your knees facing the back of the couch. Open the front of your gown and free your breasts for me."

Hands shaking with barely leashed desire, she knelt on the couch and undid the fastenings that held the bodice of the gown closed. He looked over her shoulder, resting his chin there, and slid his hands upward to cup the breasts that were now free of the dress.

"Heavy but still so high. Your tits are magnificent. Gorgeous. They make me hard whenever I just think about them." He circled the nipples with the tips of his fingers. "And these succulent nipples, Gods. Rhea, you have no idea how good you taste. Your magic coats your skin like gossamer, sweet and tangy all at once."

His hands moved to her waist.

"Hands on the back of the couch."

She felt the cool air on her ass and thighs as he pulled the skirt up and over her ass, baring her to him.

"I do so like these panties you brought back. Not so different from the ones you can get here, but just different enough." He undid the tie at the left hip and she felt the silk slide down her thighs.

Gentle fingertips traced over her ass and thighs. For the briefest moment they dipped between the lips of her pussy and tickled over her clit. Just enough to make her moan a bit.

"Spread your thighs." He helped, pushing her legs wide apart.

Moments later she felt the head of his cock nudge against her gate, pressing just inside but no further.

"You're so hot. Hot and wet, and it shoots straight to my balls." As he ended the sentence, he thrust into her in one quick movement, so hard his balls slapped against her mound. "Tight, too."

She thrust back against him, needing more. And he gave it to her. "More, Jax. Please. I need it hard and fast. Fuck me so hard all I feel is your cock battering deep into my pussy."

He groaned. "Damn it, woman! Every time I think I've got the upper hand you do or say something ten times sexier."

Her laugh ended on a strangled gasp as he began to fuck into her hard and deep. Faster and faster he pistoned into her body. She closed her eyes and rested her forehead against the couch, arching to take more of him.

"Make yourself come, angel. I need to hold your breasts."

One of her hands slid to her clit, laying her finger over it so she could caress his cock each time he moved into her.

His body bent around hers, caging her, dominating her. Large hands took her breasts, fingers played with her nipples, each tug echoing with a throb of her clit. She did little more than leave her finger there, not wanting to come just yet, but the percussive movement of the slap of his balls against her and the bump of his cock against her cervix was enough to draw her inexorably closer each time he thrust into her.

She knew it was just about to explode through her. "Don't leave me alone. I'm going to come."

He heard her whispered words right as her cunt clamped down on his cock when she came. Wet muscles fluttered and gripped him. Her nipples hardened and stabbed into his hands. She was suddenly creamy and swollen around him as a flush worked up her back.

"Shit..." He grunted and thrust into her hard and deep, his hands moving to her waist to hold her back against him as he came.

He stood behind her, still embedded within her, when she turned to look at him over her shoulder. "Yeah, I think I'm ready to kick some ass now."

Grinning, he shook his head. "You're trouble, you know that? Thank Gods you're mine."

* * * * *

Rhea spent the next hours poring over the books in her family library, reading everything she could about negative magics. She'd never tried a spell of that type before and it terrified her. At the same time, they had no other real options at that stage of the game. It was go big or go home in a coffin.

She knew her father and Jax both worried about her but both men also believed in her and that helped.

Some hours before she and Jax planned to leave to go into the mountains they ate a meal and slept.

Against the harbor of his body, Jax's warmth lulled and relaxed her. Made her feel safe. His scent rose from his skin and her body responded. Still, she spelled herself, knowing it would be impossible to sleep without help—a sleep that was dreamless and protected from invasion with protective magic.

Chapter Seven

ॐ

When she awoke, the tension was already heavy in the air. The Nameless was coming and they had to stop it.

Jax was already downstairs and giving orders, she heard him as she went down to join him. Katai refused to leave and sat in the dining room, drinking coffee and watching her grandson lead.

Rhea stood in the doorway and watched him as well. Her man emanated strength and leadership. She knew he'd run the Council at her side, a uniting of their two houses the way it was supposed to have been with Paul all those years ago.

As if he'd felt her presence, he turned, and smiled as he caught sight of her. "Good afternoon, angel. Still ready to kick some Nameless butt?"

She went to him, unable not to seek out his arms. "Yeah, something like that. It's not like I can go on a weekend at the shore instead."

"After this, I'll take you anywhere you want to go, angel. Mrs. Dakins has packed up some food. We should get going."

Katai stood and wrapped her arms around both of them. "You two will bring my great-grandchildren into the world. Believe in each other. I'll be here when you get back."

The way the internal wards were constructed, it was possible for them to open a rift to get there.

Timus met them at the base of the hillside that would serve as their staging area.

"We've set up a small place for you to Practice. It's an alcove at the top of the hill here."

Relief coursed through Rhea. The idea of Practicing with an audience didn't thrill her. She would have done it if she had to, but being alone with Jax on the crest of that mountain appealed to her far more.

"We've got Practitioners all through the mountains. Their power will amplify better that way. And soldiers stationed at the base of the rocks on both sides of the pass here. Emmia...I don't want her here but she insisted. She's with the soldiers."

Rhea nodded. "It's who she is, Father. And you can't deny her skill with the blades. I can only imagine she's gotten even better over the years. Let her help in her own way. She knows what's best for herself."

"And you? Are you sure about the negative magic?"

She nodded slowly. "It's our best hope. If it works we not only end it, we take the power and I'll transfer it into the wards."

"Sarai is here with the minxes, she said to send her love." Timus looked to Jax. "You keep my daughter safe, Jaac."

"I'll do my very best."

Rhea squeezed Jax's hand. "Where is Arta?"

"He's dead. They found him dead in his cell this afternoon." He looked to Jax quickly. "Your mother is fine. Your father is here with your sister on the far ridge. My brother Stephen knew Arta was conspiring but not exactly what. He's resigned and volunteered for exile. I sent him through a rift an hour ago. Treya is here."

"We need to go. I can feel it getting closer. When the day slides into another, at midnight, we'll begin. The Nameless will come then, it's when we will both draw the most power."

Timus kissed Rhea's forehead and turned. A guard would lead them up to the place they'd Practice.

At the crest of the mountain, they'd created a nest of blankets and mats in a small impression surrounded by rocks. The guard turned and left them there.

Under the silvery light of the moon, Jax pulled off his clothing and upended a container holding herb-laced water over his head.

Magic began to pulse low in her gut as she watched the rivulets of water run down over his muscled form. His hair was so long it hung past his ass when wet.

She pulled her own clothes off and did the same ritual with the water. The air was cold but their magic held out most of it.

Once she dried off, she pulled on her robe. Jax went to sit in the center of their nest and watched as she went to work.

She tied a piece of thistle in her hair and did the same to Jax's. Thistle would protect against magical attacks.

Moving around the area, she scattered salt, and then elder leaves were scattered at the head of where they'd lay, to ward off evil. She'd burned black sesame seeds earlier and bathed the both of them in the smoke, again to protect them from evil.

Rhea didn't always use all of these tools and ingredients, but taking the Nameless' power into herself in the negative magic spell would leave her open in ways she wasn't normally. Extra precaution would not hurt.

She knelt before Jax and held her arms out at her sides, hands stained with henna. The Nameless was on the horizon and she felt her Talent surge as midnight slipped into place.

Jax leaned in and kissed her chest above her heart. "I love you so you have to get through this. Now let's go."

"Do me." She raised a brow and smirked, pulling her robe off her body.

Warm lips grazed over her temple and then he found her mouth. The kiss was gentle, soft. It murmured sweet nothings and promised afternoon walks on the beach. She sighed into him, relaxing, giving herself.

His hands moved, sliding against her scalp, holding her head, changing the angle to suit himself, and he went back for more. His tongue, hot and wet, slipped between her lips and into her mouth like he owned it. And he did. She was his as he was hers and their magic twisted and bound together and began to pour from them.

His effect on her was intense and her body responded—tightening, tingling, blooming and getting slick. Hunger slid through her with a sharp edge. She needed him, not just as her partner but as her man.

Need broke from her lips as a primal cry and he bit her chin as he nibbled down her face and to her neck.

When the air was just thick enough, she tipped her head back and began to speak. The words she spoke were slightly different than the ones she normally used. They felt odd in her mouth, but the power began to pulse between them in a low bass. Back and forth with a seductive tempo that echoed in her nipples and clit.

The Nameless reached the wards and stopped, sensing their presence and their magic.

And then it began to work to unravel the layers of spells that held the wards in place—in a way that made it clear someone who'd had intimate knowledge of the wards had supplied the information.

She reached one henna-stained hand out and grabbed his cock. With a groan, he pumped into her fist. Dimly, she felt the throb of him against the skin of her palm, felt the wetness smear under her thumb as she moved it up and over the head.

He whispered words of encouragement and adoration against her skin. Words her brain couldn't focus on but knew existed anyway.

He placed her gently on her back against the cool nest of blankets there. The full moon hung heavy above their heads and the light of it glinted from her skin, her magic glimmering.

Each nipple called to his mouth and he gave into his need for her. He swirled his tongue around each tight knot of flesh until her hips began to churn.

Sliding his hand down her belly and between the swollen lips of her cunt, he found her wet and ready for him. Her clit was hard and begging for attention.

He sucked a nipple into his mouth and grazed it with his teeth. Her breath caught and her magic swelled, pouring out again in a greater volume.

An electric hum filled the air. Jax's hair rose with the static. The Nameless pushed through the wards enough that Jax heard the yell of the soldiers below. He knew a battle would ensue between their troops and those dark ones with the Nameless. He felt a general upsurge in power as Practitioners all over the area began to work their magic in various ways.

Rhea had told him before they left the house that it was likely the Nameless would get very close to her and that he could not interrupt her spell no matter what the reason. If the spell tying them together snapped, her own life force could be drained back into the Nameless.

He kept this in mind as the shadow of the Nameless, dank and dreadful, loomed over them.

Leaning down between her thighs, he tasted her. The creamy honey of her pussy coated his lips, eased the way for his fingers to slide into her.

As he slid the flat of his tongue from side to side over her clit, he fucked her with his fingers and wondered what battle was going on between his beloved and the monster that threatened their very existence.

Even if she could have spoken, Rhea wouldn't have been able to describe what happened in the ether. She coursed on her magic, up and out, and with her words, connected to the Nameless. It was a shock when its cold darkness began to fill her and she was glad she'd taken the extra precautions she had. It felt as if she were drowning in icy-cold dread, and terror threatened all around. It was hard to lock out her fears. Fear that she wasn't strong enough or powerful enough to win. Fear that she'd lose hold on this plane of existence and be lost forever in that darkness. As a counterpoint, sweet relief rushed through her as Jax's weight held her to the rocks and earth filled with power. Power she tapped into as the earth itself was her conduit.

The Nameless fought her then, trying to reverse the spell, but she'd taken it by surprise. As her pleasure built, her Talent did as well, amplified by the Practitioners all over the area and the man touching her.

Quicksilver, orgasm coursed through her as she felt the slight burn and then intense pleasure of Jax's finger pressing into her backside as he tongued her clit and stroked her sweet spot. Her body went into overdrive at the sheer abundance of sensory pleasure he visited upon her.

She felt the cord that connected her to Jax then, strong. The last bit of doubt left her and she grabbed the Nameless' life force and power with all her magical might and pulled it into herself and then back into the ground below her body. The earth would receive it and purify it and return it to the wards.

Jax's cock sliced into her, her body bent nearly in half, legs up over his shoulders. The rock beneath her bit into her shoulders through the blankets, but that only served to heighten the primal nature of the way he took her.

The Nameless surged against her and she felt its physical form icy against her skin. Fear slithered through her but Jax's fingers gripped her shoulders tight, pressing into the skin there. That brought her back to him, helped her get hold of herself again, and she struggled up to her magical feet.

The smug feeling from the Nameless receded as she began to drain power anew. Somewhere in the back of her head she knew people were dying below. Most assuredly people she knew and maybe even loved.

But she had to put it out of her mind because if she didn't finish the spell they'd all die for sure.

Jax's hands found her breasts, pinching her nipples until she made a low squeal. He bent over her as he rolled his hips to thrust deep into her. He'd never taken a woman this way before. He dominated her with his form but those long legs wrapped around his neck, her breasts bouncing and the low, rhythmic grunts that came from deep in her gut around the murmurings of her spell made him feel like a conquered man. She held his heart in the palm of her hand, he belonged to her utterly and completely.

He'd convince her to marry him if it was the last thing he did. There was no way he was going to let her avoid marriage because of the ways others had acted.

Her cunt rippled around him, the honey spreading on his balls and stomach as he moved into her was scalding hot. Her scent drove him crazy. So damned sexy and delicious. Sliding his tongue over his lips, he tasted her anew and that small thing pushed him a step away.

Gauging from the feeling in the air and her output of power, which was cresting higher and higher, the spell was coming to a close. The ground beneath them was superheated from the magic she channeled through it. Her own body was so warm that steam rose from it into the air.

He adjusted his angle so each thrust into her was also a grind of his pubic bone against her clit. Her breath hitched and he knew it was a move he'd use again when they weren't Practicing and she could react to him.

The static built and built, the hum was lower now and it hurt his teeth. The clashes below became less frenzied and suddenly she cried out as she climaxed. So much power shot from her and ricocheted back into them both and into the earth that he felt like his entire body shot through the head of his cock into her when he came.

The last bit of the Nameless washed through them and he felt nauseated as it touched them. He couldn't imagine what it felt like for Rhea to channel such evil through her magic, through her body.

And it was gone.

There were still shouts from below, and screams, but they began to die down as well.

Rhea, pale and still, lay there with her eyes closed. Jax wanted to shake her to break the spell but she'd warned him not so and so he sat back on his haunches and watched her, willing her to wake up.

And some half an hour later she did, eyes fluttering open and coming to focus on him. A cry of joy broke from him when she reached her hand out. He pulled her up and into his lap, cradling her and weeping into her hair.

"Ashes."

He pulled back so he could see her face. "What? What did you say, angel?"

"Ashes. All I can taste and smell are ashes."

"We'll get you back to the house and Katai will pour tea into you until you burst. I'll run you a bath and scrub your back until all you can taste and smell is me. You did it. You saved us all."

She nodded and sat up, letting him put the robe on over her head. They'd have to walk down the hillside. Seeing her weakness, Jax picked her up and carried her and their bags.

He met the guards, who nodded and let them pass.

The ground below was a bloody mess of carnage. The dead and injured lay everywhere.

Timus limped toward them both and he put his hand over his mouth at the sight of her. "You did it, Rhea, you did it."

"But at what cost?" Her words were close to a croak as she looked around.

"This is not a cost you exacted. All these years we got lazy and they built an army. We were caught unprepared, never thinking we'd need one. We thought of the Nameless as a single entity. It was more than that. While we dismissed it, an army built, using the power of the Nameless and our ignorance to catch us unaware. They nearly succeeded. And now we won't forget. The wards are so strong now. And my Talent is stronger. The energy you drained from the Nameless has flowed into us all—a new generation of Practitioners will be trained now."

"Is...are my sister and father alive?" Jax scanned the area, relieved to see Petra standing at a knot of people. But his heart stuttered when he looked at what she stared at.

"Jaac, your father..."

Without putting Rhea down, Jax ran over to where Petra stood. His father lay in a heap at her feet.

"He saved me, Jaac. But then the one who tried to kill me got him instead."

"Put me down, Jax. Go to Petra. She needs you." Rhea spoke softly in his ear and he nodded and reluctantly put her down to pull his sister into an embrace.

The sorrow of that day built as many loved ones were counted among the dead, including Rhea's uncle Treya. Emmia survived and it was a good thing Rhea was too weak to move or she'd have jumped on her sister in relief.

The two sisters embraced and Rhea kissed Emmia's forehead.

"I know you have to go. This couldn't have been easy."

"I had to come." Emmia shrugged. "But I've settled in the east. I can be alone when I need to be."

Rhea nodded, understanding. Still, sorrow at being separated from her sister again coursed through her.

With a last look over her shoulder, Emmia opened a rift and walked through.

Broken and grieving, Jax, Rhea and Petra headed back through a rift. Back home to pick up the pieces and start the next chapter. Hope was an ember burning deep inside Rhea as she clutched Jax's hand.

* * * * *

His arm around Rhea's waist, Jax gave his grandmother a rundown of what had happened, and she took a grieving Petra into her arms. "Pet, my sweet, you need to rest. Come with me, let's get you tucked up and with a cup of tea that'll help you sleep without dreams."

Katai looked at the two of them, sadness in her eyes. "Go on. You look exhausted. This will all be here when you've rested a while. You need each other right now. I'll hold everyone off for a few hours." Reaching out, she touched Rhea's cheek and then Jax's before turning away with Petra.

Not letting go, Jax picked her up and carried her straight into his bedroom, kicking the door closed behind him. Shutting out the world and all the carnage.

Laying her on the bed, he left to go turn on the water in the bathtub. Coming back, he pulled his clothes off and then hers. All the while, neither spoke, they only looked into each other's eyes.

Taking the hand he offered, she followed him into the bathroom and stepped into the large bathtub, settling between his thighs once he'd sat down. Nestling back into him more firmly, her back rested against his chest, her body cradled by his.

"I don't know what I would have done if I'd lost you today, Rhea." The emotion in his voice tore at her heart. "When you were unconscious for so long I thought...I didn't know if you'd ever come back. You said you tasted ashes when you woke up. I'd have tasted them for eternity without you at my side."

A tear rolled down her cheek as she turned her head to put her ear over his beating heart. "I'm here. And I'm not going anywhere. I'm done running. Today above all else has taught me the true value of what I have. What you and I are, Jax. You fought for me, when I needed you this time you were there. I couldn't have succeeded today without your help. I'm sorry you lost your father."

His breath hitched. "I am too. But he died doing the right thing and that's important. It would have been important to him too."

And without words, with soft caresses and gentle kisses he washed her back, ministering to her body and spirit, drying her off when they'd done.

Sorrow mixed with hope as they got into bed and tried to sleep. Knowing that they'd have to deal with much more pain when they walked out of that room, they also knew they'd have each other.

"We'll make it. And you'll finally marry me. Then we can think about a baby or three in a few years."

"Leave it to you to get me when I'm tired." Rhea sighed, laughter in her voice.

"But you love me."

"Yes. I love you."

WHISPER OF THE BLADE

Anya Bast

∞

Author's Note

I used the Two of Swords from the standard Ryder-Waite tarot deck as a basis for this story. It depicts a woman sitting in a chair with a waxing moon in the sky, rocks and a body of water behind her. She is blindfolded and balances two crossed swords.

I wanted to write this note to explain how I interpreted this card. The crossed swords I take as conflict, which the woman must balance on her shoulders. She must do it blindfolded, perhaps carefully weighing the solution to the conflict with logic and intellect, rather than force, and with neutrality. The waxing moon in the sky symbolizes a new beginning arising out of the solution to the conflict. The water represents emotion, and the rocks signify hindrances to the flow of that emotion.

Chapter One

❧

The blade could injure the wind itself.

Emmia stood in the middle of her grove, her blindfold in place. Around her, birds twittered on branches and leaves rustled in the trees. There was not one person for miles around her.

This was heaven. This was the place she most loved to be. She took a long, cleansing breath of air and slowly let it out, enjoying the emotional quiet around her.

Then she lunged and turned, driving the blade through the air at an imagined enemy, enjoying the heft and feel of the fine weapon in her hand. Each day she practiced for three hours in the woods and she often trained blindfolded. Taking away her vision helped sharpen her other senses and she needed every advantage in a fight.

Perspiration beading her brow and breathing heavily, Emmia turned, lunged, leapt and arched, feeling the delicious stretch and pull of her muscles. Just her and the blade. It was how she liked it best. No one around to batter and buffet her emotions. No one around to bombard her with their unwelcome feelings.

Her Talent was empathy. That meant she could feel the emotions of others. It was a rare Talent and she was particularly strong in her abilities. The downside was that it had been difficult to train. Emmia had tried numerous techniques since she'd been too small to filter the emotions she felt, but nothing had worked. Stemming her ability had been like trying to stop a river with a butterfly net. The only thing that worked for Emmia was long periods of solitude. That's the only thing that made the emotional bombardments she must endure bearable.

After the showdown with the Nameless in D'ar, Emmia had returned to her home in the Eastern Mountains, ravaged by the turmoil she'd been forced to absorb. All she wanted for a while was the peace and solitude of her cottage, her woods, her training grove and her bathing pool.

Emmia hoped no one came to enlist her services for a while. She stopped, pulled her blindfold off and watched the dappled sunlight gleam along the blade and tang of the sword. Although her new sword was definitely a beauty, the finest famed blacksmith Ma'hor in Galenstown had ever made. Seemed a pity not to put it to immediate use.

The blade itself was curved a little and etched with a sun and moon, mated. The grip and pommel were wound with fine cured leather to provide an excellent handhold. The ricasso was not leather-bound and instead was bare unsharpened metal, roughed a bit to make the sword more wieldy in close combat. The blood grooves etched into the blade near the guard allowed air into the inflicted wound and made for an easier pull out.

It was, in a word, *perfect*.

Yes, she was a fine sword. The very best friend a justice mercenary like her could have. Sorrow squeezed her chest. Since she didn't seem to be able to have any human friends, perhaps it was the best friend an empath could have as well. She stood, breathing heavily in the oppressive heat of the day and considered that, the slight smile she wore fading.

Her joy at the blade now somewhat diminished at the thought, she sought her scabbard and walked through the trees toward her bathing pool. She would take a swim to cool off and to bathe and then seek her dinner.

This was her life, best to accept it.

* * * * *

Magnus guided his horse past the thick covering of bushes and trees of the old forest he traveled through. He'd left the main road through the Eastern Mountains some time ago to indulge himself in a solitary ride back to Ravensbridge. He knew the way and, if he ever lost it, he had a compass and a map tucked into the saddlebag of the chestnut brown stallion he rode.

The journey would take longer cross-country, but he had no pressing need to be back at Ravensbridge. Indeed, he did not even have a desire. Rolf, his castellan, could take care of things until he returned. Everyone much preferred him gone these days, anyway. Many of them wanted him dead.

He wouldn't go easily, though. They'd have to lynch him. Magnus refused to be punished for a crime he never committed.

The evidence was damning. Magnus knew that to every man, woman and child at Ravensbridge it appeared he'd committed murder. It even looked that way to Quinn. Sorrow clenched in his chest and throat when he remembered the look of shock, then doubt in his best friend's eyes.

Even the person who knew him best in the world thought he'd done it.

Magnus knew that Quinn was even now on his way through these forests to seek the aid of a justice mercenary. That was the primary reason Magnus had gone cross-country. He wanted to get a glimpse of the woman who might stand in judgment of him, the woman likely to be his executioner...if she could manage to kill him, that was. Since he was innocent, he wouldn't go down without a fight.

A full four weeks had passed since the crime had been committed. Four weeks of hell in which he'd been accused, had protested his innocence and finally laid down the law because he'd felt he'd had no other choice. Unable to exist at Ravensbridge amid the whispers, suspicious glances, and outright fear of him, he'd left to travel to his sister's keep.

A messenger bird, keyed to his location by someone who had the Talent, had reached him yesterday, letting him know that Quinn could not take the uncertainty of Magnus' guilt any longer and had gone to employ a justice mercenary.

The woman was well known in the Eastern Mountains and he knew she dwelt in these leaf-laden hills. No one could pass through these woods without her knowing it. As an empath, she could sense the whereabouts of anyone because of the emotions they emitted. She would never sense him, however, because he was also an empath. The rare talent canceled out in two people face-to-face. Well, theoretically, anyway. There were so few empaths in the world, it had rarely, if ever, been put to the test. Mostly likely, he would not be able to feel her emotion, nor her his.

The idea of meeting someone like her was an attractive one…even if she might want to kill him. He'd take the risk.

Further into the forest, he heard the splash of water and a woman's voice swearing low. Silently as he could, Magnus slipped from his mount, tied him to a tree and stepped carefully through the trees, trying not to break any branches. She wouldn't be on guard for sounds in the forest. He knew that for certain. No, she'd been open to sensing emotion, not listening for noise, just as he would be in her position.

From his place in the undergrowth, he caught a glimpse of her in a large, still pool of water. She stood with her back to him, lean, lithe body moving as she bathed herself. The sunlight sprinkled her skin through the canopy of trees overhead and caressed her short, curvaceous body. Long, dark hair hung damp down to the small of her back, twisted into a braid that lay like a heavy rope along her spine. A pity her buttocks were concealed under the water. He had the sense they were as luscious and sweetly curved as the rest of her.

She turned a little, revealing the tender swell of a breast topped with a pinkened nipple. Her profile revealed her to be a beauty, but her features were set with an intense expression, almost sorrowful.

But the most wonderful thing was that he didn't know how she felt. The absence of foreign emotion while he viewed another person felt like a balm to his often-battered soul.

Magnus stared. He'd never expected beauty, not from all the tales he'd been told about this woman. He'd expected her to be strong, mannish, but while it was clear she was muscled, her body well-toned from physical exertions, she appeared small, almost delicate. She seemed barely able to hold a sword, yet she'd gone up against some of the worst scum Molari had to offer and had come away the victor.

Magnus took a step toward her before he remembered himself. To court a conversation with Emmia, the most deadly of justice mercenaries, was to court death.

And he was already doing that.

She stilled in the water, listening. His heart shot up into his throat. Had she heard him or sensed him in some way?

Magnus took a step back, careful not to break a branch under his boot. He would meet her soon enough and she would judge him. After the hell he'd been through in the last month, he welcomed her visit. Perhaps, by some wild twist of fate, she would discover his innocence. Or perhaps she would look at the evidence mounted against him and come to the conclusion so many others had, that he was guilty.

Either way, there would be closure. Magnus thirsted for that.

* * * * *

A blade appeared at his throat, making Quinn stop short. His horse reared in surprise behind him and came back down on his already lame foot. Poor beast.

"What do you want?" came a low, steady female voice to his right.

"For you to drop your weapon?" Quinn answered quickly.

Silence. Apparently levity was not called for in this situation, nor charm. Bad news for him.

"Are you Emmia, the justice mercenary?" He tried to turn toward the voice and got only the pressure of the blade against his throat. It pricked and he felt the warm, slow slide of blood down his flesh.

"I am."

"My name is Quinn. I come seeking you. I have business to discuss."

She held the weapon a moment longer and then dropped it. Quinn let out a breath of relief and turned toward her, only to catch his breath again. She stood before him dressed in faded brown hunting leathers and a white tunic. The pants hugged her shapely legs and hips closely, though the tunic concealed her upper body. She met his eyes with her dark brown gaze. They were pretty eyes, set in a pretty face.

So this was the famed Emmia. She was lovely. How unexpected.

"I'm not taking any jobs right now," she answered brusquely. She turned and walked into the brush. "Go home."

The lovely didn't come with good manners. Pity.

"No, I can't. Emmia, I very much need to employ you. I've come offering a large sum of money."

"I don't require money," came her voice, now going fainter as she retreated from him.

Anger rose up in him, swift and immediate. "I've traveled four days to reach you," he yelled. "My horse has gone lame. I need a meal, a bath and a good night's sleep. At least hear my case. I come to avenge a woman I cared for and perhaps save a friend."

"This is not my problem." Her voice sounded farther away.

"Please! I need your help! I'll beg, if you like!"

Silence.

"Have you no compassion at all?" he yelled.

More silence.

"Damn," he swore under his breath. He clenched his fist. He couldn't go back to Ravensbridge without her. They had to cure the poisoned environment they lived in. She was the only one who could make that happen.

The bushes to his left rustled and Emmia emerged. "I have so much compassion, sir," she said icily, "that I am numb with it." Her eyes were dark with anger, perhaps a kind of deep grief. It was there, then gone. "Follow me. I will hear your case, but that doesn't mean I'll take it. Understand?"

He nodded.

She turned and continued down the horse path he'd been following. Eventually they came to a cottage, though *cottage* may not have been the right word. In the darkening twilight, he could see that it was made of expensive gray stone and stood two stories tall with a well-thatched roof and at least three chimneys. It was not large, but it was obviously well appointed and probably snug in the wintertime. A well stood outside and nearby a large stable had been constructed.

Regardless of her of remote location, she didn't deny herself luxuries. Quinn liked that. It made her seem more accessible.

In any other situation, he would have joked about the justice mercenary business being lucrative, but Emmia didn't seem like the joking type. In an odd way, she reminded him of Magnus. Perhaps it was because they were both empaths.

Carefully cultivated flowers grew in profusion everywhere. Quinn had a hard time picturing this woman tending them, but he knew she lived alone. In the small, well-kept courtyard, she turned to him. "You said your horse had gone lame? Put him in the stable and tend him if you like. Then come into the house. I'll have stew warmed and some fresh bread with butter, if you're hungry."

"Thank you."

Unsmiling, she turned and left him, disappearing through the front door of her strange home here in the middle of nowhere.

Quinn led his horse into the stable and found one other mount already there, a fine black stallion that whickered low when they entered. He examined the hoof that had taken a sharp rock the day before. The tender frog was still raw and red, but it was nothing that wouldn't heal. He brushed him down and got him some feed and water from the well, then settled him into one of the stalls for the night.

Following the scent of food, Quinn entered the cottage and found himself in the kitchen. To his left was a sitting room and directly in front of him was a staircase, leading up to the second floor. She had a fire going in the kitchen hearth to heat the stew, making the already warm room even warmer. Emmia sliced bread at a long table in the center of the room. Perspiration shone on her forehead and the fine skin of her throat and upper chest. A long strand of her dark brown hair had freed itself from the tight braid she wore down her back.

He set his saddlebags down and let his gaze linger on her a moment, admiring her beauty and wondering what her upper body looked like under that loose tunic. It seemed horrible to be thinking carnal thoughts about this woman a scant month after Caith's death, but Caith wouldn't have minded. He could hear Caith's lilting voice in his head even now, telling him to take pleasure where he could...she did. Theirs had never been an exclusive relationship.

In any case, he couldn't help being attracted to this woman. She was incredibly intriguing.

"I'm not going to sleep with you, if that's what you think," she said curtly, without even looking up.

Hell, he'd forgotten momentarily that she was an empath. "I never assumed that. It's just that you're beautiful and I'm a man who appreciates such a quality in a woman." He shrugged. "There's not much more to say."

She just grunted and glanced up at him. "Sit there." She jerked her head at a smooth wood table in the corner where a place was set with a plate of butter, silverware and a bowl of strew. His stomach rumbled. "I've got your bread for you and a glass of ale. Then you can tell me your sad story. I warn you, though, I've heard many of them and I'm not easily swayed."

He sat and she brought him the bread and ale, then sat down in a chair near him. Quinn dug into the food immediately. The stale flatbread and water he'd been eating for the last two days hadn't done much to assuage his hunger. Emmia watched him with her dark, inscrutable eyes.

When he'd filled his stomach enough to speak, he launched into an explanation for the reason for his journey.

"I come from Ravensbridge, in the westernmost part of the mountains. I am advisor to a great lord, or he was a great lord, anyway, named Magnus. He was a friend, a good friend." He fell silent a moment, mastering his emotions before he continued. "We were both involved with the same woman, the niece of a lower baron. Please understand it wasn't any deep romantic love we held for her. It was just affairs for all of us, the lady included. Though Magnus and I did care for her deeply and were very fond of her."

"Let me guess, this woman does not now live?" she interrupted.

He drew a breath. "She was slain, yes, and I believe possibly by Magnus' hand. I don't want to think it, and it's hard for me to believe, but he was seen with her last. They went into the woods together and a scant time later she was found run through several times. The castellan conducted a search of the castle and found Magnus' blade covered in blood."

"Seems straightforward enough, but I can tell you're not truly sure Magnus killed her."

"He denies it, and I can think of no reason he would do such a thing. He is a man of violence, a strong man and a

139

sometimes cold man, but I know him well enough to understand that he would never harm a woman or child, never. He especially had no reason to harm Caith. She pleased us both well and was a very good friend."

"But you don't know everything that went on in their relationship, I suppose."

"I likely did," he replied, but said no more. There were certain things he wouldn't reveal unless he absolutely had to.

Her eyes blazed for a moment with speculation and he wondered what she was thinking. She glanced down at the table. "So you want me to travel to Ravensbridge and determine his guilt."

"Or innocence." He paused. Yes, he still hoped. "He is lord and master of the keep and the law of the land. No one but you could render justice against him." He stared at his bowl and realized he'd lost his appetite.

"You are conflicted in your emotions regarding this man, but you are resigned."

"I don't like any of this, but I want to see justice done. No matter the outcome or the pain it might cause me, Caith deserves her murderer punished."

"Tell me, is this man Magnus stupid? Careless?"

"Hardly. No, he is neither."

She scratched her fingernail over the top of the table. "Confident in his divine right as lord of the keep, then?"

"No, he's not that way, either. He's a fair man, sometimes hard and exacting in his justice, but never acting presumptuously or entitled in his rule."

Her shapely lips twisted into a half smile. "You talk so well of this man you've traveled here to have condemned."

"I only want to see justice done." A tumult of emotion roiled in his stomach. He pushed the bowl away and took a long drink of the ale. The liquid couldn't wash away the now-familiar taste of bitter guilt pooling on the back of his tongue.

"If he's not stupid or overly arrogant, then why, I wonder," she said slowly, "would he leave his bloody sword lying around where the castellan could find it?"

Quinn sighed. "That has occurred to me too. Out of shock over his crime, perhaps? Maybe he wasn't thinking clearly."

She looked up at him, still scraping her nail over the tabletop. The hank of dark hair that fell over her cheek looked like silk. He fought the urge to find out if it felt that way against his fingers. "Could be," she answered.

"Does that mean you'll accept this job?"

A muscle worked in her jaw and she glanced away. "No, I'm sorry. I cannot."

Quinn pushed a hand through his hair. "Why not?"

She stood and walked to the table. "I recently returned from fighting the Nameless. I'm sure that battle did not go unmarked in far away Ravensbridge?"

"It didn't go unmarked anywhere in Molari, Emmia."

She nodded and folded her arms over her chest. "I'm still recovering. Truthfully, I don't know how much good I would be to you."

Quinn turned in his chair, letting his gaze skate up her body. For a strong woman, she seemed fragile in a way. He nearly got up and went to her, drew her into his arms. Likely he'd incur serious injuries if he tried that. "I won't leave without you," he said simply.

Anger flickered in the depths of her eyes.

"I am not a man easily dissuaded." He paused. "When I see something I want." She was likely aware of the double entendre.

Anger turned to apprehension and…fear? She was easily read and he was not even an empath. "I should throw you and your lame horse out right now." Her voice shook slightly.

"I still won't leave this area. I'll camp nearby and bother you every day. You'll have to run a sword through me to rid yourself of my presence."

She raised an eyebrow. "Think I wouldn't?"

"I think you're not the type of person to kill someone who wasn't guilty of a heinous crime. That's what I think."

Emmia stood staring at him for a long moment, her gaze going icy. He'd seen that same look a hundred times in Magnus' eyes. It was the armor of an empath. They wore it thick in order to shield themselves from the torrents of emotions around them. He understood Emmia because he understood Magnus...or thought he had, anyway.

"You had better bank on that assumption," she answered in a low voice. "There is a bedroom at the top of the stairs on the left. You may stay there for the night, but you *will* leave in the morning." She turned on her heel and left the room.

Quinn rubbed his hand over his chin, feeling stubble. The woman had the ability to drop the temperature in a room to near freezing. She needed some warming up.

And he wasn't leaving in the morning.

He got up, took care of his dishes, gathered his saddlebags and then climbed the steep set of stairs to the second floor. The bedroom was of medium size and appointed sparsely with a large feather bed, a dresser and a wardrobe.

The door across the hallway was closed. Likely that was where Emmia slept.

He'd seen a washroom down the hall, so he took what he needed from his bags and then went down there to wash up. The water was drawn through pipes from a large water tank and heated by some method not readily apparent. Quinn didn't care much about puzzling it out. He could barely form a coherent thought when faced with the prospect of bathing in hot water after so many days of dunks in cold rivers.

He filled the bathtub and shed his traveling clothes. Then he slipped into the bathwater with a deep groan of appreciation. After a few minutes of just soaking, he lathered his hands and ran them over his chest and shoulders, massaging away the tension in his muscles. It felt good. The only thing that would've felt better was Emmia's hands on him. He thought about her stroking his skin, working his muscles, and it made him hard. Quinn wrapped a soap-slathered hand around his cock and pumped it until he groaned.

When he'd finished in the bath, he drained the water and stood at the sink with a towel wrapped around his waist to shave and trim his hair. Then he cleaned up after himself, balled his clothes up and opened the door to go back to his room.

Emmia stood in the hallway. She looked taken aback and Quinn didn't miss the slow head-to-toe perusal she gave him before she finally completely addressed him to his face. Her expression went from surprise to irritation. "Making yourself right at home, I see," she snapped.

He smiled. "I thought you'd appreciate a houseguest who didn't stink."

"I'd appreciate no houseguest at all," she grumbled, and disappeared back into her bedroom and slammed the door.

* * * * *

Emmia leaned against her bedroom door and closed her eyes for a moment. There was no reason for her to have such a reaction to a man's body. She'd seen enough of them in her days, even ones as fine as Quinn's. Still, having a man in her home, his scent, and the sounds of him...all of it was very intimate.

It had been far too long since she'd had sex and the times she'd had it had been too infrequent for a woman of her age. It was true she avoided it in general and had turned down many opportunities. Perhaps that had been a mistake. She was a healthy woman, after all, with needs like any other woman, empathic ability or not.

Now it appeared she was paying the price for her neglect of her sexual wellbeing.

She listened as Quinn walked into the other bedroom. He was definitely a strong, excellent specimen of manhood. She'd seen that when he'd been fully dressed, but clad in only a damp towel, it had been readily apparent. Broad shoulders led to capable looking arms and a hard, muscled chest. His hips were narrow and his thighs solid. He was a man who labored physically often, not some weak, well-fed eastern nobleman. He was a man who could make her feel like a woman and that was something, although she hated to admit it, that she craved from time to time. It was all made worse by the fact that she knew he was powerfully attracted to her. He wanted her. If she wanted him, he was hers for the taking.

The door across the hallway closed and her heart rate gradually returned to normal.

Chapter Two

೮೧

Emmia woke the next morning at the moment dawn slivered the sky. Her eyes fluttered open and she frowned, hearing the sound of wood being chopped.

"What?" She bounded out of bed and went to her window. Below her, in the area where she normally kept her firewood stood Quinn in all his shirtless glory. Muscles rippled as he raised the axe over his head and brought it down on a fallen tree trunk. Something tightened in her stomach at the sight, and it wasn't only because he formed such an enticing picture…it was anger.

He glanced up at the window, did a double take and smiled a little, wiping the sweat from his brow.

She disappeared and ran downstairs and out the door. "What do you think you're doing?" she demanded.

He hefted the axe over his shoulder and looked up at the sky. His rib cage rose and fell with his breathing, labored from his exertion. Emmia tried not to become overly fascinated with his strong build, the way the muscles in his arms bunched and flexed as he moved, and how the faint light filtering though the trees made his skin gleam. "It's getting colder," he said. "Winter's setting in. You don't have nearly enough firewood stored." His breath showed in the cool morning air. He pointed at her admittedly meager pile of wood. "I found some deadfall and I'm stocking it for you. Paying you back for the food, water, horse feed and the room for the night."

"I didn't ask you to do that."

"I don't leave debts unpaid, Emmia." He paused, looking at her speculatively. "You don't get much help, do you? You don't know how to handle it when you do."

"I don't need you to try to understand me, Quinn."

"Seems to me that you might need someone to take care of you a little, sometimes. Since you take care of so many others."

"You don't know what I want or what I need." Her voice was shaking a little. She tried to read his emotions, but failed. That happened sometimes when her own emotions ran high. She wasn't sure why she was so offended by Quinn taking the initiative in chopping wood for her, she just was.

He stared at her for a long moment. "I know exactly what a woman like you needs."

Anger flared through her hard and fast. His meaning was not lost on her. "That's a very high-handed comment to make."

"Out here in the woods, on your own so often," he continued. "I'll bet that even when you're working and you're around people, you keep them at a distance. I bet men pursue you, but you put them off. You don't want to be close to them because you can feel their emotions. You can tell when they're just in it for the sex, or worse, when they've grown bored with you."

"I've used men for just sex before too, Quinn."

He nodded. "We all have needs. Empty, though, isn't it? One night of sex appeases us for a short time, but we all need relationships, connections and intimacy."

"You aren't the one to talk. You admitted last night you used Caith for sex."

He shook his head. "No, it wasn't like that. Our relationship was seated in deep respect and caring, if not love. We weren't using each other, we were enjoying each other."

"A fine line." She shook her head. "I'm not having this conversation with you. I want you to leave here now. I'm very well on my own." She turned to walk away. "I don't need anyone—"

She heard the axe *thunk* to the ground and felt Quinn's strong hand on her upper arm. He spun her around to face him.

"You're lying to yourself," he growled. "I can see it in your eyes. You're lonely, Emmia." He rubbed a tendril of her hair between his fingers and then hooked it behind her ear.

His touch felt good to her, though she tried to deny it. She tried to deny his words too, but couldn't.

"So what if I am," she whispered. "That's the lot I drew in this lifetime."

He shook his head. "It doesn't have to be that way. I'm here. I'm intrigued by you, attracted to you."

"You're trying to seduce me, poor pathetic, lonely woman out in the woods, just so I'll agree to travel to Ravensbridge," she spat. "You think I don't know?"

"No! Emmia, this has nothing to do with that." He sighed heavily. "I'm genuinely attracted to you."

Emmia did feel that from him. Grudgingly, she admitted he wasn't lying.

"And I recognize things in you because Magnus is also an empath. I see things in you that I've seen in him." He shrugged. "That's all."

She stilled. "Magnus is an empath?"

"Yes. I know the Talent is rare."

"You didn't mention that before."

"I didn't know it was relevant."

She blinked. "I've never met another empath before," she replied quietly, almost to herself.

"Come to Ravensbridge and you will."

She shook herself out of the shock. "I wouldn't be able to feel his emotions. I'd be blinded in that way."

"I know. You'd have to use your other reasoning abilities to discover the truth." He paused. "Does this mean you're thinking of accepting the job?"

"I don't know." Although the fact that Magnus was an empath did change things. She pulled out of his grasp with an impatient jerk. "Give me time to think," she replied, glaring at him.

He raised his hands, palms out. "All right."

She raised her gaze to his. His dark eyes regarded her with a nice, even warmth. Quinn was attracted to her and he understood better than anyone she'd ever met, likely because of his relationship with Magnus. He confused her, set her on edge.

"Emmia," he said slowly. "Give me tonight with you. Just one night. I'll leave in the morning…with or without you."

She didn't answer. She only turned and walked away.

Give me tonight with you. Just one night.

Emmia closed her eyes for a moment. Was it horrible that she was tempted by the offer? One night of physical contact with another person, his hands on her body, his mouth on her skin, hard body moving over her, his cock filling her, moving inside her… It had been so long since she'd had that. Her body nearly ached at the thought of it being so close.

She honestly didn't know if she'd able to not take him up on the offer.

Trying to put it out of her mind, she went back into the house and dressed for the day. Avoiding Quinn seemed the best option, so she threw herself into her work, doing chores, training in the woods. Every time she sensed he was near, she moved away, doing her best to completely insulate herself from him for the day.

At twilight, when she finally returned to the cottage for the evening, he was gone. The house felt empty and when she checked the stable for his horse, she found it gone.

Suppressing a twinge of disappointment, she went into the house and took a bath. When she came back downstairs, dressed in a comfortable nightshirt that hit her about mid-thigh, he was back. She'd begun to sense him when she'd been about halfway down the stairs. He was feeling tired, sexually aroused and a little hopeful.

She breezed past him, walking toward the main part of the kitchen. "Thought you'd left," she mumbled. She couldn't suppress the tiniest bit of happiness that he hadn't.

"Not yet. Not until you either agree to the job, or you give me one night."

She stopped in front of the counter, resting heavily against it.

"Give me tonight with you and I'll leave in the morning, with or without you," he repeated.

She stepped to the side, ready to turn around, ready to flee, but he moved to block her, arms on either side of her on the countertop so that she was caged. The heat of his body radiated out and warmed her. Emmia closed her eyes for a moment. If she wanted to get away, she could, but she didn't move. She couldn't deny that the contact felt good, almost better than sex.

Just simple human contact.

Quinn lowered his head, placed his mouth at her ear. The motion pressed his body against hers, pushed her against the counter. "One night," he whispered. "From now until dawn."

She didn't say anything. Didn't utter the word yes or no. But she didn't protest when he dragged the hem of her nightshirt up to her waist either. The feel of his fingertips on her skin made her shiver. He delved his hand between her thighs, felt her bare neediness, where she was wet and warm and creaming at his touch.

Quinn made a contented sound in his throat even while Emmia gasped. He splayed his other hand against her abdomen and stroked her softly between her thighs until an animalistic moan issued from her lips. He pressed his index finger to her clit and rubbed. Emmia felt it grow under his touch, swelling and becoming sensitive.

Through the haze of pleasure that had descended on her, she heard the sound of Quinn's belt buckle being undone. He eased her thighs wider apart and set the smooth, broad head of his cock to her slick opening. Quinn flexed his thighs, pushing up and into her. A ragged groan escaped her throat at the feel of him sliding up to fit within her. She curled her fingers around the edge of the counter and held on against his slow, steady thrusts.

It had been so long.

Emmia closed her eyes and bit her bottom lip, enjoying the sensation of having a man inside her, his body cupping hers, his warm breath on her skin.

"You feel good, Emmia," Quinn murmured as he thrust steadily into the welcoming heat of her body. "Does it feel good to you too?"

She nodded, trying not to whimper and failing.

"Been a while, hasn't it?" he asked softly. She found she couldn't answer him.

Quinn stroked her clit as he thrust into her and Emmia felt her climax building and building. Pleasure seeped through every pore of her body as he took her against the counter, driving her harder and faster until it exploded and she cried out as the force of her orgasm overwhelmed her. Her body shuddered and gently convulsed under the power of it and she felt Quinn, jerk a little and groan as he released his seed within her.

She collapsed against him, feeling weak and sated. Emmia could feel his heart beating against her back. "Come, this was no place for that," he murmured into her ear. He bore her back away from the countertop with strong arms.

Seemed like a fine place for it from Emmia's perspective.

He adjusted his pants and led her to the stairs. She stopped at the foot of the stairs and looked at him sharply. "I feel regret coming from you," she accused.

"Emmia. Do not misunderstand." He cupped her face in his hands. "I feel regret only because I took you against the counter, fast and hard, when I meant to take you in a bed, slow and soft." Quinn leaned in and kissed her.

His lips slid over hers like silk, making her knees feel like jelly. He tasted her, peppering her mouth with short and then long kisses, sometimes delving between her lips to rasp his tongue against hers, sometimes dragging her lower lip gently between his teeth.

Emmia gripped his shoulders, feeling herself growing warm and wet once more. Quinn slid a hand to the small of her back, the other to her nape and then slanted his mouth across hers hungrily for a deeper kiss. He inserted his thigh between hers and rubbed against her bare pussy, making her shudder.

Quinn broke the kiss and muttered an oath. "Come, let's go find a bed before I take you against the stairs."

* * * * *

Somehow, they made it to the second floor and into Emmia's bed. They undressed each slowly, kissing and exploring each other's body at leisure.

He stared at her for several heartbeats and then pushed her down onto the mattress. Bracing himself above her, he dipped his head and laved a nipple. With his other hand, he covered the small mound of her breast with his hand. Her breasts were small, but sweetly curved. He could probably fit the whole of one in his mouth. Staring at the sweet curve of one, he decided to try and found it fit, then set about treating each of her nipples like succulent pieces of candy. Gods, he thought he could snack on her breasts alone for the entire night.

151

She bucked beneath him and let out a little sighing moan that made his cock go rigid. Then he remembered that she had more than one tender place that deserved exploring. Quinn wanted to love them all thoroughly before dawn lit the horizon. He definitely wanted to feel her bare sex on his hand and tongue before he felt it wrapped around his cock.

He lifted his head and stared down into her pretty, shadowed face. "Spread your thighs for me," he demanded in a low, soft voice.

She parted her legs for him and he leaned back and took her in, lying there against the pillows, completely naked. The soft light filtered in through the window, caressing her small, pert breasts and their tightened nipples. Her pink pussy was plumped and aroused. She'd creamed nicely for him, more than ready to take his cock. Emmia lay there looking up at him, spread out like a five-course meal. He hardly knew where to begin, although he definitely knew he wanted to consume his fill of her. She was a beautiful woman.

Magnus would appreciate a woman like this, he thought, before he remembered. He squelched the thought, squelched the moment where he'd lived in a world where Magnus wasn't suspected of murdering their lover and centered his complete attention on Emmia. He leaned down and kissed the smooth skin above her navel and enjoyed the shiver of her stomach beneath his lips. Slowly, he trailed his tongue through her short, curly dark pubic hair and licked her swollen clit.

Emmia gasped and buried her fingers in his hair.

He raised his head and grinned. "Do you like that?"

"Yes," she hissed. "A man has never done that to me before."

"Mmmm, stupid men." He settled down between her thighs and, with his thumb, spread her folds apart to examine all the beauty that was Emmia. Gods, she was so lusciously creamy. He licked her from her perineum to her clit with long, sure strokes and pulled her labia between his lips, gently sucking.

Emmia shuddered beneath him, her breathing becoming deeper and heavier. He could feel the tenseness in her muscles and then the sweet give of her body as she gave herself completely over to him. He groaned at the sweet taste of her spreading over his tongue as he lapped at her.

Her clit was engorged and had pulled all the way out from its hood. It looked like a small luscious piece of ripe fruit and he sucked at it, treating as such. She arched her back, stabbing her nipples into the air in the semidarkness.

He toyed with her clit, feeling it grow larger against the tip of his tongue. He circled it and drew into his mouth and back out, enjoying the sensation of the small bundle of nerves against his tongue and enjoying her reaction even more. He rubbed over it repeatedly, holding onto her waist as he worked her clit to a fever pitch. Her hips bucked forward, as though looking for something to fuck. It was a lovely gesture and it made his cock harder than steel. He stroked a finger idly over her folds, rubbing and caressing them with his fingertip.

"Ah, yes," she moaned.

"Do you like that?" he purred. "I know I do." He set once more to spearing his tongue in and out of her until she keened for him.

"More," she cried.

He grinned for a moment at her carnal greediness and toyed with the entrance to her pussy, stroking over the sensitive skin there, while he sucked on her clit. Finally, he slid a finger into her.

Quinn threw his head back and groaned at the feel of her muscles gripping his finger. She was so hot and tight. Emmia had spread her thighs as wide as she could. She whimpered and moaned as he drew his finger out and slowly pushed it back into her softness. He slipped another finger down and added it to the first. His fingers slipped in easily because of how wet she was, but her muscles were tight and clamped down around him.

"Faster. Harder," Emmia gasped.

He drew his hand back and thrust into her. She gripped the blankets on either side of her and moaned. He could tell she was growing close to orgasm. Her body tensed and she cried out as she climaxed. The muscles of her pussy spasmed around his fingers and her hips bucked again.

"Ah, that was beautiful," he said as he raised his head. He could see the answering curve of her lips in the dim light.

Quinn climbed up and curled his body around her. He felt her give a shuddering sigh as the post-climax languor settled over her body and ran his hands over her, exploring her curves and enjoying her soft, soft skin. She was lovely.

"I needed that," she sighed and gave a quiet laugh.

Had she just *laughed*?

Chapter Three

ॐ

She rolled over, her twined her arms around his neck, compelling his head down for a kiss. "I want more," she murmured, when they finally broke the kiss.

He tipped her face up to his with his index finger. "Patience. We have all night and I intended to use every moment of it. There's no reason to hurry. Slow"—his eyes went dark—"slow is better."

He lowered his mouth to hers and kissed her, his lips sliding warm and soft over hers. Then he parted them and his tongue slipped into her mouth. With a sigh of pleasure, she explored every inch of his torso that she could reach, drawing her fingers over the gorgeous flex of his muscles and his silk-over-steel chest. She drew her hands up his arms, over his biceps and shoulders, down to his back to his lovely, lovely buttocks.

Quinn wrapped one arm around her waist and placed his other hand to her nape and kneaded the muscles there with strong fingers. When he pressed her up against him, she felt the hardness of his chest against her nipples, his bare skin next to hers. It was a sensation she'd not felt often in her life and it was one she could definitely become addicted to, were she not careful.

He pressed his hands flat on either side of her head and straddled her hips. She wanted him inside her again—the kitchen had been too short—but Quinn was taking his time with her. He was making every moment, every breath count. He slanted his mouth to the side and deepened their kiss until she could feel only his lips on hers, his tongue in her mouth.

Her breath caught when his mouth closed over one nipple, laving it and biting gently. At the same time, his fingers found her other breast and caressed it, running the calloused pad of his thumb over the nipple. She arched her back and let out a small moan.

He lifted his head. The smoldering look in his eyes heated her blood to the boiling point. "Touch yourself for me, Emmia," he murmured.

Surprise jolted through her at his request. "Touch myself?"

He nodded. "I want to see you excite yourself before I fuck you."

Lust tingled up her spine at his words. They were coarse, but they excited the hell out of her. "I'm already excited," she replied in a breathless voice.

His lips curved in a feral smile. "Show me where you want me to touch you, where you want me to fuck you. Show me where you touch yourself when you're all alone. I want to watch." He settled on his back beside her, propped himself on one elbow and settled in to watch her. "Go ahead."

She bit her lip, watching him take his cock in his hand and stroke himself—his big hand around his big cock, pumping. Emmia remained fascinated by the sight for a moment before she slid her hands up her sides to cup both breasts. His pupils dilated as he watched her. Tentatively, she plumped her breasts, unsure of what he wanted.

He groaned and his cock jerked in his hand. "More. Give me more. Spread your thighs for me," Quinn said in a rasping voice.

Now that she knew the rules of the game, Emmia relaxed and became completely aroused. She did as he requested. She bent her knees and brought her heels up touch her butt, letting her thighs fall open. In this position, she was utterly and completely exposed to him and she loved it.

Quinn ran his gaze over her sex, groaning.

"Touch me," she moaned.

"Not yet. I want to see you touch yourself, first."

She closed her eyes, kneaded her breasts and pulled at her nipples, enjoying the little bit of pain that seemed to make the pleasure seem even sweeter.

He made a sound in his throat that was caught somewhere between a growl and a groan. "Sink your fingers into that beautiful, creamy little pussy, Emmia."

Her breath caught in her throat at his words. She wanted to drive him as crazy as he was driving her. She stroked her hands down her breasts a last time and slowly, oh, so very slowly, down over her stomach to her pubic hair. He stared at the progression of her hands down her body with a strained expression on his face. It was clear, even when she didn't read his emotions, that he was holding himself from her with effort.

He had the control here and she'd given it up to him with pleasure, and yet, in reality, she was still the one with the power. She was the one driving him crazy with the touch of her own hands on her own body. The power she wielded over him made her feel a little dizzy, a little intoxicated, and a whole lot aroused.

His cock jumped visibly in his hand as he stroked himself, waiting for her to touch herself. She threaded her fingers through her pubic hair and dipped down to stroke her clit. Pleasure skittered through her body at the contact. "Oh God," she groaned, her hips bucking.

"Does it feel good?"

"Yes. This is where I want your cock, Quinn," she said breathlessly. Teasingly, she ran her fingertip over herself. She whimpered as she imagined him fucking her there. Her hips thrust forward. Emmia rubbed two fingers around the entrance of her pussy, and then slipped them inside her. She gasped at the feel of her muscles clamping down, then rippled and pulsed. She'd had no idea it would feel that way, so warm and wet. She thrust in and out, the way a man would do. At the same time, she rubbed the base of her hand against her clit. "Oh, Quinn. I'm going to come."

"Let it go," he purred. "I want to see you climax."

Her hips bucked and her back arched as pleasure spread out from her sex and consumed her world. It drove all thought away, drove everything away and her reality was suddenly awash in white bliss.

Quinn moved her hands away and his hot, hungry mouth came down on her while she was in the grip of her orgasm. Her climax stuttered, and then flared to life once more. Emmia screamed as another, harder climax slammed into her body. Under the onslaught of his masterful hands and mouth, she couldn't resist it.

Her pussy still tingled when it was over, when the spasms of her double climax were finished. She'd never come twice in a row before. He hovered over her, a needful look in his dark eyes. "Quinn, please, fuck me," she whispered. "I need to feel you inside me."

Quinn guided the head of his cock to her entrance and eased in an inch. "Your wish is my command, love." He let out a shaky laugh. "As if you could stop me." He pushed in another inch, then another.

"Yes!" she cried out as the wide head of his cock pressed into her. He stretched her muscles so deliciously. He slid into her inch by mind-blowing, delicious inch. She felt completely possessed by his shaft, totally filled up. Every square inch of her pussy seemed touched by him. Slowly, so she could feel every little vein of him, he slid out, and then back in.

Quinn paused for a moment, hovering over her. "Are you all right?"

This time it was her turn to give a shaky laugh. "Quinn! I'm perfect. Please don't stop!"

"Perfect." The look in his hooded eyes almost stopped her heart. It definitely wiped the smile off her face. "Yes, I think you may be that, Emmia."

He dipped his head down and kissed her as he moved slowly in and out of her. She parted her lips and mated her tongue with his, tightening her hands on his shoulders as the pleasure of the experience overwhelmed her.

He brushed her hair away from her face and held her gaze as his cock tunneled in and out her. The half-light seemed to cling to his handsome face lovingly. His thrusts became surer and longer and harder with every stroke he made. Emmia let a moan rip from her throat as she arched her back. Her entire reality had narrowed to only feeling him. He lowered his head to hers and swallowed the sound of it, kissing her ferociously, as though he meant to brand her or mark her in some way.

She went to pieces beneath him as a climax washed over her. Her reality seemed to momentarily break apart under the pleasurable racking spasm that dominated her body. She felt the muscles of her cunt grip and release his cock over and over as the climax rushed through her. At the same time, Quinn groaned and she felt him spill within her.

Once their climaxes had ebbed, he rolled to the side and gathered her against him. Together they lay tangled together, breathing heavily. They stayed that way for a long time, basking in the aftermath of their shared pleasure.

She turned and tucked her face against his chest, happy that his emotions were even and nice. He was content now, sated. He liked her a lot and when he'd told her that she was perfect...he'd meant it.

She hadn't been with a man like Quinn...ever.

Usually the aftermath of a sexual encounter was awkward, sometimes even painful for her. But Quinn had an honesty about him, a guilelessness, a sort of clarity of spirit that she'd never run into before.

He was a good man, straight down to his bones.

Tears stung her eyes. For once after sex she didn't have the sweet sharp tang of regret resting on the back of her tongue. "Thank you," she whispered.

He stilled for a moment and she felt confusion emanating from him, then understanding. He forced her chin up so he could meet her gaze. "Don't say such things to me, Emmia. I was not doing you a favor."

"I—"

He lowered his mouth to hers and kissed her soundly, then settled her against his side and pulled the blankets over them both. "I am here for completely selfish reasons, love. A sexy, sweet, strong woman like you? Catnip to a man like me." He paused and she felt wistfulness coming from him. "I only wish we had longer together. Now rest, love, I'll want you again soon."

In the darkness, Emmia grinned, and then closed her eyes.

* * * * *

She awoke immersed in a lovely languor, her body twisted in the sheets of the bed and the new morning sunshine streaming through the window. She turned over, searching for Quinn and found him standing above her, half dressed. Emmia sat up a little and looked at him questioningly.

He leaned over her and kissed her. "I am leaving now, my lovely Emmia. Will you not come down to say goodbye to me?" He paused. "I will miss you." Quinn withdrew with obvious regret, gave her a lingering look and then continued dressing.

She could feel that it wasn't an act. He truly would miss her. And, damn it, she'd miss him too. Emmia had been reluctant at first to join with Quinn, but he had selflessly and, yes, lovingly, given her pleasure over and over during the night, never once emitting a negative emotion to ruin the experience. Quinn was a man like none she'd ever met before.

She swung her legs over the side of the mattress, holding the blanket to her. "You're going to leave without me, then?"

He stilled and then turned toward her with a puzzled expression on his face. "I thought you didn't want to take the job."

"He intrigues me, this man...Magnus. I've never met another empath before." She gave him a sidelong look and then said forcefully, "I wouldn't take the job at this time were it not for that." She didn't want to admit she was equally intrigued about Quinn and didn't want this to be the last time they saw each other.

Quinn regarded her for a moment, and then gave her a beaming smile. "In that case, I will wait."

* * * * *

Ravensbridge loomed on the horizon. It was a place of gray and black, a fortress that seemed to morph even the storm clouds that roiled above it.

She and Quinn rested their horses on the hill a distance away. Thunder boomed loudly and a light pattering of rain began. It looked like a forbidding place from this vantage point, like a building where they housed prisoners in one of Molari's large cities.

"It looks threatening, I know," Quinn said, flashing a smile at her. "But it is...well, *was*, a very good place to reside."

She heard the note of sadness in his voice and also felt it within him. Emmia reached across and squeezed his hand. "And hopefully we can clear this up and make it that place again."

"I hope so." A smile flickered across his lips. "Let's get going before these skies really open up."

They started down the hill and it was no time before they'd reached the keep, since Quinn's mount, now recovered from his injury, sensed he was home and there was feed to be had, and so traveled at a much quicker pace. Her horse met his strides. The keep's walls rose from a weed and briar-choked tangle. The massive wooden doors were open and Emmia could hear the clamor of the residents within. She could also feel their emotion, an awful tangle of it that rasped against her mind. Quickly, she threw up all the shields she could and braced herself to endure the rest.

Thunder boomed over their heads and the rain began to fall when they reached the outer walls. They passed under the portcullis, the horses' hoofs clopping on the cobblestone past the entrance. In a wave as they made their way into the courtyard, people stared and immediately began whispering to one another.

Quinn.

Magnus.

Justice mercenary.

So she was expected, then.

The courtyard was filled with whispering, muttering Ravensbridge residents, who held loaves of bread in their arms and other packages and foodstuffs. They'd all stopped in the drizzling rain, halting their daily errands to watch her make her way to the stables. Emmia felt the press of their emotions immediately. It made her head ache and her stomach roil in that familiar way she hated. Her fingers curled around the reins and she had to forcibly stop herself from turning her mount and heading back the way she'd come. One would think she would have grown accustomed to this horrible invasion of other people's feelings, but she never did, *never*.

Once they reached the small building standing in the shadow of the keep, a young boy ran out with eyes only for Emmia. "Are you really a justice mercenary?" he asked, his eyes shining bright.

She dismounted, pushing away a momentarily wave of dizziness, and handed the happy, curious brown-haired child her reins. "I am," she answered with a laugh. "And this is a real justice's mercenary's mount. Can you make sure he's treated well?"

The boy nodded enthusiastically.

Quinn handed over the reins of his mount and gave the boy instructions while Emmia looked on. Feeling the heavy weight of a gaze, a palpable pressure on her back, she turned around and looked up. In the one of the high windows of the keep, framed in black, stood a man. He was handsome, well-made, dark of hair and eye. They held each other's gaze for a moment and Emmia felt nothing from him, only a deep vacuum of non-emotion.

Magnus. It had to be him.

Quinn came to stand beside her and followed her gaze upward. Magnus took a step back, into the shadows. Quinn stood for a several heartbeats, saying nothing. Then he turned away without comment. Despair and guilt rolled off him in a wave so thick she nearly choked on it.

"Come, we'll find you quarters," said Quinn. "I hope you're amenable to them adjoining mine." He flashed a charming grin that she was coming to recognize well. She couldn't help but return it.

They picked up their bags and made their way through the well-appointed keep, passing common areas laid with thick rugs and comfortable-looking divans and chairs. Artwork graced the gray walls and the wings of the building were connected with open-air walks which looked down onto the blooming gardens and cheery looking courtyards. Ravensbridge, aside from the emotional turmoil of its inhabitants, was, indeed, a very nice place.

Quinn deposited her at a room next to his. They were in the back part of the keep, away from the general population of the building. It was something she deeply appreciated, giving her a small respite from the seething emotions she was currently being buffeted by.

Looking as exhausted as she felt, Quinn kissed her lingeringly after he'd led her into the large chamber and left her to take a nap. She was happy to close the door behind him and take some moments of alone time. Emmia leaned against the door and allowed the press of the keep to ebb away. It would not totally leave her while she resided here, but it was marginally better when she could lock herself away in seclusion. A room at the back of a building was always a requirement of her employment.

She opened her eyes and briefly took in her surroundings. The bed was a large, canopied four-poster, hung with burgundy velvet draperies. A large trunk stood at the end of the bed. Across from the bed was a fireplace and a small table, and next to the fireplace was a large wardrobe. In the corner of the room stood a clawfoot tub with faucets. *Excellent.*

She turned the water on and let the tub fill while she unpacked her bags. After she'd bathed, she'd call for some food to be brought to the room. Washing the travel grime off her body took precedence over all else right now.

As she pulled a pair of leggings from her bag, a deck of cards fell out onto the floor. Emmia scooped them up and considered them. They were called *tarot cards*, according to her sister, Rhea. She'd brought them back as a gift from some strange place called Earth. Her sister had been forced to live there for some time. The cards were used to tell fortunes, apparently.

On a lark, Emmia settled at the table by the fireplace and pulled the deck from its box. It seemed that, with the introduction of Quinn into her life, she was at a crossroads. There was no sense in ignoring anything that might give her an indication of what fate had in store for her.

After shuffling, Emmia cut the deck and chose one card. She flipped it over, revealing a blindfolded woman balancing two crossed swords. She sat in a chair with a waxing moon in the sky, rocks and a body of water behind her.

Emmia stared down at the image for a time, feeling a certain kinship with the woman. She, indeed, would soon be balancing two swords of her own, in the forms of Quinn and Magnus. That was something she could tell already. The water was like emotion, drowning and changeable, always so prevalent in her life.

And blindfolded.

As, yes, she did feel blind. Despite the clarity she had into other people's emotions, she'd spent much of her life groping in the darkness of her own life. Not to mention in this case, she would be blind to the suspect's emotions. The tarot card seemed accurate.

Heart heavy, she slipped the card back into the deck.

* * * * *

Emmia leaned forward and studied the castellan, Rolf, tasting the man's emotions on the back of her tongue. She'd brought him to a room in the recesses of the keep to be interviewed because the crush of feeling in the structure was nearly overwhelming. She'd had a nonstop headache from the first day she'd arrived, quelled only by Quinn's procurement of herbal remedies. Her head still ached a little, but now at least it was manageable.

"Tell me about the day Caith was killed," she said.

Sorrow. A bright, shining note of love. Then blinding hatred.

Emmia's mind reeled for a moment from the intensity of the emotions that Rolf emitted and how quick they were in succession.

The middle-aged, brown-haired man tried to force an expression of blandness onto his face, tried to control his inner turmoil.

It didn't work.

Well, she hadn't been expecting *this* reaction at all. She'd been expecting this interview to be fairly straightforward, not fraught with unexpected and confusing emotion. However, such was the way of these investigations and such was the nature of her gift. Nothing was ever predictable.

"I was about my castle duties all day long. I was busy and didn't much keep track of Lord Magnus' whereabouts or that of Quinn and Caith." *Love – shiny and clear.* It had flared when he'd said Caith's name. "But I did notice that Quinn was in the lists practicing swordplay and I did see Caith leave the keep's gates in the morning." He paused. "Lord Magnus was with her."

Love. Love. Love. Hate. Hate. Hate. This time he couldn't keep the vicious tumult of the feelings from his face. He twisted his dry, gnarled hands in his lap.

"And Lord Magnus' weapon?" she prompted.

"At his side. It's always at his side." *Hate.*

"When did you find the bloody sword?"

"In the evening, after the day was done. I went in to badger a servant about laying a fire in Lord Magnus' room and there was the sword stashed behind a chair, covered in Caith's b-blood. Lord Magnus staggered into the room, covered in blood, right after." *Sorrow – deep and painful.* "It wasn't long after that," Rolf continued, "they found her body in the field beyond the keep."

Yes, Magnus did appear to be guilty beyond a shadow of a doubt per Rolf's telling of the tale, but Rolf's strong, conflicted emotions cast uncertainty upon his words.

"I see. And would someone else have had access to Lord Magnus' sword?"

He shook his head. "Lord Magnus guarded that sword at all times. It was a gift from his father. That was the first time in the fifteen years that I have served as Ravensbridge's castellan that I have ever seen the sword without Lord Magnus near at hand."

"What was your relationship with Caith?"

He colored to the roots of his hair and smacked his thick lips twice. "Nonexistent."

She tipped her head to the side. "Is that a regret of yours?" It was. She could feel it emanating from him in powerful waves. She just wanted to hear what he had to say.

He inclined his head, equal parts of sorrow and hatred flowing from him. The mixture was so strong, it nearly made her tumble from her chair. "She didn't want me," he responded in a forced-sounding voice.

Emmia blinked. "Did that bother you?"

He raised his head and glared at her. A sudden surge of hatred tasted bitter on the back of her tongue. "I loved her."

"Yes, I can sense that. So how do you feel about Magnus?"

More hate. The bitterness nearly made her gag.

"He killed her. How do you *think* I feel?" He stood with an impatient air. "May I leave now? This is taking me from my duties."

Emmia also stood. "For now. But I may call upon you later for more information."

He bowed stiffly and left the room.

She sat for a while longer in front of the flickering flames, letting Rolf's emotions pass through her as much as she could and concentrating on not retaining them.

Well, that had been an interesting development. Rolf had been in love with Caith, and deeply, if his emotions had provided any sort of clue. He'd had to watch Quinn and his master both in a relationship with the woman he'd wanted. That must have been painful.

Painful enough to drive him to murder and make it seem as though Magnus had done it? Perhaps. Rolf was Ravensbridge's castellan. She didn't believe that he wouldn't have access to Magnus' sword at times. That was worth looking into a little more closely. The whole issue needed further exploration.

She shifted on the seat and sighed. This did not appear to be one of the easier investigations she'd ever undertaken, but she wasn't averse to new challenges.

When she left the room and walked down the corridor to the keep's gardens, she was soon confronted with an older man with black hair, graying at the temples.

He squinted blue eyes at her. "You're the justice mercenary." He felt curious to her and a little irritated.

She blinked. "I am."

"You gonna find my daughter's killer, then?"

Surprise rippled through her. "Are you Caith's father?"

"I am. My name is Arhild. It was my child found slain in the woods."

Love and contempt. Both emotions were very strong. No sorrow. No grief. *Interesting.*

"I'm very sorry for your loss, sir."

His face twisted and she caught a strong sense of regret from him. That was as close to grief as he got. "Thank you. If you need my help, need to know something about Caith, come to talk to me. I want to see this monster caught and punished."

She studied his face, wondering why he wasn't implicating the prime suspect immediately. "So you don't think Lord Magnus is the murderer?"

He stared at her for a moment and she caught another definite whiff of regret. "No, I meant Magnus when I said monster." He turned on his heel and stalked away and left behind a puzzled Emmia.

* * * * *

Magnus assessed the woman from afar, watching as she walked down a corridor with Quinn. She wore hunting leathers and a long, white linen shirt. Her long dark hair she often wore braided down her back, though sometimes she wore it long and loose. She seemed often to have two finely made swords, both sheathed on either side of her. Although, after a few days at Ravensbridge, she didn't wear them so often now. Did that mean she felt at ease here, perhaps?

She didn't seem to own a dress, the mode of fashion typical for females in this part of Molari. Still, no matter what she wore, she always looked attractive. He could see why Quinn was smitten with her. She was taken with him as well. It was all over their body language. It was in the way they leaned toward each other and smiled at each other. Plus, he could feel Quinn's emotions for the woman. He had to admit they pinched him a little.

She had been in the keep for three days, but had not yet sought him out. He was fully aware she was working, however. She'd been questioning the people of Ravensbridge — the castellan, the groundskeepers, the falconers, everyone she could find who knew himself and Caith personally. It was only a matter of time before she sought him out. Perhaps she was trying to make him nervous by deliberately ignoring him. The thought had crossed his mind once or twice. Justice mercenaries likely employed many tricks to manipulate the subjects of their investigations. However, Magnus didn't take well to being manipulated.

Perhaps it was time he introduced himself.

He watched Quinn and Emmia turned a corner. After hesitating a moment, Magnus altered his course and headed in the other direction, intent on deliberately meeting them head-on down the other corridor. As he progressed down the hallway, several people glanced at him and quickly looked away, suddenly finding the stone walls or something down in the courtyard incredibly fascinating. The emotions that battered him were confused, bitter, betrayed and angry.

Magnus sighed and buttressed his defenses in order to not feel them as acutely. Though, sadly, he was growing used to it. Although it still upset him that so many people should think so ill of him. Had no one known him at all? Did everyone think him capable of such cold-bloodedness? Of course, there were still some who refused to believe he had killed Caith, but most of them...

And Quinn. Out of everyone in the keep, his opinion mattered most. Quinn hurt most of all. They'd loved each other, had shared everything. Even worse, Magnus still loved Quinn...and he suspected that Quinn returned the sentiment.

Since thinking of Quinn was like poking a sharp stick in an open wound, Magnus backed away from the thought of him and continued to make progress down the corridor. Magnus had loved Caith. Nothing in the world would've made him hurt her. He missed her every day, thought of her every day.

He wished he wasn't an empath so that Emmia could feel all that inside him, feel his innocence in this matter. She would know in a heartbeat if she were able to peer inside his emotions that nothing in this world would have forced him to hurt Caith. Unfortunately, Emmia would have to judge him blindfolded.

Gods, he was so weary of this ordeal! He wished to be free of people's suspicions and he wanted nothing more than to find Caith's murderer and take his vengeance...for Caith, not for himself.

"Lord Magnus," came a cool, detached female voice.

Startled, he looked up. He'd been so caught up in his thoughts, he'd forgotten he'd put himself on a collision course with Quinn and Emmia. Now he didn't even have to feign surprise. Magnus looked down into the justice mercenary's dark brown eyes, suddenly at loss for words. Quinn only glared at him, his jaw tight.

"Emmia," Magnus finally answered. "It is good to meet you." He nodded at her companion. "Quinn."

Quinn inclined his head a degree, but said nothing. His emotions were tightly clamped down from Magnus, even when Magnus opened his shields completely in order to deliberately sense them, though it was clear that Quinn was sad. Quinn had been sad since Caith had been killed.

Her eyebrows lifted. "Truly? You are happy to meet me when I may be here to take your life?"

He let a smile flicker over his mouth and relaxed a little. "*Truly*. I don't think you'll find me guilty, Emmia. I don't think you err when you take on a case to judge. I trust we will talk soon? I very much wish to discuss things with you."

Her returning smile had a touch of malice in it. "We can talk now, if you'd like. I have nothing left on my agenda for today."

"Very well." He gestured back the way he'd come. "My rooms are in this direction."

The three of them turned and made their way there, amid the more curious stares and open whispering at the sight of Magnus and the justice mercenary together.

Once within, Magnus sent his servants away and closed the heavy door against prying eyes. Quinn and Emmia had found chairs near the fireplace. He took a third and sat across from them.

Quinn emitted two parts sorrow and one part curiosity. The justice mercenary emitted nothing at all that he could feel. The woman only watched him with her wide chocolate-colored eyes. Magnus wondered if she was thinking what he was thinking. It was strange...*nice* to be around someone and not sense his or her emotion. It was peaceful, a void in the constant battering of the defenses he'd learned to put against other people's emotions.

"So," he said, spreading his hands. "Have you come kill me, then?"

Emmia leaned forward. "I haven't decided yet. Quinn thinks you didn't do it. That confuses the issue a great deal for me. One would think that since he is the one who sought me out, that he would believe you to be guilty."

"I haven't said I thought Magnus innocent," Quinn said woodenly. "Nor have I indicated I think him guilty."

She glanced at him. "I can feel the truth from you. You don't truly believe Magnus capable of cold-blooded murder, especially of someone he cared about. You simply want an end to the situation here at Ravensbridge. You hope that I will declare Magnus innocent and things can return to what they were." She paused. "You miss Magnus. You care deeply for him and you feel guilty for doubting his innocence for a moment, yet you cannot help it."

Quinn blanched.

Emmia smiled. "That's what they pay me for, Quinn. That's what *you're* paying me for."

Magnus held Quinn's gaze, tried not to lose himself in the blue of his eyes. He'd always loved the color of Quinn's eyes. Once he'd loved everything about him. He still did, though he wasn't certain Quinn felt the same. Not anymore. It was hard to get an accurate reading on Quinn at all, in fact. "You don't think me guilty, Quinn?"

Quinn glanced away. "You're an empath, the same as her. Can't you look into my heart and see for yourself?"

"You're too close to my heart for me to see objectively," he answered honestly. "Your feelings are often cloudy when I try to look." For the most part, anyway. He lowered his voice a little when he spoke next. "You are too close to me, my friend. Even still."

Magnus felt a flash of deep pain from Quinn. He made a frustrated sound. "Of course I don't think you're capable of murder, but the evidence... The evidence is —"

"Damning," Magnus answered. "If you went by the evidence alone, one would come to the conclusion that I murdered Caith. I was seen leaving with her in the morning. The next time anyone saw me, Rolf was holding the bloodied murder weapon, which he'd found in my quarters, and I was covered in Caith's blood." He paused. "Except I *did not kill her.*

I had no reason to do such a thing and even if I did have a reason, I would not have done it. I am surprised certain people in this keep have entertained the idea that I might." He tried to keep a note of reproach out of his voice and failed. It had hurt him deeply that Quinn, of all people, had judged him even possibly guilty.

"You were the woman's lover and the murder weapon with her blood was found in your chambers by the castellan. Not to mention that you are the law in this place," answered Emmia. "That means you are the only person here capable of murder without repercussion. It's no mystery why your people think you guilty."

"I don't think you murdered Caith, Magnus. I will admit to suspicions, but in my heart, it's true that I don't believe you're capable of such a thing." Emotion surged from Quinn as he said the words, filling the room with a complex mixture of love and sorrow that stung the back of Magnus' throat.

Emmia must have felt it too, since she reached over and covered Quinn's hand with hers and squeezed. Quinn held onto her hand like a drowning man and Magnus watched them exchange a look of heat and caring. A surge of feeling came from Quinn as he gazed at Emmia, deep regard and lust. The emotion edged love, flirted dangerously with it.

So that was how it was.

He should have known that Quinn would never be able to resist a woman as beautiful as Emmia. Magnus was also attracted to her, not only because of her beauty, but also because of the fact he could not sense her emotion.

"Quinn, please give me a moment alone with Magnus," said Emmia.

"Of course." Quinn kept his eyes on Magnus as he got up and walked out of the room.

* * * * *

Once Quinn was free of the room, it was as if a heavy weight had been lifted. Emmia sighed in relief and noticed that Magnus' eyes grew a little less dark. He had obviously also experienced Quinn's intense emotions where Magnus was concerned. From the man opposite her, she felt nothing. Blessed, peaceful nothingness.

"So." She leaned forward. "How long have you and Quinn been lovers?" Best to get right to the point. She'd suspected it for some time, but had known it for certain when he'd reached Ravensbridge and she'd sensed Quinn's emotions every time he'd seen Magnus. It had been a combination of intense love, uncertainty and passion.

Magnus showed no reaction. He didn't even blink. He only answered smoothly, "For about five years now." He probably expected that she, as an empath, would've picked that up from Quinn, even though Quinn had never told her.

"So it was a threesome, then? You, Quinn and Caith."

"That's correct. We were in a loving relationship, the three of us. Though it was only myself and Quinn who could've been said to have anything that went beyond the physical relationship and friendship."

"Interesting." She leaned back.

"Why is that?"

She had to hide a smile. It was interesting because the thought of Magnus and Quinn together made ripples of pleasure course up her spine. But now was not the time for such thoughts or imaginings. Especially not about a man who stood accused of murder. She chose not to answer his question and was grateful for their inability to sense each other's emotions.

"Tell me what you remember of that day," she said.

He sat back and sighed. "We woke up together, the three of us. We had breakfast and took a walk in the keep's gardens. Afterward, Quinn left to practice some swordplay and Caith

174

and I decided to go riding. In the afternoon, we stopped the horses and dismounted —"

"Where?"

He frowned. "Not far from the road to Hia, but not within view of it. We made love in the sun and then fell asleep wrapped in each other's arms on a horse blanket."

"Sounds idyllic."

His lips twisted. "Up until that point, it was. I awoke with a lump on my head and a raging headache." His face grew pale. "I was covered in blood and Caith was-was *gone*." He paused, seemed to gather himself, and went on. "The horses were still tied to the tree and while I searched all over for Caith, I never found her. I went back to the keep and had just staggered into my quarters while Rolf was pulling my bloodied sword out from behind a chair."

"Hmmm. What do you know of Rolf?"

"My castellan?" he asked in surprised. "Why, is he a suspect?"

She shrugged, not wanting to give too much away. He was, indeed, after that messy emotional display at his initial interview. Plus, she did think the timing was rather convenient. Rolf had pulled the sword out just as Magnus had entered the room. "Were you aware he was in love with Caith?"

He frowned and rubbed his chin, which was covered with stubble. Shaving wasn't high on his agenda these days, Emmia was sure. Magnus was an excessively handsome man with a powerful body, long dark hair and eyes. He had a face that any woman with half a libido would appreciate and his body was like Quinn's — strong, honed from sword work and battle. She shifted her seat and forced those thoughts from her mind. "Sometimes I felt intense emotion from him when he saw her, but I never thought it went past lust."

"What I felt from him wasn't lust, it was *love*. It was strong and true even now, after her death. Along with the love, there was hatred. That also was very strong." She paused. "These emotions give him motive, to my mind. At the very least, he deserves a deeper look. Oftentimes, these crimes are the result of passion, committed in the heat of the moment. That is why, as an empath, I am so good at sniffing out the perpetrators. So very much of it is emotional. Also, do not forget that Rolf was the one to find your sword, Magnus."

"Are you saying he committed the crime and then planted the sword to make me look guilty? Impossible! Rolf is loyal. He would never do such a thing."

She smiled. "When you have seen all that I have seen, sir, you quickly learn that anything is possible. He is definitely on my list of suspects at this moment." She drew a breath and schooled her expression. "As are you." Less so now that she'd conducted her interviews, though she didn't want to advertise that information.

"If it must be. I trust your judgment. I trust your abilities as an empath, Emmia, to come to the correct conclusion. I believe, as an empath, you are far superior to me. Count yourself lucky to have such skill."

"It isn't always a blessing," she muttered, turning her head away. "It's more like a curse most days." Goddess, she had no idea why she was saying such things to this man. Perhaps because he was also an empath, and who else could better understand her plight? It had been a long time since she could talk to someone about how she felt about her Talent, let alone to someone who might actually understand.

Magnus leaned forward. "Is it truly so strong for you that you would count the ability ill?"

She scoffed. "Don't you?" Emmia gestured toward the room. "How can you stand to reside here, among these people? All their emotions whirling around like a tempest, always pushing at you, demanding your attention. I must live deep in the woods, away from everyone, in order not to go insane from it. Even now, even with herbal remedies, I feel sick from it."

Magnus leaned back in his seat and frowned at her. "Sometimes it can be a little overwhelming, but I regulate my exposure to it, a little like opening and closing flood gates in my mind. Surely you have mental barriers erected to stave off the most powerful emotions you encounter? Doesn't every empath?"

She shook her head. "I have tried a million ways to acquire this skill. I don't mean to boast, because I don't consider it an advantage, but I think my ability is far too strong to allow me to build barriers."

He sat silent for a moment. "Nonsense."

She blinked in surprise and then smiled. "Nonsense?"

"Let me help you, Emmia. I think together we can find a way. It took me a long time to build my barriers too, but I was able to do it because I found the key inside me." He stared at her speculatively for a moment. "I may know your key, too."

She chewed her lip for a moment. As much as she was tempted to take him up on the offer, it wasn't right she should align herself so closely with a suspect. It was against every justice mercenary code she knew. Anyway... "I don't think there's any technique you could show me that I haven't already tried."

She stood.

"Well, we'll never know if we don't explore it, will we?" His smile was slow and sure and seemed to refer to things that had nothing to do with the building of psychic barriers and everything to do with sex.

It was wrong on so many levels, but she couldn't stop her body from reacting to him. She felt strongly drawn to this man on a physical level. She had felt this attraction from the moment she'd seen him in the courtyard when she'd arrived. Magnus had what she could only describe as *presence*. He had the aura of a leader—power, strength and fairness.

And Emmia truly didn't think he'd killed Caith. It was a gut feeling she had and her gut feelings were rarely wrong.

Her intuition was the second tool she used in her investigations.

She felt a blush creep into her cheeks. "I must go."

He stood and walked her to the door. "I look forward to meeting with you again soon, Emmia. I trust in your skill and your intelligence."

He was so close to her that she could scent his bathing soap mixed with the smell of warm, worn leather. She mumbled something nearly intelligible and slipped out the door.

Quinn stood a short way down the corridor, leaning against the wall and wearing a brooding expression. She could feel that he was deep in thought. Emmia approached him and put a hand to his arm. He startled and looked at her. He held her gaze for a moment before his expression changed from surprise to knowingness.

Quinn smiled and his eyes went half-lidded. "Yes, he's very charming, isn't he?" His voice was low and smooth, like melted chocolate. "Good-looking too."

"Don't be ridiculous." She glanced away. Was she so easy to read? Her face did still feel a little flushed. She cleared her throat. "We had a good talk."

"You don't think he did it, do you?"

She licked her lips and glanced around to make sure no one could overhear her. "My primary suspect right now is Rolf. Rolf had the motive, whereas I can't see Magnus did. Magnus had what he wanted from Caith—a friendly, casual relationship. Rolf did not and may have been guided by jealousy. However, I haven't yet ruled out the possibility that Magnus committed this crime." She paused, chewing her lip. "Who had more of a relationship with Caith, you or Magnus?"

Quinn thought for a moment. His emotions spiraled quickly, almost too fast for Emmia to follow, as he remembered. "Magnus...I think."

She nodded. "That would explain why, if Rolf is responsible, he went after Magnus and not you."

"And me? Why I am I not on your list of suspects?"

Emmia allowed her expression to soften. She reached up and cupped his cheek. "Because I can look into your heart and what I have seen there is good—love and compassion. I have never met a man like you, Quinn, not ever. I know you didn't kill Caith."

He took her hand and kissed it. His eyes darkened. "I think that if you could look into Magnus' heart, you would see the same thing."

She shrugged. "Perhaps, but I cannot. We'll have to let this play out in another way."

He pulled her against him, dragging her up against his chest. "Speaking of playing..."

Feeling the weight of disapproving stares, she whispered, "Let's go somewhere a little more private. In any case, I need some solitude. I need to escape these pounding emotions for a time."

They retreated to Quinn's apartment in the keep. It consisted of three rooms in total—a sitting room, his bedroom and a bathing room complete with a large tub and a commode. He shut the door behind them and pulled her into his bedroom, yanking off her clothing as he went.

"I want you," he growled into her ear as he pulled her shirt over her head.

As he said those words, Emmia felt emotion course from him. He wasn't sure what he meant. He wanted her sexually, that was certain, but there was something more there and he wasn't sure what it was yet.

Neither was she, but it was beginning to feel a lot...like *love*. Oddly, it didn't frighten her. It only made her want more. It was a salve for her whole life, when she'd had to hold herself away from everyone.

Anyway, her feelings for Quinn were growing daily too.

"How do you want me, Quinn? Your emotions feel oddly confused right now."

He paused and looked down at her. "I find you very attractive, Emmia. Not only physically, but…" He swore under his breath and kissed her hard. His tongue penetrated her mouth and swiped up against hers.

With one powerful swoop, he had her up in his arms. Emmia threw her head back and laughed as he walked to the bed and threw her down onto the deep, soft mattress. Giving her an evil little grin, he pushed her thighs apart and fastened his mouth over her cunt.

Her laughter became a gasp and then a moan as Quinn's skillful tongue licked her and then settled in to tease her clit. He kept her thighs braced wide apart as he feasted on her, so she couldn't move away…not that she wanted to escape this.

* * * * *

Magnus pushed the heavy tapestry to the side and glimpsed the erotic scene on the bed. After their conversation, he'd wanted…no, *needed*, to speak with Quinn in private. Unable to bear the looks and emotion of the keep's inhabitants, he'd traveled via the secret tunnels within the keep, taking a chance that Quinn had returned to his room.

He had returned, but he wasn't alone. Magnus should have expected that, but now it was too late to change course.

Lust twisting low in his gut and making his cock grow hard, he watched Quinn's head bob between Emmia's long, creamy legs as he suckled her pussy. Emmia's back was arched and her eyes were closed. A look of erotic rapture made her face even more beautiful than it was ordinarily. Her breasts stabbed up into the air, pinked and hard from her excitement.

Magnus' fingers curled as he imagined pulling them and teasing them as Quinn licked her cunt to climax. Together, they could make her scream…just as they had Caith so many times.

The thought of Caith instantly made Magnus feel guilty for spying. He should leave them. He should go back to his room and continue to mourn the loss of one his best friends. Anyway, it was wrong to invade their privacy like this, though it used to be a game for Caith, Quinn and him. It was unfair to Emmia that he watched them in private, at the very least.

He turned away, but heard his name whispered...*Magnus*...and turned back. Quinn was now between her spread thighs, hovering over her with his magnificent, hard cock pressed against the opening of her cunt. He frowned. Why were they saying *his* name at a time like this? He pitched his hearing to catch their soft conversation.

"Have you ever been with two men at once?" Quinn asked.

Emmia squirmed under Quinn, pressing her hips upward in an effort to force his cock inside her. "No. Quinn! Please, you're killing me."

He grabbed her wrists and pressed them down on the mattress at either side of her head. "I know you find Magnus attractive. I *know* you do. Can you imagine what it would be like to have both us in the same bed at the same time, love?"

"Quinn, please fuck me! I'm so close to coming!"

He teased her clit with the head of his cock, dragging a groan from Emmia's throat. "Answer my question and you get my cock. Answer it honestly. Has the thought crossed your mind? Have you imagined Magnus in this bed with us?"

"This isn't right. This isn't proper!"

"Oh, and what do we care about that? Right and proper? How boring. Give me your answer, Emmia and I'll fuck you until you can't think."

"Yes," she gasped. "Yes, I've thought of it. Goddess help me, I'm thinking of it now."

Quinn flexed his ass and slid his thick cock into her cunt. They both groaned. "Good girl, Emmia. Good girl for telling me the truth. I knew it all along, love. I knew it and could see it in your eyes, on your pretty face."

Magnus gripped the tapestry, now totally unable to make himself do the right thing and turn away. He watched as Quinn fucked her, his long cock glistening wetly with her juices on every outward stroke. Emmia moaned and bucked as he took her harder and faster. Her body moved on the bed every time he pumped into her, seating himself deep inside her cunt.

"Think of it," he whispered to her. "Think of four hands on you, two pairs of lips. Think of two cocks inside you, two to pleasure you."

Emmia tossed her head and panted. "I'm going to come."

Just then, Quinn raised his head and looked directly at Magnus. Holding his gaze he said, "Yes, love, come for me. Come thinking about me and Magnus fucking you."

Emmia cried out and Quinn tipped his head back, likely enjoying the feeling of her rippling cunt around his length as she orgasmed. She thrashed on the bed beneath his ever-pistoning cock, caught in a powerful climax.

Once her orgasm had eased, Emmia reached up and tenderly touched Quinn's cheek. "What did you mean *two* cocks inside me?" The words were a little satisfaction-slurred. "At the same time? That's not possible."

Quinn threw his head back and laughed. "That's one thing I like about you, Emmia. You're incredibly jaded and world-weary in most ways." He shook his head. "But not in *all* ways." He pulled his still hard cock from her body. "On your hands and knees."

She gave him a quizzical look.

"I'm going to show you how, love."

As Emmia changed position, Quinn got up and retrieved a bottle of liquid Magnus recognized as a sexual lubricant. As Quinn turned and went back to the bed, he looked again straight at Magnus. It was almost a look of challenge and it left Magnus feeling a mixture of emotions he couldn't sort out.

Quinn's cock still stood at painful erect attention as he eased Emmia to her stomach and squeezed some of the viscous liquid lubricant into his palm. He massaged it into her shoulders and down her back, drawing a groan of pleasure from her. Magnus watched Quinn work, tracing the lines of his fine body with his gaze and longing to stroke his lovely cock, to take it into his mouth.

"Mmmm, Quinn, you're going to put me to sleep," murmured Emmia.

"So you're relaxed, then?"

She nodded.

"Stay relaxed, love. Know I would never do anything to hurt you, all right?"

"Mmmm," she mumbled in response.

Magnus watched Quinn's hand skate lower and lower over the curves and valleys of Emmia's fine body. He knew what was coming, because this was the same way they'd introduced Caith to the possibilities of having two lovers at the same time. Quinn eased his hand between the cheeks of her buttocks, urging her to spread her thighs. Quinn eased his fingers over her little rosebud of an anus and Magnus heard Emmia's quick intake of breath.

"Say stop and I will," Quinn said softly. "But if you want true pleasure, you'll allow me to play." He pulled her up to her hands and knees and stood beside her.

Magnus had a clear view from where he stood, something he was certain Quinn had orchestrated for whatever reason. Quinn's emotions were too centered on Emmia to get a clear read. Quinn slid his other hand down her front, letting it disappear between her spread thighs to tease and caress her clit. In the same moment, he pressed a finger softly and easily into her nether hole.

"Oh Gods," she cried. Her fingers curled into the bedding.

"Mmm, it's good, isn't it, love?" His finger thrust in and out of her as his other hand stroked her clit from the front.

"Yes," she gasped breathlessly.

He pushed his fingers deep into her cunt as he continued to thrust into her ass. "This is how you would take two men at once," he purred. "See? You were made for it."

"I've never had a man...ah!...do...this before." Her body looked tense and a look of lust had overtaken her features. She looked even lovelier than normal, intoxicated with pleasure and passion, her perfect features slack.

Quinn added a second finger to her ass, stretching her slowly and easily, making her ready for his cock. "Poor baby. You've been neglected by your lovers, then. Do you want more?"

"More?" she choked out. "There's more?"

A low, masculine chuckle came from Quinn. "There's more, love." He added yet another finger into her rear, widening her muscles back there even more. Slowly, he thrust his thick fingers in and out of her cunt at the same time. "So much more."

She tossed her head. "Yes," she hissed.

"Does it hurt?"

She said nothing for a few moments, then finally said, "A little, but the pain is slight and feels...good in a strange way. I never knew..." She trailed off.

"That this was a place of pleasure? Oh yes, love. It is. I can't wait to take you here," he groaned. "You're relaxing back here enough for me to fit. You're going to feel so good around my cock."

Magnus' hand slipped down and he stroked himself through the fabric of his trousers for a moment. His cock was harder than his sword. It had been so long since he'd had sex.

Goddess, how he wanted Emmia. He wanted Quinn too. Seeing them together like this was like taunting a starving man with a four-course meal. It was torture. He sank his teeth into his bottom lip and returned to watching...only because he couldn't bring himself to look away.

Emmia bucked against Quinn's hand and lowered her head to raise her ass up, offering herself to him without restrictions. "Quinn," she gasped. "Take me."

"You want it, love?"

She nodded. "Take me before I come again."

"You're going to come again, Emmia? Well, then, let's see how fast we can make you." Magnus watched as Quinn repositioned his hand, probably so he could stroke the spot deep inside a woman's cunt where it was so sensitive.

"Quinn!" Emmia cried out, her hips bucking as she climaxed. Magnus could practically feel the way her pussy spasmed around Quinn's fingers and how her slick, hot juices drenched his hand.

"Ah, that's what I wanted," Quinn purred. Are you ready to take me into your sweet little ass?"

"Yes!" she sobbed.

While she was still caught in the tail end of her climax and her body was relaxed and pliable, Quinn shifted position, setting the head of his cock to the entrance of her ass. He uncapped the bottle of lubricant again and dowsed himself in it. If Magnus had been there, he would have spread it on his cock, worked it in well before Quinn took her rear.

"Remember, I'd never do anything to hurt you, Emmia," whispered Quinn. "Stay relaxed."

She took a deep breath. "I know."

He grabbed her hips, holding her in place, and then brushed the head of his cock across her opening. "Gods," he groaned. "Your body is completely ready for this. You're aroused, nice and open."

"Take me, Quinn," she murmured. "I can't wait to have you in there."

"The crown will be the worst," he said through gritted teeth. Quinn placed his broad hands on her hips. The head of his cock pressed into her, breaching the tight ring of muscles of her anus. He pressed inside her slowly, oh so very slowly.

"More," she gasped. She pushed back, trying to impale herself. "It's so good." Her words were slurred again. Gods, but Emmia was eager in bed. So lush, so ripe and perfect for sexual experiment. Magnus' fingers curled to stroke her satiny skin, feel the heat of her cunt. At the moment, he wanted her with a bone-deep yearning that was hard to explain. Magnus wanted her with an intensity that almost entered insanity. He had to force himself to stay behind the curtain, to keep himself hidden.

Quinn groaned and held both hands on her hips, stilling her movement. "Emmia, you're going to make me come before I've even hilted." He eased her back against him and slowly thrust his shaft deeper into her. "You're so sweet and tight."

Finally, he seated himself within her to the base of his cock. His hips pulled back and thrust forward as he set up a relentless rhythm. With every thrust, the penetration grew easier. "I can't hold back," he groaned as he picked up speed, pushing her harder and harder.

"Don't stop," she moaned. "Please, don't stop, Quinn."

He slid his hand around her front, stroking his fingers through her dark pubic hair. She bucked her hips when he thrust two fingers into her creaming pussy. She moaned out his name and tossed her head like a wild thing being mounted against her will.

"Gods, you feel so good," Quinn groaned. He extracted his fingers from her dripping pussy and slicked her cream over her clit as he worked the sensitized bundle between two fingers, pushing her harder and faster toward orgasm as he rode her ass.

Emmia cried out again, lost once more to climax.

"*Emmia.*" Behind her, she heard Quinn's deep groan as he came. Magnus watched him thrust balls-deep within her and climax, his head thrown back and his eyes closed.

Magnus passed his hand over his cock once more and then melted back into the shadows, leaving them at least a little privacy.

In that moment, he vowed he'd have Emmia. He'd have Quinn back too.

Chapter Four

$\wp$

Quinn pulled Emmia against his body and glanced up to find Magnus had retreated. He wasn't sure what had come over him when he realized that his old lover had followed the secret pathway they always used to use to get to one another's rooms and had found himself watching Quinn make love to Emmia.

Magnus had been a part of him for so long. Quinn had shared everything important with him for years now. Emmia was becoming important to him and Quinn was finding that he couldn't leave Magnus out of his relationship with her, even if Magnus was only an outsider in the shadowed corner.

Even though he stood accused of murder.

Emmia tucked her head between his cheek and collarbone and sighed. His heart squeezed as he admitted something to himself that he'd been having trouble acknowledging since this ordeal had begun. He loved Magnus. With every inch of his being, he loved him.

She raised her head. "What? Am I feeling this emotion correctly, Quinn? Do I feel love coming from you?" There was a slight sheen of panic in her dark eyes. "Quinn?" she repeated.

He reached out and touched her cheek. "Are you truly so afraid that someone might love you, Emmia? Why is that? I find you very loveable."

She pulled away from him. Wrapping herself in the sheet, she sat on the edge of the bed with her back to him. "I don't know. I feel...conflicted on the issue."

He sat up and rubbed her back. "I do have very strong feelings for you, love. They get stronger with every moment I spend in your glorious, strong, fragile presence. However, in this case, it was Magnus I was thinking of when you felt the love coming from me. It's Magnus I love irrefutably."

She looked at him and he tried not to be offended by the look of relief in her eyes. "Magnus? Well, I already knew that, although before now your feelings for him have been quite confused. What I felt just now from you was a pure, brilliant and clear note of love."

"Yes."

She leaned over and kissed him. "You're a special man, Quinn. I care deeply for you, as well."

He wrapped his hand around the back of her head, pressed her mouth to his and then rolled her beneath his body. She laughed and squirmed as he attempted to kiss her senseless. He loved it when he could make her laugh. Quinn wanted to hear her do it every single day.

* * * * * *

"Magnus?"

Magnus jerked, startled by the sound of Quinn's voice. He spilled the container of ink he was using to write a letter all over his desk. "Damn it!" He leapt up as black ink trickled over the edge of the desk and into his lap.

Quinn's boot heels sounded on the stone floor as he approached to help him. "I'm sorry I surprised you. You didn't answer when I knocked, but I could hear you muttering to yourself in here."

He wiped his pants off with some scrap paper. "It's all right. I guess I was distracted by the letter I was writing to my sister."

"To Caroline?"

Magnus nodded and dropped his ink-stained hands to his sides. "I was telling her about Emmia."

Quinn smiled. "You tell her everything." He laughed. "I think she knows more of your secrets than I do." He instantly sobered once he'd realized what he'd said. For a moment, it had seemed as if everything had been back to normal. But, of course, the world was far, far from normal these days.

An awkward silence fell.

"What did you need?" Magnus said impatiently. He couldn't stand this tension between them. He'd rather they have no contact at all if they were meant to suffer this way every time they came face-to-face. "Have you come to discuss what happened several nights ago in your chamber?"

Quinn took a step forward and then stopped. "I'm not sure what that was. When I saw you there in the corner, I guess I needed for you to be a part of what was happening between myself and Emmia."

"You care about her, don't you?"

He nodded. "She's tough, and while she is strong, mostly it's an act. She's been damaged by the strength of her empathic abilities and she's been forced to keep herself away from people." He paused. "I want to see her happy."

"I haven't spent much time with her, but I'm also drawn to her."

"Even though she came here to possibly kill you?"

Magnus nodded. "Strange, isn't it?"

"Not really. You always did like a little danger with your sex."

They held each other's gazes for a long moment, each clearly caught in their own memories. Magnus wanted to close the distance between them, wanted to crush Quinn against him and kiss him deeply. He wanted to slip his hand down his pants and touch his cock, arouse him the way he would have before this mess had begun. Magnus wanted to tease him to a fever pitch, then lean him over the desk and take Quinn right here and now.

Heat emanated from Quinn, sexual heat and love in a heady mix that had Magnus taking a step forward. Then Quinn's emotions changed, grew cooler and more confused.

And the spell was broken.

Magnus froze in place. They stood looking at each other for another long moment. "You never said why you decided to stop by, Quinn." Magnus' voice sounded clipped and cold to his own ears. He just couldn't take this anymore.

He shrugged in response. "I guess I wanted to talk to you."

"I'm surprised. I would've thought you'd want to stay far away from Caith's murderer." The tone of his voice was bitter, but he couldn't force it to be any sweeter. The fact that Quinn had abandoned him after he'd been accused still cut deeply.

"I told you I never thought you did it, not deep down."

"But you did think there was a possibility."

"The evidence—"

"The evidence! Come on, Quinn. You're my best and dearest friend, as well as my longtime lover. You should know me better than to think me capable of such a thing."

Quinn went silent for a few moments before measuring out his words, "Your sword had her blood on it, Magnus. Your clothes had her—"

"You abandoned me, Quinn."

Regret came off Quinn in a wave. "I know," he said quietly.

They stared at each other for a long heartbeat. There was a knock on the door and Magnus called *enter* in a sharp, bitter voice.

Emmia stepped into the room, assessed the situation at a glance and pulled Quinn back toward the door. "Quinn, I've been looking for you. Do you have a moment?"

Quinn held Magnus' gaze a moment longer. "Magnus—"

Magnus turned his back to them both. "Just go." Bitterness soured the words. He could taste it on the back of his tongue. He loved Quinn, but so much lay between them. He hoped they would both be able to get through this, but at the moment it wasn't looking hopeful.

"Of course, Emmia. Let's go," Quinn answered sadly.

Together they left. Magnus watched the door close behind them with sorrow curling through his stomach...and relief that Quinn was gone.

* * * * *

"Are you all right?" Emmia asked as she led Quinn down the corridor.

Quinn started to answer, snapped his mouth shut and then simply said, "Yes." It was a lie and Quinn knew that Emmia could feel it. He simply didn't want to talk about what had just happened.

Emmia nodded and thankfully changed the subject. "I need to speak with Arhild again. "I'd prefer not to do it alone."

"Why?"

She grimaced. "Arhild feels...*icky*."

He nodded. "I never liked him and I can't even feel his emotions."

She hooked her arm through his. "Thank you for coming with me."

He smiled at her, warm regard filling his being at the mere sight of her. "Emmia, you crook your finger, I obey."

His nerves were shot from his encounter with Magnus moments before. So he was grateful that Emmia had sought him out before he'd done something he would've regretted. He and Magnus been ready to fuck for a moment...then ready to fight. His heart had whiplash and his mind reeled from the web of conflict they'd been caught in. He didn't know how to unravel the tangle. Now he had something to take his mind from the incident and he was glad of it.

They found Arhild in the stables, where he was saddling his horse. When he glimpsed them, he grumbled something unintelligible at them and went back to his task.

"Are you going somewhere, Arhild?" Emmia asked.

He turned to her, gripping his horse's bit in one hand tight enough to turn his fingers white. Quinn wondered what sort of emotion Emmia was getting from him. "Have you found my daughter's killer yet?"

She took a step forward. "You didn't answer my question."

He squinted. "Nor did you answer mine." He shifted and glanced to the left. "I'm leaving, aye. Going back to see to my estate for a time."

"Did you get leave from Lord Magnus for that?" Quinn asked.

Arhild's grip on the bit tightened impossibly further. "I'm not asking leave of my child's murderer!" His voice sounded like a whip in the small building. His bay mare stamped her feet and snorted, likely sensing her master's disquiet.

"I would prefer if you did not leave just now," responded Emmia calmly.

"Why? Am I a suspect?"

Emmia paused for a heartbeat and then said, "Yes."

Arhild stared, his face purpling. Then he threw the bit down to the straw-covered stable floor. The mare danced to the side, startled, and Quinn had an urge to gentle the poor, skittish beast. To his horseman's eyes, she'd been mistreated.

"I do not have time for this trouble!" Arhild yelled. "I have lands to keep in Hia and farming tariffs to collect. I cannot remain here and wait for you to do your job. Why have you not taken Magnus for the murder yet? The evidence clearly indicates him."

"The investigation of a justice mercenary encompasses more than just evidence. I need to dig deeper than just the surface, into the heart of those concerned. *You* are one concerned, Arhild."

Quinn thought Emmia was acting with admirable restraint. He wanted to punch Arhild, personally.

Arhild stood fuming at her for a moment and stormed out of the stables muttering to himself.

"That was interesting," Quinn commented.

Emmia frowned. "I didn't even get to ask my questions."

"Well, Arhild always had an unpredictable character."

"I see that. How was his relationship with his daughter?"

"Nearly nonexistent, from what I could tell. Arhild never wanted much to do with her, nor she him."

"Hmmm."

Quinn watched that expression steal over her face that meant she needed to think. As much as he enjoyed spending time with her, the job came first. He took the hint. "Well, I need to go over to the armory."

"Mmmm."

"I'll see you later?"

"Mmmhmm."

He leaned in and gave her a lingering kiss on her cheek which he wasn't sure she even felt, then took his leave.

* * * * *

Emmia watched Quinn walk away, still trying to sort through and interpret the tumult of emotion Arhild had emitted. She supposed it was normal that he should be confused, considering his daughter had been brutally murdered, but what Emmia didn't understand was the lack of grief. There was love, sorrow and anger, lots of anger.

There was no grief.

Frowning, she walked away from the stables and back into the keep. Rolling the complex blend of feeling around on her tongue, she found herself just walking and hardly paying attention to anything or anyone around her.

Soon she found herself sitting on a plush chair somewhere in a part of the keep near her room. She'd chosen it because of the lack of people around to confuse her thought process about Arhild and Rolf.

Rolf had the motive, not Arhild. So why did she consider Arhild suspicious? Why was her intuition telling her to pay closer attention to him? Was it simply because she found him grating and unpleasant? If that was the case, she needed to separate her personal distaste of Arhild from the investigation and make certain that she was on task. She owed that much to Caith.

"Emmia?"

Her head jerked up to see Magnus staring down at her with a frown on his face. He'd shaven, finally.

"I said your name three times before you noticed me."

"I'm thinking," she responded impatiently.

"I apologize. I'll leave you alone." He turned to leave.

"No, wait. Stay. I'd like to talk to you a little."

He turned back toward her. "Well, in that case…thinking about what?"

She chewed the edge of the thumbnail. She'd been thinking that Magnus looked less and less guilty by the day. She glanced up at him and let a smile flutter over her lips. "It still amazes me how you can approach me that way and I can't even tell."

He smiled. "It's nice, isn't it?"

She nodded. "I like it more than I ever imagined I would. In fact, honestly, I wasn't going to take this case."

"Truly?"

She shook her head. "I'd just returned from the battle with The Nameless, at my sister, Rhea's, side, and was exhausted. I didn't think I'd be at my best on an investigation like this one, but once I found out you were an empath, I wanted to come. Come to meet you, that is.

"I'm flattered, but I'm sure Quinn played at least a small role in your decision."

She blushed a little. "You caught me. Mostly it was you, though." She motioned at the place beside her. "Please sit down."

They sat for a moment in silence, but it wasn't an uncomfortable one. Emmia thought he probably felt like she did, simply happy to be with someone and have things be...*noiseless.*

"I liked to spend time with Caith too," said Magnus after a time. "If only because she was so carefree and kind of...detached."

"Quinn mentioned that she was very sexually adventurous and didn't want to have any kind of deeper, emotional relationship with either of you."

"That's true. She was young in so many ways. She was simply content to live in the moment and enjoy every aspect of life as it came to her. Her emotions were always a joy to be around, never heavy, never a burden to bear." He paused. His voice cracked. "I miss her."

Emmia didn't need to psychically sense his emotions to know that he was being sincere. From all accounts that she'd heard of Caith, what Magnus said was true. "I'm truly sorry that you lost your friend."

He didn't speak for a moment. "Yes, me too."

"I will find her killer."

"I know you will." He drew a tired-sounding breath.

She turned to him and said exactly what she shouldn't say, but felt a need to, "I don't think it's you."

He nodded. "I hoped you'd cross me off the list."

"Formally, you're still on it, but..." She chewed the inside of her lip for a moment. "What do you think of Caith's father?"

"Arhild?" He sounded surprised she'd asked about him. "I always felt strong love come from him regarding Caith, yet he berated her at every turn. He didn't approve of her lifestyle and wanted her to find a husband, settle down and have children. Caith didn't want any of that. Why? Is he a suspect?"

Motive. Maybe. She shook her head and then shrugged. "I haven't decided yet. There are several people in the keep with motive enough to have committed the murder. There's only one person who had both the motive to murder Caith and the opportunity to plant the sword in your chamber, however."

"Rolf."

She nodded.

He shook his head. "I don't think he did it."

She gave him a sharp look. "Shouldn't you be eager to have me latch onto someone other than you?"

He smiled. "I just want you to find Caith's killer and I want you to be right when you do, that's all."

She returned his smile and then turned back around, sighing. They stayed that way for a long time, simply enjoying each other's presence.

* * * * *

"I see why you like her."

Quinn turned from his place at one of the long dining room tables to see Magnus. He fought the rise of emotion that always accompanied the sight of him and took a bite of his sandwich, chewing and swallowing before answering.

The man could wait.

"I do like her. Very much," he answered finally. He scooted to the side without looking at his former lover, giving him an invitation to sit. Magnus took it, making Quinn's stomach tighten and his cock twitch at the scent of him so close.

"How much do you like her?" Magnus' voice was deep, smooth and intimately close to his ear. It brought back memories of long, hot sweaty nights.

Gods, how he missed those nights. Would there ever be another one?

Quinn dropped his sandwich to the plate and pushed it away. "Enough that for the first time in a very long time I'm actually considering being in a serious relationship again."

"I think I'm a little jealous." Magnus was quiet for several moments before asking, "How long has it been since you considered such a thing?"

"Don't play with my emotions, Magnus. That's not fair when you can feel them." His voice sounded low and threatening to his own ears. "I can't hide anything from you. Never could. It's irritating."

"You haven't answered my question."

Quinn sighed. "Since you, of course."

"I just needed to hear it." He waited a heartbeat and then said, "I still love you, Quinn. Despite everything, I still love you. I just need for you to know that."

Quinn glanced at him. "I can't do this right now." His voice was heavy with emotion. He wanted to scream at him that he still loved him as well and that he'd never stopped loving him and that he was sorry for not standing by him after Caith's murder.

That he'd made a mistake.

That he'd never be able to forgive himself for giving up heaven, trading it for mistrust and suspicion. Gods, what had he been thinking? Magnus hadn't killed Caith. Not even Emmia thought he had. Why hadn't he stood by Magnus' side the way he should've? Had it been pure shock? Had it been grief? Quinn just didn't know.

"Fine," answered Magnus in a clipped tone. "I just wanted you to know that. I also need you to know that I want Emmia."

"She and I have no formal commitment." Still, it pricked a little. He'd never felt jealous over Caith, but Emmia was different. However, he had no idea how Emmia regarded him. His feelings for her were deepening, but she probably didn't feel the same for him. She was probably too afraid to let her feelings for him go very deep. Sometimes where Emmia was concerned Quinn wished he had the Talent of empathy. The woman was difficult to read.

"I just want you to know that I don't want her because of her connection to you, although that does make her more attractive to me. I can be honest about that. But I want Emmia for Emmia. Because I find her very attractive on many levels."

"I'm not standing in your way."

Magnus placed his hand on Quinn's thigh under the table. Quinn started, and then relaxed under Magnus' familiar touch. He'd missed the warm, heavy weight of that hand, missed the taste of Magnus' mouth and the feel of his cock.

"I want you to know that not only am I going after Emmia, I'm also coming after you, Quinn." Magnus paused. "I want you back. I want things the way they were...before, between you and me."

Quinn just shook his head. "Too much has happened —"

"Don't you think I know that?" Magnus' voice was like the lash of a whip. "Doesn't change the fact that I still have feelings for you, Quinn."

Quinn stared at the table until Magnus had left. Magnus would forgive him for what he'd done? Magnus still loved him after he'd suspected, along with everyone else, that Magnus may have killed Caith?

Gods, was there still hope?

* * * * *

Emmia and Magnus had taken to playing *lochart* in the afternoons in Magnus' chambers, a board game of strategy.

She was still interviewing the suspects for Caith's murder, letting their emotions sit in her mind, allowing herself to study them, live with them. This was how she worked. Oftentimes, a person could only shield and hide their emotions from her for a certain amount of time. Eventually, they slipped under the stress of her constant presence and then she had them. Sometimes time told the truth when the perpetrator would not.

Magnus was still officially still on her list, but he was the last one in terms of ranking.

Anyway, she liked playing *lochart* with him.

She moved her knight to the side and captured his king.

"By the Gods, Emmia, you're going to beat me again," Magnus groused, leaning over the board to consider his next move. "You're too good at this game by half."

"I used to play it with my sister, Rhea, when we were young. I used to get angry because she beat me all the time, so I studied the game until I could play very well."

"Curse your determination," he murmured, then caught his tongue between his teeth and frowned down at the board. Magnus made his move.

So did Emmia.

He stared down at the board for a moment. "Blast it!"

Emmia laughed.

He leaned back in his chair and smiled. "Well, at least if I must lose, I'm losing to someone pretty."

Emmia's laugh faded and she self-consciously touched a lock of her hair. Men usually didn't regard her as such. Quinn was the first one who'd repeatedly told her over and over how attractive she was. If Magnus started it too, she might just start believing it.

"Did I say something wrong?"

"No." She glanced away. "I'm just tired, I guess. Having to live with so many people and their emotions for so long this way is very wearing. Especially since I'm just coming off the battle with the The Nameless."

"I heard you had a large role to play in that."

"Everyone did. It was very…draining."

Magnus chuckled. "You're the only person I know who would refer to nearly having their world destroyed and almost dying as merely *draining*."

She let a smile flicker across her mouth.

Magnus stared at her for a moment, then stood and held out a hand. "Come."

Emmia stared at his broad hand with a confused look on her face.

"I know you said you tried everything there was to try to build up your shields, but how you do you *know* everything there is to try?"

"Magnus…"

"There is no harm in *trying*, Emmia. Please. Humor me. I don't like to see you suffer so."

She glanced up at him sharply. "Why should you care?"

"So prickly! When I spend so much time being beaten at *lochart* by someone, I tend to get attached, all right?" He motioned with his hand again. "Now, please, Emmia, take my hand."

She hesitated for a moment, and then put her hand in his. He helped her to stand and led her to the center of the room. His body was warm—it seemed warmer than Quinn's for some reason, like Magnus' body temperature was naturally higher. In addition, she could smell the scent of him—leather from his horse's saddle and the now-familiar spice-scented soap he used. The combination of his scent, his warmth and the aura of his masculinity made shivers run down her spine.

She'd been fighting her attraction for Magnus because of the investigation. It wasn't right that a justice mercenary become involved with a suspect, even one she believed innocent. Such a situation might not ruin her career, but it could damage her reputation.

Being able to abstain from Magnus was made easy by the steady and satisfying supply of sex she received from Quinn. Quinn was a wonderful man, a giving and supportive man. He was a man she thought she could grow to love. He had awoken her sexuality, something she'd repressed since it had first been stirred to life within her for a fear of aligning herself forevermore with another person's emotions.

And Quinn had turned out to be no great burden in this regard. Emmia found that aligning herself with Quinn's emotions was actually more a pleasure than a pain. He liked her very much and love flickered from time to time. She found she minded those flickers less as time passed. She even kind of liked them.

Perhaps it was because she had such flickers for him as well.

Magnus pulled her into his arms and she went stiff at first, and then relaxed into him. He threaded his fingers through her hair and she allowed it. It was...nice. She liked having physical contact with him.

"Now, close your eyes and feel all that emotion that batters at you."

Dutifully, she did as he requested...but sighed.

"No sighing with resignation. Give yourself to this exercise, Emmia. Give yourself to it completely and open your mind. You must *want it* for it to work." His voice was low and silken.

She pushed away from him. "Of course I *want it*!"

"Do you?" He smiled. "Do you really? Are you sure? Maybe there's a part of you that truly doesn't want to sever your ability to sense all emotion. Way deep down inside."

"Ridiculous."

He raised an eyebrow. "Is it? Really? Search your heart. I know that for myself, that need and desire is what initially prevented me from erecting shields for my Talent."

She frowned, licked her lips and glanced down. Could it be true? Was there some part of her that craved the contact with others? Some part far deep within her that kept her from erecting the psychic walls she needed to protect herself?

All her life she'd held herself back from people, even her own family, in an effort to reduce the rasp of raw emotion against her most tender psychic flesh. And yet, she'd always longed for the contact of others...for as long as she could remember.

She looked up at him. "Maybe."

"Ah. Yes, *maybe*." He touched her cheek. "I know you, Emmia. I know you because you so closely parallel me." He held out his arms. "Now, please, do as I request."

She stepped forward and allowed him to embrace her. She closed her eyes and searched deep within to find that part of her that wanted the abuse, the part of her that craved it because it meant contact with others...no matter how unbearable and violent at times.

"There's the way," Magnus crooned. "Take your time. Find the root. Don't pull it out, though. It needs to be there. It's healthy, that drive to connect. Instead, acknowledge it. Make friends with it. Pull it out into the daylight of your consciousness, so that you can deal with it, manage it and make it yours."

She squeezed her eyes shut as though it would help her concentrate better. Her fingers found purchase in the sleeves of his shirt and fisted. Memories from her childhood flitted through her brain—the first time she could remember being overwhelmed by emotion, the first time she pushed someone away because of it, the first time she mourned the loss of that person in her life. She took all those memories and rolled them around in her mind as though tasting a dish that was both bitter and sweet at the same time. In the back of her throat, she made a whimpering sound.

"You found it, didn't you?"

"Yes."

"Good. Put it away in a safe place, somewhere you can find it again whenever you want to. Now let's start building the walls. But before we start, assure yourself that just because you erect them, you still will be able to have contact with others. Know that because of the walls you build, you'll actually be able to have *more* contact with others, deeper relationships. You'll be happier with the shields in place."

Together they worked, doing things that Emmia had already tried before. She felt it was more successful this time because she had acknowledged what had been blocking her.

When she'd finished building up the psychic walls around her ability, the ever-present pressure of the keep's inhabitants had eased. She opened her eyes, took a step back, blinked and smiled.

He stared at her. "Beautiful."

"Excuse me?"

"Well, you were beautiful before, to be sure, but without that tension in your face and shoulders..." His voice held a note of awe. "Do you feel better?"

"Yes." She inclined her head a degree. "Thank you."

He reached out and pulled her against him once more and she allowed it. "I want to touch you," Magnus said somewhere near her ear. She shivered against him.

Emmia knew she shouldn't want him to touch her, but the *shoulds* of her world were rapidly fading in the face of her desire. She couldn't help but wonder what it would be like to have sex with Magnus and completely allow herself to succumb to the purely physical experience of it, without any distraction from the other person's emotions at all.

Apparently, Magnus wondered as well.

It was wrong, seeing as he was still on the list of suspects, formally, but...her body didn't seem to mind. Her breasts had grown sensitive and her cunt slick with the mere possibility of having sex with him.

He eased his hand to her upper thigh. His lips found her ear and she closed her eyes, feeling goose bumps rise along her body and her pussy grow warmer and damper.

"Emmia? Let me touch you."

She couldn't respond. Her lips parted and he rubbed his thumb along her lower lip. He murmured that he was going to kiss her, and then he did.

She snaked her hand between them and pushed him away. He looked at her with questions in his eyes, his mouth only a breath away. "This is a mistake, Magnus. This isn't right. I should leave this room immediately and put a mile between us," she whispered.

He stared at her lips. "I know." He pressed her into him while his mouth descended on hers.

Emmia went stiff at first, but then relaxed, curving to fit Magnus' body perfectly. Her lips rested against his for a moment until a need stronger than anything she could combat rose up within her. She returned his kiss with a sudden urgency, allowing him to coax her lips apart. His tongue slipped within to explore.

Her hands came up, sliding over his biceps to his shoulders. He was a bit taller than Quinn and she suddenly felt a little shy, realizing that this was not her current lover she now kissed. This was a different man with a different feel and a different taste. Finally, she curled the fingers of one hand into the hair at the nape of his neck. The other she pressed tight against the back of his shoulder.

Her tongue found his and moved against it, stroking it the way she kissed Quinn. Magnus groaned in the back of his throat and held her closer, so close every breath she took dragged her hard nipples against his chest. It made her want fewer clothes between them.

As if reading her mind and knowing exactly what she wanted, he brought a hand around and cupped her breast through the material of her shirt. He brushed his thumb back and forth over her erect nipple, making her moan and arch into him. At the same time he pressed his hard cock against her so she could feel what she was doing to him, and how much he wanted her.

Emmia found his hand on her breast and pushed it beneath her shirt. She guided him upward until he found her bare, unbound breast. He made an appreciative sound in his throat and worked it with skillful fingers until Emmia felt weak in the knees and felt herself cream between her thighs. Then he let his hand roam down. She helped him get down her pants in the front and he guided his hand between her thighs, where he found hot, aroused pussy and cupped it.

Emmia made a low, satisfied sound in her throat and spread her legs to give him better access. He pushed the material of her panties away and dragged his fingers over her sex. He shuddered against her and she felt a sudden flicker of power at the way the touch of her seemed to be affecting him.

Magnus slanted his mouth over her and hungrily sank his tongue into her hot mouth over and over, as if trying to consume her. The way he kissed her, like he'd been starving and she was his first meal in months, made her breath come in short, sharp puffs. He teased and stroked her clit until her body tensed, and he slid first one thick finger up inside her, and then added a second, and slowly, surely began to thrust into her with them.

He worked them in and out of her, still kissing her deeply, until her interior muscles spasmed and she let out a low moan into the interior of Magnus' mouth. An orgasm skittered through her body, teasing her, then crashed into her at a force so strong it made her knees weak. The muscles of her cunt squeezed around Magnus' thrusting fingers as she came.

He caught all her soft cries against his mouth. It hadn't taken long to make her climax. It was almost embarrassing how excited he made her with merely the stroke of his fingers deep inside her pussy.

She groaned into his mouth, catching and gently dragging his lower lip between her teeth. Magnus' whole body shook in response, revealing how excited he was. All she wanted in the world right now was for this man to take off all her clothes and take her so hard she wouldn't be able to see straight for a week.

He re-intensified his kiss and she snaked her hand between their bodies, feeling out his long, hard cock through his clothing and stroking him. Being kissed by this man was like being battered with pleasure. His lips worked magic over hers, making love to her mouth and to her tongue with the same skill he'd likely employ to her entire body.

Gods, how she wanted to find out if that was true.

Magnus made a sound deep in his throat, snaked his arms around her and lifted her. Emmia gasped at the ease with which he hoisted her. She grabbed his shoulders, feeling his muscles work as he moved. He turned and took several steps to the bed and laid her down on the mattress. Then he came down on top of her, slanting his mouth hungrily over hers. Every little movement he made rasped her shirt across her stiff, sensitive nipples. Finally he reached between them and ripped the offending garment off her, allowing her bare breasts to spill free. The ache between her thighs intensified as the material of his shirt rubbed her sensitized nipples, then he palmed her breasts both in turn.

Magnus slid his hands down her back and cupped her buttocks, lifting her cunt to press against his hard cock. She cursed every thread of material that still lay between them and ground against him needfully, pressing herself up against him as if trying to climb his body.

Magnus broke the kiss with a heartfelt groan. "Emmia, you don't know how much I want you."

"I do, because it's as much as I want you." She curled her fingers into the fabric of his shirt. "What's holding you back?"

He stared down at her for a moment, breathing heavily. "I don't know. I-I don't want to damage anything between us."

Emmia let out a little laugh. "I'm here to investigate you for murder. How much more can we damage things?"

He smiled. "Good point."

"Then fuck me, Magnus. Please."

Magnus held her gaze as he reached down and yanked the waistband of her pants down and cupped her bare buttock. She felt the rasp of his calloused palm against her skin. Her pussy seemed to grow hotter and wetter, anticipating the feel of him touching her more intimately.

"Touch me, Magnus," she whispered. "Touch me before I lose my mind."

"Like this? Is this how you want to be touched?" He dragged a finger along her exposed, swollen labia and then over her anus.

Emmia tensed and shut her eyes, trying to get past the sudden tang of fear and more fully into the pleasure. She liked it when Quinn had taken her there. It had been surprisingly good. "Yes," she breathed. "Like that. *More.*"

"You feel like heaven," he murmured, his voice shaking a little. "I will give you *more*, sweet Emmia."

She reached up, unbuttoned his shirt and he pulled it over his head, revealing a chest made powerfully strong and scarred by sword practice and war. She traced her palms down his satin-over-steel skin, incredulous she should be given the delicious bounty of both Quinn and Magnus in such a short span of time. How lucky was she? She was definitely making up for lost time, that was for certain.

His gaze focused on her face as he ran his palms up her thighs and waist. She spread her legs for him, slipping them around his hips and arching up at him hungrily. "You're beautiful, Emmia. Irresistible. I wanted from you from the first moment I saw you in the courtyard, even though your presence perhaps meant my death." He slid down her body, parted her thighs and licked her.

"Magnus!" She grabbed on to the blankets on either side of her and held on under the swell of a near climax that rippled through her body. Gods, how embarrassing it was that this man could make her orgasm so easily. She felt like some untried virgin in his arms.

Magnus groaned and lifted his head briefly. "You taste so good. Just like I imagined."

"You imagined?" she gasped out.

He raised his head and groaned. "Too many times to count."

His hands found her hips and clamped down, holding her in place. The erotic sight of his dark head between her thighs, his strong hands gripping her and the muscles of his shoulders working as he licked and sucked her was nearly enough to drive her to the edge of another orgasm. His thumbs pulled her labia apart, revealing the heart of her. Magnus studied her for a moment, then groaned and dropped his head to devour her once more. He toyed with her sensitive clit with the tip of his tongue and then slowly licked her labia, easing into every fold.

She arched her back and moaned. Her orgasm rose, tingling through her body. He kept it at bay, managed it, until she teetered on the razor's edge of a climax.

"Look at me, Emmia," he murmured.

She tipped her head forward and let her eyes flicker open. She felt like she'd been drinking wine, intoxicated on the carnal pleasure of it.

"Look right into my eyes. I want you to know who it is that's making you come."

"Magnus," she breathed, unable to make any other kind of response. She held his gaze as he lowered his mouth to her clit and sucked it between his sensual lips. He kept his gaze focused on hers, up the line of her body. Ecstasy skittered through her body as he teased it, driving her to the brilliant, sharp edge of another orgasm.

With his finger, Magnus stroked her sensitive entrance, massaging the area around her labia. Then he eased his skillful tongue up into her and thrust in and out. At the same time, he stroked her clit with the pad of his thumb, rubbing the small bundle of nerves to climax.

"Come for me, Emmia," he demanded.

Emmia's climax exploded through her body. She cried out as it washed through her body. She couldn't breathe, couldn't think, couldn't even form words. Magnus had made it more powerful by withholding it, building it up and then skillfully sending it to crash down over her. Magnus drew it out even longer by gently caressing her clit.

"Magnus," she breathed when she finally could. "Gods, Magnus."

He climbed up her body with a hungry, almost dangerous, look in his eyes. Magnus sealed his mouth over hers once more impatiently. At the same time, he thrust his still fabric-clad pelvis against her cunt, rasping over her sensitized and aroused clit.

Emmia arched her back and wrapped her legs around his waist, grinding her cunt against him. Holding her hips, he settled himself between her thighs and ground back until she cried from the hard edge of the pleasure of it. His rock-hard, huge cock jutted against her tender folds, rasped against her and made her feel empty inside. Why was he making her wait so long for his cock?

"I want to ease inside your sweet pussy, Emmia," Magnus whispered.

She slipped her hand between their bodies and undid his pants. "Then don't make me wait any longer." She pushed at the waistband of his pants and he slipped them down and off.

Thanks the Goddess and all the Gods, he was finally naked.

And, ah, but he was pretty. Long, broad and hard. She rose up, pushed him down and closed her mouth around him.

Her turn.

"Gods, Emmia!" His back arched and his fingers tangled in her hair.

She suppressed a grin and licked the length of him instead. He felt good in her mouth. His back arched again when she sucked him deep into the recesses and then slowly drew him out again, all the while letting her tongue play along the length of him.

Emmia loved this most, loved doing this to Quinn as well. Loved the fact that she could bring these men to their knees with only the swipe of her tongue. Men were slaves to a woman's mouth around their cock. Quinn reacted the same way. For a moment, she imagined having both them in bed with her. That night when Quinn had made her imagine it, it had made her come. It made her cunt damp now to even think of it.

Magnus' fingers twisted in her hair as she worked his cock in and out of her mouth. Then, abruptly, he slid out from beneath her. "You keep doing that and I won't last much longer."

"Would that be so bad?"

He came over her, muscling her thighs apart and settling between them. "Yes, Emmia, because I want to feel your sweet cunt around my cock and I don't know if this is my only opportunity. By this time tomorrow, you'll have come to your senses and you won't want me anymore."

She thrust her hips up at him. "I want you now, Magnus. Please."

"I want to make this last. I don't want it to go quickly."

She reached up and cupped his cheek. "Why?"

"It's like dessert, Emmia. You're like fine chocolate from D'ar in eastern Molari. I know you're rare and I want to savor you." He took her hand and guided it between their bodies to her pussy. Taking her fingers in his hand, he made her pet her own clit, finger her creamy labia and finally sink her own fingers deep into her cunt.

"It's like heaven in there," Magnus whispered. He eased her hand away and brushed the head of his cock against her. "What are you thinking about right now, Emmia? Are you thinking about Quinn?"

Her eyes fluttered shut, and then opened. She looked up and caught his gaze. "Yes, I'm thinking about Quinn. When I'm with Quinn sometimes I think about you."

"Do you think about having us both at the same time?"

"Yes," she breathed.

"It excites you." It was a statement, not a question.

"Yes, now give me more. You're making me insane with this slow pace."

He slid the smooth crown of his cock past the lips of her cunt. She arched into him, wanting more. The way he stretched her muscles felt exquisite. Magnus groaned and slid in another few inches.

"More?" he asked her.

"More!"

Magnus thrust until he hilted. He remained motionless for a few moments, allowing her body to adjust to his length and width, then pulled out and thrust in again so slowly she could almost memorize every vein of his cock as it glided inside her. Her breath hissed between her teeth at the sensation of it. He held her hips, keeping her from writhing as he shafted her slowly.

"Faster," she whispered. She could feel the rising edge of a climax, a powerful one that grew closer and closer.

Magnus pulled back and drove into her hard and fast, all the way to the base of him. Then again and again. He took her fast and hard, possessing her body with every masterful stroke.

Emmia came. The waves of her orgasm washed over her, nearly drowning her with their intensity. She felt her sex spasm around his still thrusting cock, her muscles contracting around him.

His big body tensed and he thrust all the way up inside her. "Emmia, Gods, I'm coming." She felt him shudder and his cock jump deep inside her. He whispered her name and then groaned low as he climaxed.

He collapsed on her and held her tight, his cock still thrust deep into her body. They stayed that way until the waves passed, then Magnus rolled to the side. Her body felt sore in places, but it was a delicious soreness. It was the kind of soreness that declared her body well loved. Emmia lay on the bed, her body still tingling from pleasure. She cupped her breast, feeling the press of her still hardened nipple against her palm.

When her breathing had returned to normal, Emmia looked over at him. His cock glistened with her juices and was still hard as a rock.

He glanced at her, noticing where her gaze had landed. "It's been a long time," he explained. "I haven't had sex since..." he trailed off, as unwilling as she to bring that subject up now.

"It was wonderful," she murmured. "It was *incredible*." She gave a little laugh of pure satisfaction and joy. She always felt this way with Quinn after they'd joined as well. Sated. Bone-deep happiness.

He reached over to pet her cunt. Leisurely, he slid a finger into her and, using their combined juices as a lubricant, slowly fucked her with it until she moaned. "Are you sore?"

She spread her thighs a little farther, giving him better access. "A little."

"I love the way you feel." He leaned over and slanted his mouth over hers. "I love to make you come. I love the way you sound when you do it. How you call my name." He stroked his finger over and over that knot of nerves inside her. Masterfully. Perfectly. Magnus knew how to touch her, the right pressure, and the right place.

"Umm." That's all she was capable of saying in response. She closed her eyes and gave herself over completely to the pleasure he exerted over her body.

"Are you going to come again for me, Emmia?" he whispered into her ear.

"Yes," she breathed, closing her eyes. Just then it exploded softly over her body, making her cry out. This one was longer, almost gentle. Magnus kissed her, eating up her groans, as he drew the climax out longer and longer.

When it came to its shuddering conclusion, Emmia felt every muscle in her body relax. She threaded her fingers though his thick hair and kissed the side of his head, realizing only afterward what an intimate gesture it was. It had seemed like such a natural thing to do.

He rolled to the side and pulled her against him, cradling her against the hard curve of his body. Together, they lay and breathed heavily, enjoying the aftermath of their pleasure.

Her face shielded from Magnus' view, Emmia smiled. It was so magnificent to lie in his arms, in perfect peace, in perfect satisfaction. No emotional distractions marred her enjoyment of his moment and the poignant memory of his body moving with hers. She didn't know how he felt about any of this, and he didn't know how she felt.

And that was a good thing.

She snuggled back against him, allowing all other concerns to leave her mind for the moment. His arms tightened around her and he gave a contented sigh. "I'm glad you came to Ravensbridge," he whispered. "I'm glad you came to my bed."

She laughed softly. "You're a strange man, Magnus, but I'm glad too."

"Did you leave anyone behind? Anyone you care about?"

She drew a careful breath. "No. I live alone. It's...easier that way." She paused. "But maybe, just maybe, if what we did this night works, perhaps I can learn eventually to live among others." The seething emotions of the keep were still being held at bay by the walls she'd built with Magnus, but she still doubted they'd hold. It just seemed too good to be true that they would.

Magnus urged her to roll over and she slid onto her back. He braced himself on his elbow and stared down into her face. "I think you are a magnificent woman, Emmia."

She felt her cheeks color. "Thank you."

"You need to give yourself to the world more often." He touched her cheek and then slid his hand down her throat, over her collarbone to tease a nipple. "And I love your body." He grinned wickedly. "I think you need to give it to me more often."

Her laugh came out a little raspy as he touched and gently squeezed her nipple. Her cunt responded, growing warm and soft with her honey. She shifted on the mattress, suppressing a moan.

"And you're lush," he continued, trailing his hand down her stomach, over her mound and to her pussy. She spread her thighs to allow him to play. "So sensual and sexual. Gods, I want you again."

Indeed, his cock had begun to harden once more against her thigh. Magnus stroked her clit over and over, pushing her to one more gentle and long climax. She shuddered in his arms and Magnus ate up her sounds by placing his mouth over hers as she came against his hand.

Then he pulled her against him once more and they slept.

* * * * *

Emmia closed the door of Magnus' room in the wee morning hours. The keep was quiet and dark. She'd slept full into the middle of the night in his bed. It had been a good sleep, untroubled by excess emotion that wasn't hers. It had been the best sleep she could remember having and she had to wonder if it was because of the walls that Magnus had helped her to build, or if it had been Magnus himself.

Just the fact that it was a question in her mind bothered her, but there it was, all the same, defying logic and her wishes.

Deep in thought, she turned to head down the corridor to her room...and ran smack into a broad chest. Startled, she looked up into Quinn's darkened eyes.

Emmia grabbed his arms. "You frightened me!" she exclaimed in a surprised and excited voice.

"I'm sorry."

"No! No, you don't understand. I didn't know you were there!"

He just stared down at her with a funny look on his face.

She sighed in exasperation. Magnus would know exactly what she meant. "I couldn't feel your emotions!"

"Have you learned to manage your ability?"

"Yes...no." She shook her head. "I don't know. Magnus had a fresh perspective on the matter. He may have helped me to get over the mental block I didn't know I had. Only time will tell if it works or not."

In the cool, dim light, Quinn blinked slowly. "You've been all this time with Magnus?"

Gods...

There was a note of jealousy in his voice and she dropped her guard a little to see if his emotion matched. It did. She built the walls back up and frowned. "Why are you jealous, Quinn? Why be jealous of Magnus' time with me? You and I have no understanding of monogamy in our relationship." She inhaled swiftly as understanding struck. "You're not jealous of Magnus' time with me, you're jealous of *my* time with *Magnus*. That's it, isn't it?"

Quinn took her shoulders and eased her back against the wall behind her. He placed his hands to either side of her head, pinning her there. "You misunderstand how swiftly my regard for you is developing, Emmia. You're only half correct. I *am* jealous that you spent the evening making love to Magnus, but I am also jealous that he made love to you."

"Quinn—"

"I can smell him on you and his scent on your flesh—the two of them mingling—is the best thing I can think of. I could lick every inch of your body right now and be happy." He grabbed her hips and pulled her up against him. She could feel the press of his cock against her stomach. "I want both of you and I want you at the same time."

Emmia's breath came swift and shallow at the thought of it. Was it wrong that she wanted that too? She closed her eyes as he nuzzled her ear. "Magnus still…cares for you, Quinn."

He stilled. "I know. But much lies between us now. I don't know if it's surmountable." He paused. "And it's my fault."

She kissed him on the lips, long and hard. The pain Quinn felt was in his eyes and in his voice and she wanted to take it away. "Come," she said, leading him down the corridor. "Let's go sleep."

* * * * *

From the other side of the door, Magnus listened to them progress down the hallway. His heart ached to go to Quinn, but part of him still hurt.

Gods, he wanted Quinn back so much.

Chapter Five

ℛ

"Where are you taking me?" Quinn asked, his voice raspy with good-natured annoyance.

Emmia only glanced back with a smile and continued to drag him down the hall. On either side of the wide, open corridor that looked down on the courtyard, people stared. Their curiosity and wonderment pressed against her psychic barriers, but her new walls held up and sheltered her against the worst of it.

"Emmia!" Quinn grabbed her wrist and pulled her backward against him.

She laughed as he dragged her into a nearby alcove and pressed her against the wall. There they were sheltered from all prying eyes.

He slipped his hands to her waist and pressed his mouth to hers. His breath smelled of sweet mint and warmed her lips. "Tell me where we're going, or I'll take you back to my room and torture the information from you."

She tilted her head to the side and smiled. "Promise?"

She felt him smile in return. Then he kissed her breathless. His tongue slid between her lips and played restlessly with hers, making her body tighten. Her fingers curled into his upper arms.

He broke the kiss and rested his forehead against her. "Would it scare you if I said I were falling for you, Emmia? In ways not physical? In ways that might even involve the word...*love*?"

She bit her lower lip and suppressed a smile. It was nice to be desired, nice to be in a relationship, *nice* to be cared for.

She felt so light today, so free from the heavy emotion that normal plagued her that it didn't scare her at all. "On the contrary. I care deeply for you too, Quinn. In any case, do you really think you can hide your emotions from me? I *know* what you feel for me." She paused. "I think I love you back, Quinn."

A smile spread over his face. "Oh good. Then tell me where you're taking me."

She laughed and slipped under his arm, dancing away from him into the corridor.

Quinn stared at her for a moment in disbelief and then smiled broadly. "Who are you and what have you done with Emmia?"

"Magnus freed her." She crooked a finger and continued down the corridor. "Come on now."

He fell into step beside her. "I'll go anywhere you lead, even if I don't know where it is. Although I am a little jealous that it was Magnus who helped you overcome your problem and not me."

She stopped short in the corridor. He took another couple steps before he realized she'd halted and turned to her with questions in his eyes. She took a step toward him and caught his hands in hers. "Quinn, you have no idea what your presence in my life means to me. Please understand how much you've helped me and how much I care for you. If it weren't for you I would still be on my cottage in the woods. I never would've discovered that I could be in a relationship despite my Talent. You showed me I could." Tears pricked her eyes. "I care so much about you."

He pulled her into his arms and kissed the top of her head. She inhaled and the scent of the soap he used filled her nostrils. "Likewise, my little love. Likewise."

She pulled away from him. "Now, come on. You keep slowing us down."

Emmia continued down the corridor and he followed. They approached a set of heavy, elaborately carved wooden doors and Emmia pushed them open. The room within was dark, lit only by a fire in the hearth. It was the way Magnus mostly spent his days, away from the pressing suspicion and seething emotion of the keep. She could hardly blame him.

He turned from the hearth. "Emmia," he greeted warmly. Then he got a glimpse of her companion and his voice took on a note of uncertainty, "Quinn."

Emmia stood to the side to let Quinn enter the room first. She'd set up a meeting between herself and Magnus in this room, not telling her either her true objective. "Now, I want you two to talk. I'll be back later." With that, she closed the doors, took the key from a chain under her shirt and secured the lock.

With a final, satisfied smile at the door, she turned and walked away.

* * * * *

Quinn tried the doors. "She locked us in."

"That minx."

Quinn stared at the doors for a long moment before turning. He had no idea what to do or say in this situation. Magnus gazed back, mute. Apparently, he didn't know what to do or say either.

So, inevitably, an awkward silence fell that seemed to last forever, but really only spanned a few seconds. Quinn shifted his weight and cleared his throat.

Magnus motioned to a small table near the fire. "I have some ale. Would you like a little?"

Quinn nodded and went to the table where Magnus poured him a glass. They sat down together and both took a drink. The cool, sweet ale cleared his mind a little so that he could think again. Didn't have anything to say? Wrong. He had lots to say.

"Magnus," he started, stopped, and then started again, "Magnus, I'm so sorry about these last months. I'm sorry that I ever doubted your innocence, even for a moment. I loved you then...as I love you now and I should have stayed by your side through everything—" He broke off, his chest filling with a warm mixture of emotion that he knew Magnus sensed. "Damn it, Magnus, I made so many mistakes. I wouldn't fault you for never forgiving me."

Magnus reached over and put his hand on Quinn's leg. His body reacted instantly to the other man's touch, his cock hardening. "I admit that it was...difficult." He paused. "But I love you too, Quinn, and that love is unconditional."

Quinn stood and paced to the fire and back. "How can you forgive me when I can't forgive myself, Magnus?"

Magnus rose and walked to him. In the dim light, he could see a familiar look on his face. Lust. Love. A heady combination of the two emotions. It was an expression that Quinn liked to see, or had...*before*.

Quinn's gaze traced the lines of Magnus' upper arms and chest as he approached. Then his gaze descended to Magnus' cock. It strained against the zipper of his pants.

"I can forgive you," said Magnus in a low, steady voice, "because I can feel what is in your heart right now." He reached out and placed his palm flat to Quinn's chest. The heat of his palm bled through the material of his shirt and into his skin. "You do still care for me, don't you, Quinn?"

Quinn closed his eyes for a moment, trying to quell the sexual response he felt. "With everything that I am."

"I still care for you, Quinn, and I want you right now." Magnus hand drifted down his chest to his groin, where he cupped Quinn's hardness in his hand. "And you want me too, don't you?"

"Yes." Quinn felt his heart rate speed up as Magnus stroked him through the material of his pants, making him harder. He stared into Magnus' eyes, feeling the need to dominant him rise up. "And I will have you."

Magnus' mouth curled in a satisfied smile. They often took turns taking the lead in sex, though Quinn was more often the more aggressive of the two in this regard. It was a game they played and Magnus knew he'd just pushed all of Quinn's buttons...and Magnus liked it.

He pulled away from Magnus and circled him, his eyes heavy-lidded. As he stalked around his former lover, he took in his gorgeous male body. They'd been dancing on the knife's edge of this for a long time now. It was time they gave in. He wanted to take Magnus, and take him forcefully. He wanted to assert his connection to him once more and make him his. In this one blessed moment it was as if nothing had happened and they were the same two lovers they'd been before Caith's death.

Quinn stopped behind Magnus and traced over his shoulders and down his arms. He inhaled the scent of his skin and enjoyed the warmth of his flesh under his hands. "Gods, I've missed you," he said on a groan. This moment was just about perfect. The only thing that would have made it better was if Emmia had been present. He greatly desired to see that happen sometime in the near future.

Magnus covered his hands with his own. "I've missed you too."

Quinn dropped down to the button and zipper of Magnus' pants and undid them. His pants fell to the floor and Magnus' cock sprang free. Anticipation building within him, along with a huge dose of impatience, Quinn wrapped his hand around it and pumped. This time, it was Magnus who groaned.

His cock was long and thick and heavily veined. Right now, it was very, very hard—like silk-covered steel. He ran his fingers teasingly over the broad tip and then down to stroke his shaft. Magnus still had his hand over Quinn's and he moved with Quinn, pumping his cock against Quinn's palm until Magnus' breath came fast.

"I need you," Quinn rasped out. "I need you now."

In response, Magnus kissed him roughly, his tongue spearing past his lips and tangling. They wrestled each other to the floor, each pulling at the other's clothing until they were both half undressed. The buttons on Quinn's shirt popped and flew, while Quinn undid his fly with shaking hands. Quinn's need to join physically with the man he loved was like nothing he'd ever experienced.

Quinn flipped his lover to his stomach ran his hand down Magnus' ass. He pressed a finger into his anus, eliciting groans from them both. Magnus' cock jumped and he let out a guttural groan as Quinn skillfully manipulated his body into relaxing and opening.

When Magnus was ready, Quinn slipped the head of his cock within him, and then fed the length to him slowly, inch by inch. Magnus splayed his hand flat on the floor and pressed back against him on every thrust.

Quinn reached around and took Magnus' cock in hand, stroking in time as he thrust. He knew Magnus so well, knew that when his breathing hitched and changed that he was ready to climax. His cock jerked in Quinn's hand, he groaned his name and then came.

Quinn went right after him.

Panting, they collapsed to the floor. Quinn rolled onto his back and gave a short bark of laughter. "Emmia told us to *talk.*"

After a moment, Magnus rolled over and grinned. "I'm glad we didn't just talk."

Quinn leaned in and gave him a lingering kiss. "That was explosive. Gods, I wanted you so much." His heart felt lighter than it had in a long time, looking into Magnus' smiling eyes. *This* was where he belonged. Anywhere Magnus was, that was home for Quinn. If one good thing had come out of their recent ordeal, it was that Quinn had truly realized how much he loved him.

Magnus tangled his hands through his hair. "I forgive you, Quinn."

His smile faded and he looked away. In the heat of the moment, he'd forgotten about that. Magnus' grip tightened in his hair, forcing his gaze back to his face. "No. *Look at me.* I forgive you." He paused. "Please. Please, just don't ever leave me again."

Quinn pulled his body against his. "Oh Gods, I won't. I promise that I'll never leave you again. I love you, Magnus." Their arms twined and they hung on to one another as if drowning.

They lay tangled together on the floor, listening to the fire crackle and pop and watching the shadows play along the walls. For the first time in a very long time, Quinn felt almost at peace. He was missing just one thing for perfect contentment.

They heard the lock on the door turning. Sunlight from outside spilled in, haloing Emmia's head as she peeked in.

And there it was now.

"Hello?" she called. "I hope you haven't killed each other while I've been gone."

Magnus chuckled.

Emmia closed the door behind her and caught a glimpse of them lying on the floor once her eyes adjusted to the dimly lit room. Her footsteps sounded on the floor as she walked to them. "Well," she said, standing over them with a hand to her hip and a superior look on her face. "I see there was no murder after all. Just some sexual mayhem. I hope you two had fun—"

Quinn moved fast as a snake, reaching up and pulling her down into his arms. She let out a squeal of surprise which he quickly swallowed as he sealed her mouth with his and rolled her to lie in between himself and Magnus.

Finally he broke the kiss and Emmia lay there looking dazed. Magnus had moved in on her other side so that she was effectively sandwiched between them. Emmia sighed and snuggled against them both. "Mmm...I was a bit chilled. Not anymore."

Magnus shared a look with Quinn over her head. It was one of hunger laid bare. There was no question they would try to get Emmia into bed with them. It was definitely an objective they shared. Quinn didn't think it would be all that hard. He knew well she was fascinated with the idea.

Emmia closed her eyes and murmured, "So, I take it you two kissed and made up."

"We did more than kiss," Magnus said, running his fingers through her hair. "But yes, we made up."

"Good," she murmured. "It was painful watching you both pine away for one another."

"Although," continued Magnus. "We should put you over our knees for locking us up in this room that way."

She gave a soft, throaty laugh. "It was the only way I knew how to do it and, anyway, I'd probably like being put over your knee. Not much of a punishment, that."

Quinn traced his index finger down her cheek, to the full plumpness of her breast and brushed her nipple. It hardened instantly beneath the fabric of her shirt and her breathing quickened. Her eyes flew open and she struggled to stand. "Oh no, you don't, Quinn. I have work to do and you two don't need me right now—"

"I'll always need you, love," answered Quinn right away. He propped his elbow on the floor and rested his chin in his palm. "Come back down here. I don't mean for anything major to happen, just a little petting. Nothing wrong with a little petting." He flashed a wicked grin. "Never hurt anyone."

She shook her head. "No. You two need time to be alone."

Magnus went to grab for her and she stepped out of his way, laughing. "I'm leaving now," she called as she went toward the door. "I won't lock it this time, though."

* * * * *

She closed the doors behind her and walked to the edge of the balcony for a moment, smiling and enjoying the deepening twilight.

Life had suddenly started to get good.

"Where is Lord Magnus?"

She jumped, startled and turned to find Arhild squinting at her. "He's in his chambers."

Arhild turned and stalked toward the doors. Emmia dropped her shields, wanting to know how Arhild was feeling, and quickly followed him.

"You can't go in there!" she said, pulling at his arm.

Annoyance. "I need to speak with his lordship immediately." He reached for the doorknob.

"No! He's not alone. He's with…he's with Quinn."

Hatred. Disgust. Murderous rage.

The sudden burst of dark feeling socked her in the stomach and made her take several steps back from him.

Arhild turned toward her. "Revolting." He pointed at the door. "It's an abomination what they do. T'was an abomination what they did with Caith!" Then he turned on his heel and stalked in the opposite direction, leaving Emmia at loss for words or thought, swimming in the backlash of Arhild's abhorrence.

Chapter Six

&)

Two days later, Emmia sat in her room contemplating all she knew. She had narrowed her list of suspects to two—Arhild and Rolf. With no concrete evidence, she was going on pure emotion to make her determination.

And she couldn't.

Before the episode with Arhild outside Magnus' chamber, her main suspect had been Rolf. Then Arhild had unleashed that heavy stream of violent emotion at her over the fact that Magnus and Quinn were lovers and that had made her uncertain about Rolf once again.

She stared into the low burning fire in the hearth with her eyes unfocused and curled deeper into the blanket she had snuggled into against the morning chill. A steaming cup of coffee sat next to her on a small table. She thought best in the morning hours, when most of the keep—and their emotions—still slumbered. The shields had been a huge boon, but they didn't block everything, just made it more manageable.

Right now she simply couldn't make a determination one way or another. She had to wait for one of them to implicate themselves. Usually it happened that way. The perpetrator would break under the stress and scrutiny of the ever-present justice mercenary and do something to out himself.

The tension had seemed to have grown steadily since her arrival. It was just a matter of time before things exploded. She'd seen it happen over and over.

And what happened when the mystery was solved, the bad guy brought to justice and her work here was done? That remained unclear. So much had happened to her since Quinn had first stepped onto her lands and cajoled her to come here.

227

She had changed so much. She'd made connections with other people—real, live, breathing people—and she'd never realized just how much she'd wanted them or *needed* them.

She also needed those she'd connected with, namely Magnus and Quinn.

She'd fallen for Quinn hard in the past weeks since she'd arrived at Ravensbridge. She knew how easily she could fall for Magnus as well. She stood staring at the edge of cliff where he was concerned. One little push would send her head over heels.

The thought of leaving them, going back to her secluded cottage, was nearly unbearable. At one time she'd counted that place her only refuge and her only opportunity to retain her sanity. Now that she'd managed to harness and control her gift, now that she'd fallen in love, it seemed a prison.

She felt a warm tear slide down her cheek and she wiped it away with the back of her hand. Love was a double-edged sword. She'd been so happy lately. Now she had to brace for sorrow.

Someone knocked at her door, startling her. She called for the person to enter, but knew it was Quinn before he even came into the room. Magnus was close behind him. She brushed her fingers through her long, loose hair a little self-consciously as they closed the door behind them and approached her chair. She'd hardly expected visitors this early in the morning.

Quinn kissed her lips and knelt beside her chair. "We wanted to ask you to go riding with us today."

"Yes. I'd love that." She didn't have anything pressing on her agenda today. Now it was just a matter of waiting.

Magnus knelt on his other side and slipped his hand over hers. "Why do you look so sad, Emmia?"

She glanced away from him, unwilling to reveal her feelings. What if they thought she was silly for wanting more than a sexual relationship with them? What if she scared them away with her emotions? What they rejected her? She wasn't carefree, life-loving Caith, in it just for the sex, but did they know that?

No, she couldn't tell Magnus the truth. There was too much risk. She wanted as much time with them both as possible, so she couldn't say a word about how she really felt. That path was fraught with too much danger.

Quinn's brow furrowed. "What is it, love?"

"I want you to make love to me," she whispered. "Both of you."

Quinn and Magnus exchanged a look, and then Quinn took her hand and helped her to stand. Her blanket fell away, leaving her in just the linen shift she slept in. He pulled her against his body and laid a kiss to the top of her head. "I believe that's something Magnus and I both want too. We weren't expecting it here and now, but it's a gift we'd never turn away from."

She closed her eyes when she felt Magnus press against her back. The warmth of both their bodies was a tonic for her frayed emotions and it drew a deep sigh of contentment from her. Magnus' hand grasped her shift and drew it up and over her head, tossing it to the floor at their feet. Now she was nude from her toes to the top of her head and sandwiched between two still fully clothed men.

Her breath came heavy and her heart beat as deep desire filled her. Her cunt felt warm and wet already and they hadn't even touched her yet. Quinn drew her up against his chest, kissing her open-mouthed. His tongue hungrily mated with hers while his hand delved down to stroke her sex. He teased her clit, and slid his finger inside her to prime her cunt. Behind her, Magnus ran his hand over her skin, running his fingers along the cleft of her ass and kissing and nipping her shoulder.

Emmia let out another shuddering sigh of happiness and clung to Quinn's shoulders. She felt like she was drowning in a sea of pleasure. Without a word, Magnus took her from Quinn, lifted her and carried her to the bed. He lay down on top of her, still fully clothed, his gaze intent on her face. Balancing on one hand, he stroked her between her thighs, still staring into her eyes. She shuddering under his touch, feeling a gush of warm honey as her body responded to him.

"You two never doubted that I'd want this, did you?" she murmured.

Quinn lay on the bed beside her. He was now undressed. "Not for a moment."

"We're going to tie you," said Magnus.

She blinked in surprise. That hadn't been something she'd expected at all. "That didn't sound like a question."

Quinn smiled. "That's because it wasn't."

She lifted a brow. "Have you two been discussing this?"

Quinn just gave her a sexy little smile and didn't answer.

Magnus slid from the bed and, in the trunk at the end of the bed, found two long silk scarves that she hadn't even known were there. He and Quinn each bound a wrist and tied her to the bed frame. She tried them and found the bonds secure, but not uncomfortable. They'd tied the knots so the scarves restrained her, but didn't hurt her.

Then they stood back and admired their handiwork. "She looks beautiful bound that way, don't you think?" commented Quinn with a glint of mischievousness in his eyes.

"I could stand here all day and admire her," answered Magnus as he undressed, "if I didn't want to fuck her so badly. Do you want to fuck her, Quinn?"

Quinn let his gaze slide down her body, warming every inch of her skin it touched. "Until she can't even think. I want to fuck her fast and hard, and then make love to her slow and easy."

"Excellent plan."

Together they crawled onto the bed on either side of her and stroked their hands down her body, petting her breasts, teasing her nipples and delving between her thighs to stroke her cunt. Soon she was twisting against her bonds, wanting more than just this foreplay. She wanted their cocks, both of them. She wanted to touch them, lick them, bring them deep into her body.

"Please," she whispered.

The two men exchanged another look, seeming to communicate nonverbally. It was Magnus who mounted her first, spreading her legs and setting the head of his smooth cock to the entrance of her needy cunt. Quinn settled down beside them, allowing his hand to stroke Magnus' shaft and her pussy with an easy, equal skill.

"How does she feel?" Quinn asked Magnus.

Magnus slid the crown of his cock between her nether lips, making her gasp. "Hot and silky sweet." He pushed in another inch, stretching her muscles with his incredible width. "Like heaven," he finished in a strained voice. "She always feels like heaven." With one sharp jab of his hips, he seated himself within her.

Emmia grabbed the scarves in her fists and wallowed in the intense feeling of having Magnus so deep inside her. When he began to thrust, she thought she'd lose her mind from the pleasure. Quinn leaned over and kissed her, eating up all the small sounds she made, all her sighs, and every time she murmured their names.

Magnus hooked his broad hands under her knees and spread her thighs as he took her, allowing Quinn to watch his cock tunneling in and out of her pussy. Quinn settled in to play with them both, running his fingers along Magnus' shaft on every outward thrust and petting Emmia's clit skillfully. His fingers stroked her over and over, relentlessly driving her to the brink of climax...and then pushed her right over the edge.

Emmia's body tensed as pleasure poured through her. Quinn continued to stroke her clit while Magnus took her harder and faster, driving her orgasm to a shattering crescendo that made her cry out nearly full-throated and practically see stars. She felt Magnus' big body tense as well, and soon felt him shoot deep within her with a groan that reverberated through her.

She sagged in the scarves, her body limp in the aftermath of the pleasure. "Untie me," she said to Quinn. "If I can't touch you two soon, I'm going to go crazy."

Quinn untied her and she got up on her hands and knees and crawled across the bed to Magnus. She pressed her lips to his and kissed him deeply, as they both rested on their knees in the center of the mattress. He threaded his fingers through her hair and slanted his mouth greedily over hers, delving his tongue between her lips to possess every inch of her mouth.

Behind her, Quinn pressed his body to hers and ran his hands down her back, over her buttocks. He lingered there a moment before sliding his hands between her and Magnus to cup her breasts.

Though she'd just climaxed hard and long, all it had seemed to do was prime her body for more. She'd never been with two men at once this way and it was pure ecstasy. She wanted to take advantage of every moment of it.

She broke her kiss with Magnus and turned to Quinn. Knowing her mouth was swollen and red from Magnus' kiss, she pressed her lips to Quinn's, wanting to share Magnus with him in this way.

Quinn made a hungry, growling sound deep in his throat and pressed her down onto the mattress beneath him. He placed his palms flat against the bed on either side of her head, pinning her there, and kissed her deeply. Eventually, he moved down her body, stopping to suck at her nipples at leisure and then forcing her legs apart and settling there to lick her.

In the meantime, Magnus had straddled her chest and she took his cock in hand eagerly. She pulled him toward her mouth and suckled his now flaccid flesh between her lips, tasting the musky flavor of herself on him just slightly.

Between her thighs, Quinn had gone to work, driving her back to that point of pure pleasure where she couldn't form thought anymore. He slipped two fingers inside and worked them in and out, rasping over her g-spot with every inward thrust as he set about sucking and licking her fat, aroused clit.

Meanwhile, she played with Magnus' cock, enjoying how soft it was and the texture of it against her tongue. It didn't stay soft for long, however. Soon Magnus was again growing hard between her lips.

"Emmia," Magnus breathed, staring down at her. "You're going to make me come again and Quinn has barely had a chance to touch you yet." He moved off from her.

Quinn looked up from between her spread thighs with a look so needful, so feral, that it sent shivers up her spine. "On your hands and knees," he commanded.

She went to her hands and knees and felt the press of Quinn's cock to her sex as he mounted her. He was not gentle. He'd obviously waited too long for that. Quinn grasped her hips and thrust, seating himself within her to his balls in one powerful movement. Emmia's head whipped back and groaned at the sensation of it.

Magnus moved to her head and she took him into her mouth once again as Quinn set up an easy, steady rhythm. Quinn's thrusts slid Magnus' cock between her lips every time. Magnus threaded his fingers through her hair and fucked her mouth as sure and easy as Quinn thrust into her pussy. The three of them became like a machine, all the parts moving in perfect accord. They seemed to fit together flawlessly, each giving pleasure to the other in turn.

Emmia went first, tipping into her climax so fast and hard she nearly lost her hold on Magnus' cock. Magnus went next, shooting deep down Emma's throat even as her orgasm was fading. Finally Quinn's climax exploded and he called both their names over and over as he filled her with his seed.

They collapsed onto the mattress, all satisfied and limp as noodles. Each of them was sheened with perspiration, despite the morning chill. Emmia's long hair was sticking to her skin. When the cold did finally start to bite, the two men pulled her near and cuddled her close, protecting her from shivering.

Emmia drowsed as their hands idly stroked her, unsure of the last time she'd felt so content, so…complete. "Is this what it was like between you two and Caith?"

There was silence for a moment and then Magnus said, "No. It was a little different with Caith. The mood wasn't so serious, so—"

"Loving," Quinn supplied from behind her.

Emmia turned that over in her mind for a moment. "What does that mean…exactly?"

Magnus stroked his fingers through her hair as he mulled his response. "With Caith, it was always very playful and detached. She was about the pleasure, about the sex itself. With you, it's different, more…intense. Deeper, if you will pardon the unintentional pun."

Quinn spooned her back and kissed her shoulder. "For example, Caith would never have stayed here with us afterward this way. She had her fun and then left."

"Was she frightened of connecting with someone on a deeper level?"

"No," answered Magnus. "I don't think so. I think Caith simply wasn't made for that. She wished for superficial relationships, ones she could toss aside when she was bored. She wanted to experience every aspect of life and wanted nothing to hold her back. She was very much a free spirit."

Had her love of experiencing life without regard for propriety led to her death? It was possible.

Emmia snuggled back against Quinn and nuzzled the place where Magnus' throat and shoulder met, inhaling the scent of him happily. "I can't think of anything better than this. *This* is almost better than sex."

Quinn's hand skated down between her thighs to stroke her softly. "I like it when you come, Emmia," he whispered into her ear. "You're so beautiful when you climax."

Her breath caught as Magnus kissed her, and then moved down to suckle her nipples. The two men slowly, easily worked her body to another shuddering climax. The muscles of her cunt pulsed and contracted around Quinn's pistoning fingers and her finger twisted into Magnus' hair where he laved her nipples, each in turn.

By now Magnus and Quinn were hard once more. Emmia took them both in hand and stroked them until the two men were groaning. Seeing the possibilities of having two cocks at her disposal, she urged them to their knees, side by side in front her and took turns taking each of them deep into her mouth.

When she thought Magnus was going to go, he pulled away from her. "No, in you, love. I want for us to finish inside your sweet body."

"Both of you?" Her eyes widened. "At the same time?"

"Both of us," answered Quinn. "Remember how I showed you, love?"

While Magnus lay down and guided her to mount him, Quinn sought the small vial of olive oil a servant had brought for her morning bread and returned to the bed.

Magnus jabbed his hips up into her already well-loved cunt and she gasped with pleasure and surprise. Quinn wasted no time settling behind her. He spread the olive oil on his cock and also on the opening of her ass.

She stiffened in apprehension, knowing what Quinn was about to do, even though the combination of all those little nerves being stimulated along with Magnus' gentle in and out thrusts was very distracting. Once more, she felt drunk on passion and lust.

"It's all right," Quinn murmured into her ear. He slid a finger into her, then two, widening her, stretching her for his cock. "Remember in my room that day? Remember how I took you and how much you liked it?"

She closed her eyes, bit her lower lip and nodded.

"Remember how fantasizing about how Magnus and I would make love to you at the same time made you come? It's not a fantasy now, is it?"

She shook her head slightly, lost in the dual sensation of having her cunt and ass stimulated at the same time.

"Did you know that day that Magnus was watching us from the corner?"

Her eyes flew open and met Magnus' gaze.

"It's true," said Magnus. "I watched you two and longed to be a part of your intimacy, as I am now. Gods, you were beautiful, Emmia, the stretch and lines of your body, how you gave yourself over to passion with so few inhibitions."

She should have been mad, should have left them both right then and there, but they knew her better than that. They knew this information would arouse her, and it did. "You-you watched us?" It came out all breathy sounding.

A very male, very self-satisfied smile spread over Magnus' face. "Watched and wanted."

Quinn chose that moment to ease the head of his cock into her ass. She gasped at the stretch of her muscles and grabbed the headboard above. Magnus reached up and rolled her nipples between his fingers as Quinn worked slowly inch-by-well-lubricated-inch deep within her.

It burned. It stung. It stretched. But mostly it felt very, *very* good. There was a moment when she almost told him to back out, that she didn't want to be taken this way, but her muscles relaxed a bit more and all was well.

She eased down to press her hands on either side of Magnus' body. He grabbed her hips and shafted her slowly. While, behind her, Quinn did the same.

Emmia saw stars.

Never had she thought her body capable of this much pleasure. Being filled by the two men she cared so very deeply for, having both her orifices pleasured this way, brought tears to her eyes.

The three of them moved together in perfect unison, giving and taking pleasure in equal amounts. Magnus moved deep within her, playing with her breasts and kissing her as he drove her to a shattering climax.

Quinn came first, with a shout of exaltation and both their names rolling off his tongue in succession. Emmia went right after him, like a domino, feeding off his ecstasy. Magnus went last, pulling her down against him and kissing her all over her face as he whispered sweet, loving things in her ear.

As Emmia lay sandwiched between them once more, with the scent of them both on her skin and their seed deep inside her, she knew she didn't want to leave.

Not ever.

* * * * *

It was a beautiful day, bright and full of sunshine. By the time the three of them had bathed and dressed, it was midafternoon, but the day had warmed considerably from the morning.

They each took their favorite horses from the stables and rode from the courtyard and into the meadows that lay around Ravensbridge keep. It was so nice to be away from all of Ravensbridge's inhabitants for the day. It was true she'd been able to build walls to protect herself from the rawest emotions, but the barriers weren't completely soundproof, some emotion always made its way through.

Magnus had brought a small lunch for them all, so they found a good, shaded place to stop in the forest, dismounted and secured their horses. Quinn spread a few blankets on the grass and they all sat down to partake of the bread, cheese and wine.

"I'm starving," Emmia said, biting into a thick piece of nutty bread.

"It's well-earned. You were very...*active* this morning, Emmia," answered Quinn with a twinkle in his eye. "We all were."

Magnus laughed. "I'd like to be...*active* again sometime today too."

"And now I'm hungry and exhausted, but in a good way," she replied after she'd chewed and swallowed. "I'm so happy to see you both together again. It's like I can feel *both* your emotions and they're singing at the proximity of each other. It's just beautiful."

Magnus leaned over and gave her a long, deep kiss. He set his forehead to hers and murmured against her lips, "It's not only because Quinn and I are together, Emmia. It's also because you're with us."

She smiled and held his gaze for a long, pregnant moment.

Quinn set his wine bottle to the side and joined them, pressing his body close to theirs, so that the three of them kissed.

Emmia backed away to allow the two men a moment. They took it with both hands and crushed their bodies together. Tears rolled down her cheeks as she watched Quinn and Magnus kiss. Their lips and tongue mated tenderly and their hands found purchase on each other's body as though they'd drown if they didn't have each other. It made her heart swell with happiness to see them both that way and her Talent responded, taking Quinn's love and making her heart fill with euphoria.

"Disgusting!"

The joy Emmia felt shattered into bitter fragments at the sound of Arhild's voice behind her. She'd been so focused on the emotion she felt from Quinn and Magnus that she hadn't even felt him approach. Now his hatred and revulsion rolled over her with the force of a team of workhorses. She built up her walls a little, but not completely. Something in her sensed she needed her Talent now.

"Arhild?" Magnus queried, coming to his feet. "What are you doing here?"

Arhild stood with his horse's reins in hand. "I went see to my lands, then came back through the forest and saw you *three* like that. It's an abomination! A sacrilege!"

"It's love!" Emmia shouted at him, unable to tamp down her ire. "See with different eyes. See *correctly*, Arhild!"

Arhild took several menacing steps toward her. "What I see is a little *slut* who is so deviant she can't limit herself to one man." There was a light in Arhild's eyes that Emmia didn't like.

Magnus and Quinn both rushed Arhild at the same time, having taken offense at what he'd said to her, but Arhild grabbed her first and produced a long, wickedly thin blade, which he pressed to her throat.

Emmia gasped, feeling herself pressed up against Arhild and the blade making an incision in her skin. A thread of hot red blood ran down her throat and pain burned her, making her wince.

Oh, if only she'd come with her swords. She'd left them in her room, not expecting to encounter violence on an innocent horse ride.

She was certain Caith hadn't been expecting it, either.

Sorrow for Caith welled up within her as she realized who had killed her. Goddess, she hoped Arhild had killed her in her sleep so she'd never seen the hatred in her own father's eyes.

"Back away!" shouted Arhild at the two men. "Back away from me, or I will cut her. Don't doubt me."

Quinn and Magnus both stopped dead in their tracks.

"Don't hurt her," rasped out Magnus. "I swear, Arhild. Hurt her and I'll mount your head outside the gates of Ravensbridge."

"You would kill me over this little slut?" yelled Arhild. "I'm the richest and most powerful of your retainers. You wouldn't dare hurt me."

Magnus took a menacing step forward, but Quinn stopped him with a hand to his chest. Magnus narrowed his eyes and when he spoke, his voice was low and dangerous-sounding. "I would flay every inch of your skin from your body and ensure you were conscious while I did it."

"I am Caith's father! The last bit of her you have to hang on to."

"But you killed her, didn't you?" Emmia asked. She made her voice sound weak and shaky, though the only emotion she felt now was anger, not fear. She could free herself from Arhild's sloppy hold at any time she chose, though she was likely the only one in this company who knew that. "You killed Caith because you found out about her relationship with Magnus and Quinn." It wasn't a question. Riding the waves of Arhild's emotions now, she knew it to be truth.

Arhild made a keening noise and she felt a wave of grief from him. "She dishonored our family. She had to die before she could disgrace our name even more."

Quinn's face twisted in grief and Magnus dropped his head for a long moment. When Magnus raised his head, there was a look pure malice on his face. Emmia knew she had to be free of Arhild's grip soon. Magnus was barely hanging on to his control.

"So you knocked Magnus out as he slept, took his sword and killed your daughter with it?" Emmia asked, her voice harsh with emotion and her gaze fixed on Magnus, who seethed with a rage even she could feel. "Then you put blood on Magnus' shirt and planted the sword in his chamber, didn't you, Arhild?"

"Yes." Arhild wailed. "Gods, *yes*." Relief washed through the man, almost as if his confession was a burden lifted. His body shuddered as a sob rose up from the depths of him and covered her over with grief.

Finally, she felt grief from him.

Emmia grabbed his wrist, pushed it away from her throat and spun away from him in one fluid movement. Her booted foot came up in a flash and kicked him in the stomach. He doubled over and Magnus and Quinn were on him in a flash.

Emmia stumbled backward and fell on her butt in the grass, watching as Arhild fought Magnus and Quinn tooth and nail. Quinn and Magnus battled to restrain him, but Arhild was wiry and strong.

It happened so fast it almost seemed to occur in slow motion. Arhild lunged to the ground, found the knife he'd dropped and plunged it into his own throat.

Emmia stared, watching the blood flow and trying to block the gurgling sound from her ears. Magnus and Quinn stilled, watching the dying man at their feet.

Regret washed through Arhild, poignant and deep. It was sweet and bitter and burned the back of Emmia's tongue with its strength. Then, there was no emotion and Arhild was still and silent.

Silence descended on the meadow. All Emmia could hear was the sound of the men's labored breathing and her own beating heart.

She stared at Arhild's crumpled body, pitiful on the ground at their feet. Tears rolled down her cheeks and her face crumpled as she sobbed in relief for Arhild, who had wanted death in the end, and in relief for Magnus.

It was over. Magnus was free.

Chapter Seven

❧

Emmia packed the rest of her things in her sack and sighed. It was indeed over. The keep's inhabitants had accepted Arhild's guilt and Magnus' rule without apprehension once more. When she dropped her shields, the keep felt light and joyous, instead of heavy with suspicion and fear as it had before.

Yes, her work was done and now she had no excuse to stay. In any case, neither Quinn nor Magnus had asked her to. When she'd mentioned it the night before, neither man had raised a syllable in protest.

It was no huge surprise. After all, they had no formal understanding of a relationship beyond the sexual and, while she had fallen in love with both Quinn and Magnus, she'd had no true, *clear* indication that they shared her feelings as deeply. She'd perceived love from both of them at various times, of course, but she could have easily been confusing love with lust. Anyway, they had each other now.

She picked up her bag and turned toward the door, ready to finally take her leave of his place. Slowly, she made her way down to the stables. She would make her horse ready and store her gear, then go and find the men to say her goodbyes.

She stepped off the last step into the courtyard, and raised her head to see Magnus and Quinn both astride. "Where have you been, Emmia?" asked Magnus. "It's nearly noon. We've been waiting forever."

"Excuse me?" she asked, walking toward them. "What are you talking about?"

"You said last night that you were returning home," answered Quinn. "Surely you didn't think you were leaving without us."

"Uh..."

"I thought a trip into the forests was an excellent idea," added Magnus. "I could use a little vacation from this place and Rolf is more than able to take care of things in my absence. A short vacation at your cottage, alone, just the three of us, sounds very good to me."

"Then we can talk about what happens next," Quinn put in. His face grew serious. "You have gotten over your inability to stomach human companionship, haven't you, love?"

Emmia blinked.

"Because I thought maybe we could all live here at Ravensbridge," said Magnus. "If that's all right with you, of course."

"Umm."

"Or perhaps we could travel a bit, go and see your sister Rhea. You miss her, don't you, Emmia?"

"I do, but... What are you talking about?"

Quinn slid from his horse and Magnus followed. They both approached her, getting down on bended knee and each of them taking a hand.

"Emmia," started Magnus.

"Emmia," said Quinn, with a glance at Magnus. "We love you." At his words, Quinn's love for her poured past her barriers, breaking them utterly and filling her chest up with warmth.

"*We* love you, Emmia," added Magnus. And even though she couldn't feel emotion from Magnus normally, she felt it then. The love increased by half, making joy bubble through her body and the taste of honey tease the back of her tongue.

"Live with us," said Quinn.

"Marry us," put in Magnus. He pulled a bracelet from his pocket. It was thin, gold and encrusted with rubies and sapphires. "Rubies are the jewel of my house and sapphires are the jewel of Quinn's. We had this piece of jewelry forged for you to wear as our bride, so that all who view it know that you belong to us."

"I-I don't know what to say." Her voice came out a whisper.

"Say you'll wear it. Say you'll marry us, Emmia," said Quinn. "Say no and you break our hearts forever."

Emmia fell to her knees before the two men and embraced them. "Of course, it's yes. I love you both and want nothing more than to spend my days with you."

Around them came cheers and clapping. She glanced up and realized that a crowd had formed. Then Magnus and Quinn crushed her to them, kissing her over her face.

"What do you feel right now, my Emmia," Quinn whispered into her ear.

"Happy," she murmured. "Happy and loved."

"We aim to keep you that way, love," Magnus murmured. "Forevermore."

Also by Lauren Dane

ഌ

About the Author

෨

Lauren Dane been writing stories since she was able to use a pencil, and before that she used to tell them to people. Of course, she still talks nonstop, but now she decided to try and make a go of being a writer. And so here she is. She still loves to write, and through wonderful fate and good fortune, she's able to share what she writes with others now. It's a wonderful life!

The basics: She's a mom, a partner, a best friend and a daughter. Living in the rainy but beautiful Pacific Northwest, she spends her late evenings writing like a fiend when she finally wrestles all of her kids to bed.

Lauren welcomes comments from readers. You can find her website and email address on her author bio page at www.ellorascave.com.

Tell Us What You Think

We appreciate hearing reader opinions about our books. You can email us at Comments@EllorasCave.com.

Also by Anya Bast

୫୨

About the Author

ഇ

Anya Bast is a multipublished erotic fantasy & paranormal romance author. Primarily, she writes happily-ever-afters with lots of steamy sex. After all, happily-ever-afters with lots of sex are the very best kind.

She enjoys the study of Celtic myth, dreaming, and shamanism and incorporates what she learns into her paranormal stories.

Anya got her start writing fantasy romance. Since writing a little hotter seemed to come naturally to her, she had no trouble making the move to erotic romance. She loves writing books that are heavy on plot, emotion and character development, and also have spicy, no-holds-barred sex scenes. Exploring the elements of dark sexual fantasy in her writing is what Anya does best.

She lives in the country with her husband. They share their lives with eight cats and one perplexed dog.

Anya welcomes comments from readers. You can find her website and email address on her author bio page at www.ellorascave.com.

Tell Us What You Think

We appreciate hearing reader opinions about our books. You can email us at Comments@EllorasCave.com.

Why an electronic book?

We live in the Information Age—an exciting time in the history of human civilization, in which technology rules supreme and continues to progress in leaps and bounds every minute of every day. For a multitude of reasons, more and more avid literary fans are opting to purchase e-books instead of paper books. The question from those not yet initiated into the world of electronic reading is simply: *Why?*

1. *Price.* An electronic title at Ellora's Cave Publishing and Cerridwen Press runs anywhere from 40% to 75% less than the cover price of the exact same title in paperback format. Why? Basic mathematics and cost. It is less expensive to publish an e-book (no paper and printing, no warehousing and shipping) than it is to publish a paperback, so the savings are passed along to the consumer.

2. *Space.* Running out of room in your house for your books? That is one worry you will never have with electronic books. For a low one-time cost, you can purchase a handheld device specifically designed for e-reading. Many e-readers have large, convenient screens for viewing. Better yet, hundreds of titles can be stored within your new library—on a single microchip. There are a variety of e-readers from different manufacturers. You can also read e-books on your PC or laptop computer. (Please note that Ellora's Cave does not endorse any specific brands.

You can check our websites at www.ellorascave.com or www.cerridwenpress.com for information we make available to new consumers.)

3. *Mobility.* Because your new e-library consists of only a microchip within a small, easily transportable e-reader, your entire cache of books can be taken with you wherever you go.

4. *Personal Viewing Preferences.* Are the words you are currently reading too small? Too large? Too… ANNOYING? Paperback books cannot be modified according to personal preferences, but e-books can.

5. *Instant Gratification.* Is it the middle of the night and all the bookstores near you are closed? Are you tired of waiting days, sometimes weeks, for bookstores to ship the novels you bought? Ellora's Cave Publishing sells instantaneous downloads twenty-four hours a day, seven days a week, every day of the year. Our webstore is never closed. Our e-book delivery system is 100% automated, meaning your order is filled as soon as you pay for it.

Those are a few of the top reasons why electronic books are replacing paperbacks for many avid readers.

As always, Ellora's Cave and Cerridwen Press welcome your questions and comments. We invite you to email us at Comments@ellorascave.com or write to us directly at Ellora's Cave Publishing Inc., 1056 Home Avenue, Akron, OH 44310-3502.

Cerridwen, the Celtic Goddess of wisdom, was the muse who brought inspiration to storytellers and those in the creative arts. Cerridwen Press encompasses the best and most innovative stories in all genres of today's fiction. Visit our site and discover the newest titles by talented authors who still get inspired - much like the ancient storytellers did, once upon a time.

Cerridwen Press

www.cerridwenpress.com

CPSIA information can be obtained at www.ICGtesting.com
Printed in the USA
LVOW08s1438211113

362271LV00002B/338/P